Bloody Acquisitions

REUTS PUBLICATIONS

BLOODY ACQUISITIONS

Drew Hayes

Cover design by Ashley Ruggirello
Interior formatting by Ashley Ruggirello
Edited by Kisa Whipkey and Rae Oestreich
Cover art Copyright 2015 silinias/NokieSchafe/withmycamera/Giallo86 on DeviantArt.com

Paperback ISBN: 978-1-942111-35-1
Electronic ISBN: 978-1-942111-36-8

REUTS Publications
www.REUTS.com

This book, the third in a series I wasn't sure would get off the ground beyond the first, goes out to the wonderful readers who've made this possible. Thank you for taking a chance on the strange tales of a socially awkward vampire accountant, whose stories I hope to be telling for a long time to come.

PREFACE

I ALMOST CERTAINLY DO NOT KNOW YOU; however, I shall assume you are a lovely person, and it is my loss for not having yet had the opportunity to meet you. Still, I must assume you and I are connected in some way, for the works you are about to read are selections from a journal of my memoirs. I compiled these not in the belief that the stories within are so compelling they must be told, but rather because I found my unexpected life transition to be so shockingly uneventful—at least initially. I place the blame for my aggrandized expectations squarely on contemporary media, filling my head with the belief that a ticket to the supernatural also put one on an express train toward coolness and suave charm.

This is simply not the case. Or, at least, it was not my case. I recorded my journeys in the hopes that, should another being find themselves utterly depressed at the humdrum personality still saddling their supernatural frame, they might find solace in knowing they are not the only one to have felt that way. Given the lengthy lifespan of many of the people with whom I associate, there is no guarantee they will have passed on by the time this is read. Therefore, names have been changed as I deemed necessary.

So, dear reader, whom I suspect is a wonderful person merely in need of a bit of reassurance, take comfort in my tales of uneventful blundering. One's nature is hard to change; sometimes even death is insufficient to accomplish such a task. But be assured that, while you might find yourself still more human than anticipated, you are far from the only one. You will eventually discover that under the movie stereotypes, imposed mystique, and overall inflated expectations, each and every one of us is at least a touch more boring than our images would indicate.

And that is not a bad thing.

-*Fredrick Frankford Fletcher*

A HUNTER IN THE STREETS

1.

"WHILE I'M GLAD YOU DON'T FALL INTO the old female stereotype of having lots of shoes, part of me wishes you did. I'd much prefer to be lugging around high heels than yet another box full of guns." As gently as I possibly could, I set the cardboard cube down on Krystal's empty counter. Normally, there was nowhere near enough kitchen space cleaned off to fit even a single glass, let alone a whole box of armaments, but today was different. Today, her entire apartment was almost stripped bare, with much of the furniture going off into storage or being returned to the rental locations they'd been taken from.

Today was moving day, which was why I'd been roped into helping to haul the possessions she was keeping—including what had to be an illegal amount of firearms even for an agent—off to her new home.

"Don't be such a baby. My collection is nothing. You should see the armory that Arch carts around everywhere." Krystal emerged from her bedroom, a duffel bag packed with more of her knives, batons, and other melee gear rattling on her shoulder. "Plus, like I've been saying ever since the word came down, this is ultimately all your fault. Once the Agency found out what a deal you'd gotten for Arch, they didn't see the sense in paying for me to have a more expensive, less defended apartment."

While "fault" seemed like an aggressive term, there was no denying that I had set in motion the chain of events which resulted in Krystal's fellow agent, Arch, moving into the animated house on the outskirts of Winslow, Colorado known as Charlotte Manor. On top of coming with three meals a day and all utilities included, Charlotte was also something of a magical fortress, built by a commune of insane mages and meant to repel all but the most powerful of attackers. Granted, not everyone would be thrilled by the idea of living in a home that was self-aware and always watching, but for people like Krystal and Arch, the loss of privacy was well worth it to be able to sleep with both eyes shut.

But perhaps I should step back briefly, in case those last few lines seem like the raving of a madman or incomprehensible gibberish. My name is Fredrick Frankford Fletcher, and I am a Certified Public Parahuman Accountant. Also, a vampire. Despite what film and television might have led to you believe, joining the undead does not inherently make one suave, cool, or even particularly more socially competent. What it does do, however, is thrust you into a community that lives in the normal world's shadow, a society comprised of parahumans. That very community has technically endangered my undead life several times, but it has also helped me meet a variety of friends I would never have run across in my mortal days, so it's not that bad of a trade. Krystal, my girlfriend, makes her living working for the agency that polices our kind, ensuring that all the laws and treaties of our various peoples are upheld. It keeps her on the road a lot, which is just one more reason why moving to Charlotte Manor made more sense than her previous arrangement.

We hauled our respective loads down the stairs, setting them into the back cab of Krystal's pickup truck, where she'd saved a space specifically for the weaponry. My hybrid was already filled with the more mundane objects like clothing and dishes, rather than firearms and blades. She had the security clearance to be walking around with half a riot squad's arsenal; I didn't, and even for vampires, traffic stops are still a possibility.

"And that . . . is it." Krystal slammed the door closed, causing me to jump as I waited to hear the guns go off, despite her assurances that they were all unloaded. She chuckled, but didn't call me out on being startled, likely because I was in the middle of doing her a favor. "Bubba and Amy should be about done with their load by now, so once we get the dangerous stuff inside, we can break for night-lunch."

Much as I wished she'd think of a new term for our customary meal around midnight, being my equivalent of a mid-day point, I was never going to object to enjoying Charlotte's cooking. While it's true that I primarily need blood to survive, I can still dine on human food. My body gains no nutrients from it, but that's never really the best part of eating a fine meal anyway, is it?

"I just have to swing by my place real quick to fire off an email," I told her. "Promised to have some acquisition forms sent out before morning."

"Can't Albert do that?" Krystal asked.

"You already dragged Albert and Neil into helping you move," I reminded her. "They took the first couple of boxes. And anyway, there's a bit of prep work to do, which puts it out of Albert's depth. Great assistant or not, some tasks require my personal touch."

Krystal leered at me for a few seconds—her way of letting me know I was on thin ice—before finally relenting with a sigh. "I'll let it slide this time, but don't take too long. These boxes aren't going to unpack themselves."

"I promise to be as quick as possible," I assured her.

"I'd prefer you promise to hire some more help," Krystal shot back. "Even vampires need rest, you know."

She had me there. When I first got my CPPA license and began courting parahuman clients, I'd been fearful there wouldn't be enough business to sustain the investment. What I discovered was that this was a hole in the market that desperately required filling, and over the past few months, it had been all I could do to keep up with the influx of new clients. Fletcher Accounting Services needed to expand, which was far easier said than done. Parahumans might be in ample supply, but precious few of them wanted to make their living as accountants.

"It would be nice," I agreed. "My original plan was to get Albert trained up as he grew more familiar with the practice, and then pay for him to obtain the necessary accounting degrees. But with the sword training, that's just not viable." Several months prior, Albert had pulled the Blade of the Unlikely Champion from its sheath. Technically, that didn't come with any built-in responsibilities; however, everyone had agreed it was best he get comfortable using it, just in case. Which, in fact, was why Arch had moved to Winslow and needed somewhere to stay in the first place. Despite seeming human, Arch was quite old, and renowned for his abilities as a trainer, among other things.

"I'll keep an ear to the ground, just in case I come across any good candidates." Krystal pulled open the door to her truck, then paused to lean in and give me a short, but forceful, kiss. "Don't take too long with your work, or I'll let them start night-lunch without you."

"Only a few minutes, at most." She let it be, getting into her truck and heading off before I'd so much as gotten my own car's door unlocked.

The truth of the matter was that I knew exactly how long the work would take, and it would be seconds, at most. I'd purposely left it undone specifically so I'd have an excuse to split up from her when the last load was packed. I'm not a terrible liar, but Krystal is an agent for a reason, and telling the truth made it far less likely that the real reason I was going back to my apartment would be uncovered.

After all, it wouldn't be much of a surprise house-warming party without the surprise part. Or a cake, specially ordered from a bakery back in Krystal's and my hometown of Kent. It was a favorite of both of ours, and a nice way to ring in the new with the old. But I needed to hurry. The plan was for everyone to distract her with unpacking while I picked up the cake and brought it to Charlotte Manor.

Turning on my engine, I started to floor it, then remembered my car was full of Krystal's possessions—some of which were almost certain to be illegal for a non-agent to have, dishes or no—and resumed a far more moderate pace.

2.

IT TURNED OUT TO BE A GOOD THING THAT
I was driving so carefully, because, if I'd come racing up
to my building, the spiky metal balls hurled under my
tires might have caused me to completely spin out of
control. As it was, I held on to the wheel as three of my
four tires blew out at once, foot pressing on the brake so
hard that I worried I'd snap it off, until I came skidding
to a merciful stop a few feet from the curb. Thankfully,
the late hour and lack of nightlife in my neighborhood
meant the streets were clear, so I didn't hurt anyone as I

scrambled to get my automobile halted. That didn't last long, though. I'd barely begun to reach for the door, my fingers shaking from shock and fear, when a new figure stepped out from a nearby alley.

He was tall, with close-cut brown hair and a scar just below his left eye. A large brown coat concealed most of his body, but when he moved, I could catch a peek inside, which was not a comforting sight. Wooden stakes, bulbs of garlic, the telltale shine of guns, silver chains, and several other bulges I couldn't quite make out during my brief glimpse all sent my usually anxious mind into overdrive. His hands dipped inside, coming out with a pair of pistols. Krystal could have told me the make and model, but all I knew was that they were big, and would undoubtedly punch a bloody hole in any part of me they were aimed at.

I froze, fingers still wrapped around the handle, until he motioned for me to get out of the car. With only one good tire, escape was off the table, so I didn't have a lot of choice. Besides, I was sure this was some sort of misunderstanding. Maybe an agent had been given the wrong address for a rogue vampire, one who didn't adhere to the law as carefully as me. A simple call would sort it right out. At least, that's what I told myself as I climbed slowly out of my car.

"Don't move. Don't try anything." He barked more than spoke, gesturing with the guns. Now that I was out,

I could catch a glimpse of his eyes for the first time, and I noticed how wild they seemed. Every agent I'd met was a bastion of control—even Krystal's chaotic attitude came with a carefully measured understanding of how much force was needed. But this man . . . I felt like he could begin firing at any moment. That certainty I'd had about the misunderstanding began to erode, ever so slightly.

"Empty your pockets on the ground." It struck me that I might just be getting mugged, which was an oddly comforting thought. Possessions could be replaced, and some crook was far less dangerous than a person actually keyed in to the parahuman world.

I did as I was told, dropping my wallet, car keys, and cell phone to the concrete. As soon as the last item hit the ground, he took quick aim and fired, causing me to jump back and turning my phone into nothing more than plastic debris. Undead or not, guns are scary things, especially when pointed at you, and I decided it was time to try and start extricating myself from this situation.

"I'm not sure what charges are being leveled at me, but I'm willing to go along peacefully," I told him. "If you could reach out to Agent Jenkins, I'll trust her to arrange proper representation. We do still get lawyers, right?" It had never occurred to me until this very moment, yet it suddenly seemed strikingly relevant. America's constitution did provide representation for all its citizens, but parahumans had a somewhat different set of rules. Since they helped form the country, they'd negotiated their own sets of laws to accommodate the need for things like hunting and magic. Sometimes it meant we could get away with more than normal humans, sometimes less. I imagined due process had to be factored in there somewhere, though.

"Representation?" He sneered at me, those wild eyes twitching irregularly. "You think I'm dumb enough to take you to the cops? I know what you are, and I know those cells couldn't hold you for long. Isn't that right, *vampire*?"

The way he said it, like it was a big reveal . . . I think I was supposed to react more. Like the silver chains and garlic didn't give away what he thought he was confronting. Although, now that I finally had a chance to think about it, why would an agent bring garlic? Vampires are allergic to it, but only in the sense that our lips get puffy and our throats sore. It's useless in any real capacity, and an agent would definitely know that.

"You're not affiliated with the Agency, are you?"

"Keep talking nonsense, and I'll do this right here in the street," he snapped. "No, I'm not part of whatever organization you use. Just a man who saw what was happening and couldn't stand for it any longer. Took me a long while to find this town's first vampire, until I thought to stake out the local hospital's blood supply. Your little flunky didn't want to talk, loyal one you've got there, but I got it out of him eventually."

"You didn't . . . ?" Granted, what Dr. Huerta and I had was purely a business relationship—he sold me blood and I, in turn, worked the hospital's books to keep them afloat come tax season—but I certainly didn't want the man dead.

"No, I don't kill humans. Just monsters." Slowly lowering one of the guns, the other staying tight on my center of mass, he pulled out a length of silver chain from under his coat and tossed it onto the sidewalk in front of me.

"Wrap yourself."

"And if I do, then what?" It wasn't that I was suddenly feeling brave; it was more like the rational part of my brain was finally beginning to outpace my fearful reaction to the sudden surprise. Whoever this man was, he obviously wasn't an agent. While that made him weaker, physically, it also made him more dangerous. Agents were part of something with rules; they were accountable. That seemed unlikely with my would-be kidnapper, which meant going along peacefully could be more dangerous than making a break for it. Well-prepared or not, there was no way he could keep up with the strength in my undead legs and lungs that didn't need air.

"Then we go for a drive, and when we get somewhere more private, you're telling me everything you know about all the other bloodsuckers in this area. If you do that, then I'll make it quick. If not . . . well, I've got nowhere to be, and you monsters seem to be able to take a lot of punishment."

If I'd had any lingering doubts about the value of running away versus trying to reason this out with him, those words killed them. This man was unhinged, and while someone obviously needed to deal with him, that . . . well, that was what agents were for. My best bet was to escape, contact Krystal, and let her know there was a madman who fancied himself a vampire hunter on the loose.

He was staring at me, and the longer I waited to touch the chains, the tighter his grip on the trigger grew. Getting out of here without any bloodshed seemed more or less impossible, but I could at least keep it minimized. Leaning forward, I started to reach for the chains. When I was a few inches away, I saw him relax just a bit. Little as it was, I still seized the opportunity, lunging to the side with balance precious few humans could hope to match and launching into a dead sprint down the sidewalk.

I felt the bullet hit at the same time I heard the gunshot, tearing through the back of my shoulder and wedging itself somewhere around my spine. If not for the natural toughness of my vampiric body, it likely would have carved straight through me. As it was, the bullet stung, and the shock of the impact caused me to stumble slightly.

"How's that feel, monster? The silver burning you as it rips apart your flesh? I'm still learning about what works on you things, but I've seen firsthand just how potent silver is at putting you down." He was walking toward me, no doubt expecting me to fall to the ground in a heap as the bullet did its work.

Truthfully, it was a pretty good stopping measure, as such things went. Silver acts a magical insulator and disruptor, weakening most parahumans just by touching them. Shoot us with a silver bullet, and the most we'll manage is a crawl. However, the problem with that strategy was that it only works on *most* parahumans. Some come from other realms and have reactions to different metals, like the Fey and their aversion to iron. Others, such as dragons, are either immune or so powerful that their magic can't be insulated—no one is entirely sure.

As for me, several months prior I'd allowed an ancient dragon of immeasurable power to use my body as a conduit to escape his prison. The process hadn't been a fun one, and I'd needed a lot of blood and rest when it was over, but overall, I'd come out more or less unscathed. Except for the one odd side effect that no one had been able to entirely explain: I was no longer bothered by silver.

For some vampires, that might have been a boon that made them incredible warriors, nigh unstoppable on the battlefield. I, however, used that immunity to recover from my stumble and kept on running away from the crazy man in the coat.

"Hey!" He let out a yelp of surprise as I dashed into the night, firing off a few more rounds. I felt one of them graze my back but not actually break the skin, and assumed he'd traded out for regular bullets.

Within seconds, I turned the corner, and after another minute of running, not even my enhanced ears could hear his chasing footsteps anymore.

3.

AFTER A FEW MINUTES OF RACING THROUGH town, it began to occur to me that I had no real idea of where I was going. In the initial burst of panic, my plan had been simply to get away as fast as possible. Now that I was out of immediate danger, it was time to move on to step two, which I had in no way tried to come up with.

I slowed my run, taking in my surroundings. Winslow was a large city, not quite metropolitan but far from the farming town I'd grown up in. This area wasn't familiar, which was hardly surprising given that I'm an introvert who usually works from home, but there were well-lit street signs I could use to get my bearings. The comfort of that thought lasted exactly as long as it took me to dip my hand into my empty pocket and realize my phone was in pieces on a sidewalk. Inconvenient as that was already, it was made doubly worse by the fact that I, like most people in the modern age, also used the GPS function to guide me around. Without my phone, I had no idea how to get anywhere familiar.

Taking deep breaths to try and relax—some habits refused to die even though I already had—I fought down a rising wave of panic and forced myself to think. Paper maps still existed, not that I had the money to buy one, but if I found a gas station, I might be able to figure out where I was and a route to take me somewhere safe. Or, if they happened to have a phone book, there was a chance I could look up the number to Charlotte Manor and let everyone know I needed a lift. Granted, if I remembered their numbers, I could just call direct with any phone, but of course, I hadn't needed to dial them since putting the numbers in my phone the first time. I cursed myself for becoming so dependent on modern conveniences, even as I began to jog down the street looking for any open businesses.

With nothing else to do but think and search, my natural instinct to worry soon kicked in. The concern at the top of the heap was for Dr. Huerta, who it seemed was alive, but likely in rough shape. Given how quickly the vampire hunter had gone to the torture method with me, it seemed a good guess he wasn't shy about using pain to get information, even from humans. Once this was all over, I'd make a point to check in on Dr. Huerta, mostly to see if he was all right. In my truest heart, I knew there would be a selfish component to the visit as well. Being tortured by an insane man because he was stealing blood would quite likely put a strain on our working relationship. There was a very real possibility that, after tonight, I'd have to find a new source of blood, which would be far more problematic than just dealing with a crazy man.

Luckily, I didn't get too far into a building anxiety spiral before my eyes fell upon the familiar blue glow of a Slurp Stop gas station sign. It was a bit run down, but the lights were on and I could see a clerk standing at the counter, visibly bored as he tapped away at his phone's screen. I hurried across the street, stepping into the station and causing the small bell overhead to let out a shrill jingle.

The clerk glanced up from his phone. "Welcome to Slurp Stop, how can I—holy shit!" His eyes went wide and the phone fell from his hand, clattering to the floor. "Hang on, dude, I'll call an ambulance."

For a moment, I just stared at him, genuinely puzzled. What on earth was he talking about? Then it hit me: his vantage point let him see me from the side, which meant he was at least catching a glimpse of the blood-stained tears in the back of my shirt and sweater vest. The wounds had already closed—we vampires are known for our rapid healing—but the evidence of the shooting still remained. Add in that I have the tell-tale pale pallor of a vampire, and it probably looked like I'd been shot and was on the verge of bleeding out.

"Oh, oh no, no, no." I held up my hands, though I have no idea why. It just seemed like the right motion to try and reassure him. "I'm fine. Well, not *fine* fine, I do need to use your phone if it's okay, but this is . . . for a costume party." We were nowhere near Halloween, so I'm not certain what on earth made me feel like this was an acceptable excuse for wearing a torn and bloody shirt. Strangely enough, though, it worked, and he began to nod, looking less like he was on the verge of fainting.

"Are you going as a shooting victim?" Now that the emergency had passed, he sounded more annoyed than bothered. Guess he didn't enjoy being made to think that someone on death's door had just stumbled in during his shift.

"Sure. It was what I could throw together at the last minute." The rest of the tension finally left his body; evidently, that was a sentiment he could comprehend. A small bell, different from the one over the door, drew his eyes away from mine as a pair of headlights flashed through the window. A beat-up sedan was pulling into the nearest pump, no doubt refueling for its own late-night adventures.

"Hang on." The clerk reached under the counter and hefted up a phone book that was at least three years old, a fact which would have been more concerning if Charlotte Manor hadn't been a Bed and Breakfast for several decades. He spun a large phone with a curly cord over from behind the register and pushed it to the edge of the counter. "I think I'm supposed to make you buy something before you can use this."

"That would be problematic," I admitted. "I was . . . let's say mugged, a few minutes ago. It's why I don't have my own phone in the first place."

"Sort of figured." The clerk sighed, then nodded to the phone and the book. "It's cool, man. No one really cares about what happens on the night shift."

"Thank you so much." I rushed forward, picking up the massive tome of thin pages and flipping through them. The sooner I found Charlotte's number, the sooner I could alert the others, and the sooner Krystal could get the proper authorities after that psycho. I was only inconvenienced by bullet wounds, but the next person he went after, parahuman or not, might not be so lucky.

This time, the bell I heard was the one for the door, though I didn't find that particularly odd. Someone buying gas would have to pay for it, obviously. The sound of what movies had told me was a shotgun being pumped did prick my attention, however. Even then, I might have been able to convince myself it was just a robbery, if not for the scream of "Die, you monster!" that came just before the gunshot.

I didn't bother glancing behind me; instead, I hurled myself over the counter, tackling the clerk to the ground in the process. Quick I was, I still felt some of the shotgun's blast on my leg as we fell, but the more vulnerable flesh of the clerk remained mercifully unmarred.

"Shit! I'll give you the money. You just had to ask!" Fundamentally misunderstanding what was happening (and really, who could blame him?), the clerk was yelling from our prone position even as he worked to get out from under me.

I took the opportunity to glance at one of the many anti-shoplifting mirrors that provided a comprehensive view of the store from the counter. Sure enough, it was my hunter, looking even more angry and deranged than when I'd given him the slip. He pumped the shotgun again, sending a spent casing tumbling to the ground, and I had to wonder how much he knew about forensic science. Leaving evidence all over like that, he'd soon have the regular police on him as well. And given that he'd just shown a willingness to bring down bystanders, that didn't bode well for those who came to collect him.

"I thought you didn't kill humans!" At this point, my mind was racing, trying to figure out how he'd located me and, more importantly, how to get away. At least if I could make him talk, I might buy a few seconds to work things out.

"I don't. Not intentionally." He wasn't yelling his replies, just stating them like cold facts, which only served to make me more worried. "But every war has casualties. Better one lost now than all the others you'd kill."

And now the clerk was staring at me, and my bloody shirt, in a whole new light. Hopefully, he'd write this all off as the insane screams of two mentally ill people who'd wandered into his gas station. That was the best case scenario for him, at least.

"You keep saying things like that, but I don't hurt anyone. I'm just an accountant!"

"I know what your kind does. I've seen it. Save your lies for the Devil, monster." Now I could hear the emotion in his voice—fury and loss twisted together like coiled serpents around his heart. That was when I knew, for sure and for certain, that no amount of talk would get through to him. Not from me, anyway. I needed to get him out of here and away from the clerk, lest he decide to torture someone for the sin of helping me.

"When I get up, you need to sneak out of here," I whispered to the clerk. "I'll buy you time, but you have to *go*. Understand?"

There must have been someone in the heavens looking out for me, because the clerk nodded his head and then flipped his position around, ready to move.

Moving slowly, because not even I was sure I could survive a shotgun blast to the head, I emerged from behind the counter with my hands held up. With one large step, I moved on top of the counter, then slid down the front, ending up with only a few feet between me and the hunter. He watched me with those same wild eyes, never letting a single one of my motions escape his gaze. That was exactly what I wanted, though, as it meant he wasn't watching as the clerk crawled along the floor, keeping below displays and making his way toward the back of the gas station.

"What's your name?" I'll be honest, even I'm not sure what I was hoping to accomplish, I just wanted to create noise in order to muffle the clerk's escape attempt. My ears were primed, tracking his every movement until he was safe, which would be my cue to run for it. That said, I wanted to be the only one aware of that movement, which is why I started up the small talk again.

"Trying to befriend me now? To weave a new set of lies?" His finger grew tighter on the trigger.

"Every man deserves to know the name of their executioner," I said, though, looking back, I'm almost certain I stole the line from an old noir film. Like I mentioned earlier, I was very much just running on whatever popped into mind.

"Maybe so, but you're not a man, you're—"

"A monster? You know, we don't really like that word. Lot of connotation that purposely paints us in a negative light. Some consider it a very pointed insult."

"I'll be sure to keep that in mind. When I kill the next one." He took a step closer to me, keeping the gun steady. "My name is Colin. If there's an afterlife for you things, be sure to tell the others I sent you there."

"Nice to meet you, Colin. I'm Fred." Here, a mix of fear, worry, and habit convalesced into my defaulting to professionalism. I could hear the clerk getting to his feet from across the station; it was almost time to act.

"A real pleasure, Fred." He began to lift the gun, no doubt lining up a shot with my skull. "Time for you to die."

And just like that, everything suddenly went black.

4.

IT TOOK A MOMENT FOR ME TO REALIZE
that my life hadn't ended for the second time, and that
my head was still rightly attached to my shoulders. The
clerk, that wondrous little slacker, hadn't just run out the
back, he'd also killed the power on his way, plunging the
entire gas station into darkness. For the hunter, that was
a serious issue, but vampires are made to be nocturnal. If
anything, our vision in darkness is better than in light. I
seized on the moment of confusion and darted to the side,
out of the area where he'd been preparing to open fire.

The report of the shotgun blast made it clear that I hadn't moved a moment too soon, as the hunter heard me racing through the station and realized his moment of hesitation had cost him the opportunity. Another shot, this one wild, obliterated a display of beef jerky twenty feet to my left. He was aiming blind, but eventually his eyes would adjust and I'd be in trouble again. Best to go while the going was good.

I burst through the front door, hitting it so hard I shattered the glass and knocked the metal frame out of the wall. Another shot and the sound of more breaking glass told me that he'd been able to follow at least the basics of my movement. I was about to start racing down the street again when my eyes fell upon the beat-up sedan that had pulled into the gas station. While I didn't know how he'd managed to find me, this was obviously how he'd been able match my vampiric running speed. If I could disable his ride, I might be able to shake him for good.

It would have been a simple matter half a year earlier, when a drop of dragon's blood was augmenting my strength to incredible levels. Then, I likely could have flipped the whole thing over, or put a fist through the engine. Vampire strength on its own wasn't quite up to that level, however, so I was forced to take a far more unpleasant option.

Darting to the side, I raced up to one of his tires, opened wide, and sank my fangs into the rubber. While I usually considered keeping my sense of taste a true blessing, at that moment I'd have traded all the fine cooking and wine in the world to have a dead palette. I'd bitten into fire extinguishers that were less disgusting than the mouth full of tire I had to chew on. If I were able to throw up, I doubtlessly would have, but since vampires lack that reaction, I instead pulled back, ripping out a massive chunk of tire and then spitting it to the ground. Awful as it had been, my goal was accomplished; there was no way he was going anywhere until he got a new tire, and by then I'd be long gone.

The sound of footsteps on broken glass alerted me that he'd left the station, so I didn't waste any more time. Keeping clear of the pumps, because he definitely seemed like someone crazy enough to shoot at gasoline containers, I began another sprint, running as hard and as fast as I could away from Colin the hunter. I kept up the pace for a solid ten minutes, ignoring the strange stares of the few people out and about as I whipped by them at inhuman speeds. While I usually preferred discretion at all costs, it was definitely taking a back seat to survival.

Finally, I slowed down and tried to get my bearings. This section of Winslow at least looked a little familiar, and I realized that I'd run to a part of town not far off from Richard Alderson's office. Ordinarily, that would have been as good as salvation, since the local head of the therianthropes (the general term for all were-creatures) was a client and a friend who certainly would have offered me shelter. Unfortunately, he, along with his young daughter Sally, were also guests at Krystal's surprise party, which by now had likely kicked off, cake or no. I could try and approach the office anyway, but most therians had a bit of suspicion as far as vampires were concerned. My kind had a bad history of feeding off therians to increase our own power, so I was tolerated only due to my usefulness to Richard.

Of course, there was always the possibility that Gideon, the King of the West, was still in the office. I was never really sure where I stood with him, though. The ancient dragon who masqueraded as a child didn't appear to loathe me, but I wasn't certain he'd intervene on my behalf, either. And if I strolled up to the front doors with a madman on my tail, that could put the other therians in danger. There was no way they were going to look kindly on that kind of stunt. But I might be able to talk someone into letting me use a phone, which was still my best bet at salvation.

Eventually, I decided to start heading in that direction, keeping my eyes open for better options. I didn't want to endanger another innocent person, but I still had no idea how to get to Charlotte Manor outside of using the highways, and someone racing down the road in that public of a spot was bound to be noticed. Scary as Colin the crazed hunter was, I still preferred him to Krystal's Agency being pissed that I put parahumans in the public eye. They were not well known for their kind or forgiving nature.

As the sound of my loafers echoed through the empty street, I fell into something of a pensive state, my mind no doubt trying to find some solid ground after braving the tidal wave of crazy that was my night so far. I imagined how nice it would be to finally make it back to Charlotte Manor, where everything in the world I cared about currently was. It was strange to think that all of my friends and loved ones were gathered together right now, safe and happy and nowhere near the danger that was bloodying my clothes piece by piece. The oddness was not that I begrudged their being out of harm's way—it was a far cry better than seeing them in peril—but because it was usually those friends who got me into trouble in the first place. Tonight, however, was completely my own doing. My arrangement with a hospital had been the clue Colin used to find me. If I'd never gone to my high school reunion, never met Krystal and by extension everyone else, this still would have been happening. And part of me wondered, without those friends constantly exposing me to some measure of adventure, how would the old Fred have handled things?

Truth be told, I didn't think he would have survived that first encounter. Even if they weren't actually here at the moment, the experiences my odd little family had given me were what kept me alive. It made me long to be back with them all the more, and I finally noticed that I'd unconsciously quickened my step. I was hurrying toward Richard's building, carried by feet that were too ready to be done with the evening to fear being turned away at the door.

With no other real options, I decided that perhaps it was best just to roll the dice. I needed help, there was no shame in admitting that, and without his car, the odds of Colin tracking me were negligible. Even if he did somehow know where I went, at most he'd have cause to think I went to a big building full of offices, and one garish club, to try and use their phone. At least, that was the thought process I hoped he'd have.

I could see Richard's building when I was suddenly spotlighted in the headlights of a car pulling out from the road in front of me. My body tensed, ready for Colin to point a gun out the window or try to run me down, but then I noticed the bright yellow color of the vehicle and realized it was just a cab, probably taking someone home from a late night at the bar.

Unfortunately, my tense body turned out to be smarter than my logical brain as the tires beneath the cab began to spin and it lurched forward, trying to turn me into nothing more than a smear on the road. As it raced toward me, I caught a glimpse of the man behind the wheel.

Sure enough, there were the mad eyes of Colin as he floored the accelerator, trying with all he had to run me over.

5.

WHILE IN LIFE MY REACTION SPEED WAS always somewhere between "abysmal" and "for the love of heaven don't let Fred hold anything too valuable," the turn to undead had sharpened my reflexes significantly. Granted, they were nowhere near as potent as they would have been if I were even remotely physically gifted when alive, but sometimes all you need is good enough. In this case, good enough was allowing me to leap out of the way of an oncoming taxi cab as it careened toward me, only dodging the bumper's left corner by a few inches.

The screech of tires filled the air as Colin jerked the wheel around, trying to get another run at me, but now that the element of surprise was gone, he had no hope of outmaneuvering me. I began to race up the street again, when a sound unlike any gun I'd ever heard filled the air. Pain, dull and muted but still present, filled me as I looked over at my previously unshot shoulder. Now, the tip of a large metal claw was sticking out, smaller tines already dug into my flesh. Unbidden memories of watching nature documentaries filled my head as I recognized the iconic shape.

"Did you just harpoon me?"

"Modified it a little to cling on to you slippery bastards." Colin was leaning out the window, spear gun in hand, and that was when I saw the length of metal cord running from the back of my shoulder to the butt of the gun. Not wasting any time, Colin jerked it in, bracing the gun against something unseen inside, and threw the taxi into reverse.

While I might have physically been able to react in time, I was mentally still processing the fact that someone had *harpooned* me in the middle of the street, which was why I didn't understand what Colin was doing until the cord pulled taut and my feet went out from under me. I bounced off the road once, then twice, then finally got my feet under me and ran along rather than be dragged. Had Colin floored it again, not even I would have been able to keep pace, but he seemed content to keep the speed manageable. He was leading me, trying to get me to a place without as much room to run.

I tried to pull out the harpoon, but every time I reached for it Colin accelerated, knocking me off balance if not outright sending me sprawling. It still might have been manageable, even with the shifting speeds; however, my own regeneration was working against me. The wound around the spear had almost completely sealed up, meaning that instead of just pulling it back out through the same area, I had to try and rip apart my own resilient vampire flesh.

Much as I disliked Colin, I couldn't say he hadn't come up with an effective method for ensnaring vampires.

We didn't travel far, only a few blocks down the road. Colin backed the cab into an alley behind a closed noodle shop I'd loved to order from before they went out of business, and killed the engine. He stepped out from the cab, dark coat still flapping, showing off the wide array of weapons he had tucked about inside. The spear gun wasn't one of those, as he left it wedged in the cab even as he stepped away. I was still on a line, and unless I found a way to yank the harpoon out or drag an entire cab along with me, he'd finally managed to take running away off the table.

"You are a tricky one," Colin noted, pulling out his pistol again. "Silver has stopped every vampire I've dealt with, so why didn't it work on you?"

"Kind of a long story, and honestly, I doubt you'd believe me." My hands fumbled with the harpoon, tugging at it as I tried to get free. The hooks were made to keep me from pulling it back out, which meant forward was the only option. Of course, then I'd still have a metal rope running through me, and I wasn't sure my hands alone could snap something like that. There was the option of biting through it—I'd met very little a vampire's fangs couldn't pierce—but that was a lot of steps to freedom, and Colin wasn't going to wait patiently while I did them all.

"You're right, there; I'd never believe one of your lies." He reached into his coat with his free hand and pulled out a small squirt bottle, like the kind that go on bikes for long rides. "I've hunted a couple of your kind already, but you are far and away the worst of the lot. At least the others had the decency to own what they are. You, you burrowed into society like a tick, pretending to be normal, to be human. You tried to infiltrate us, and that makes you much too dangerous to live, even long enough to interrogate."

"There is another, far more logical explanation," I pointed out. "I lived in an apartment because it's my home, I bought my blood because I didn't want to hurt people, I kept working a normal job because I love what I do. This is just me. I'm not a monster, just a guy whose life took an unexpected turn."

"Whoever you might have been is dead. I know what lives inside you creatures, and there's no goodness there. Just death and blood." He popped the top off the bottle and took a sniff, his nose recoiling slightly.

"Funny, by my count, you're the one who shot at an unarmed clerk, tortured a doctor, and, I'm assuming, stole a cabbie's car at gunpoint." My hand rested on the top of the harpoon. Maybe I didn't need to bother with the rope; if I just popped the hooked part off, I could yank the rest out and get free. That was still no easy task, but it seemed more viable than biting through the metal rope. And, more importantly, it seemed faster, which was starting to feel like a very important element in this encounter.

"Sometimes, you have to be a monster to a kill a monster." Colin stepped forward, gun at the ready, and squirted me with the contents of the bottle. Even if I didn't have an incredible sense of smell, I'd have recognized the scent immediately: gasoline. He squeezed the bottle until it only spit out droplets and empty wheezes, then dropped the plastic container to the ground.

"Have you ever noticed that not once, despite everything you've done tonight, have I attacked or even tried to make a threatening move toward you?" Panic was slipping back into my voice, and with good reason, because while I might be immune to silver, there was no reason I would have any such resistance to fire. I knew for a fact that vampires could burn to death; it was the one death I'd witnessed up close and personally. Though, at the time, Krystal had been the one doing the burning, and the vampire in question was not one I'd miss.

"You sell the lie well, but I'm not going to be fooled." Colin reached back into his coat and pulled out a silver lighter, the old-fashioned kind without safety measures to keep it from burning without a thumb on the plunger. Behind him, I noticed a shadow move beyond the taxi. It was difficult even for my eyes to see, though, and I wasn't sure it had even been real.

"Colin, please listen to me, you're making a big mistake. I get that you hate vampires, I really do, and I don't know what you've had to do to survive before this, but what you're doing right now is murder. Beyond that, it's stepping into a world you *really* don't want to be a part of. Please, go turn yourself into the cops, do your time for the car theft and the gas station shooting, and then go on to live a normal life."

"That's a unique way to plead for your life, I'll give you that," Colin replied. He flicked the lighter and a bright orange flame sputtered forth from the top. I took hold of the hook, feeling the sharp blades cut through my palms as I readied to try with all my might to snap it off. This move was a gamble, but it was the best one I could make. If I managed to get clear, there had to be a way to end this without anyone getting hurt. I just needed to think harder.

"You really don't get it," I told him. "It's not my life I'm pleading for. If you do this, there's no going back. And the people who'll be coming for you don't share my tendency to shy away from violence."

"Why would I want to go back? Especially with such a bright, warm future ahead of me." Colin reared back to toss the lighter, and I pushed down with all my might on the top of the hook. It bent down at a sharp angle, but refused to break, and in that instant, I knew I was dead.

As it turned out, however, Colin was no more successful with his toss than I with my escape attempt, as a sharp, sudden blow struck him across the back of the head. He crumpled to the ground, the lighter falling through the air for only a second before a pale, well-manicured hand snatched it up and snapped it shut.

"Wow, that guy seemed like a real asshole." The voice of my savior was soft, with undercurrents of an accent that had long since been worn away by time. She had dark hair trimmed to just above her shoulders, sported a pantsuit that would have fit right in at any office in America, and was as pale as a sheet. If that weren't enough, she flashed a small grin, just large enough for me to see an extended incisor at the top of her mouth.

For the first time since my own maker had tried to kill me, I was in the presence of another vampire.

6.

A SLIGHT GROAN BROKE THE SILENT TENSION between this new vampire and me as Colin shifted on the ground. He was still unconscious, and given the amount of blood coming from his head, it would be some time before he was fully recovered. Actually, unless he had some sort of parahuman ability I hadn't noticed, an attack like that would leave him with neck, if not brain, damage. It's hard to understand just how fragile humans are until you stop technically being one.

"Sorry about that. Let's finish this jackass all the way off." The woman leaned down, mouth opening wider as her fangs began to extend even further.

"Stop!" I darted forward, spraying gasoline from my flailing limbs as I hurried to put myself between my savior and the hunter who had tried to kill me.

"Oh, my apologies. That was rude of me." She stopped, still bent halfway toward his unconscious form, then began to rise once more. "You're the one he attacked and stabbed, of course you should get to have the privilege. Not to mention, it looks like you could use the blood."

She had me there; the hooked head of the harpoon was bent but still lodged in my chest, tethering me to the car. What's more, my efforts to rip it off had reopened the wound, which was slowly oozing a darker blood than normal. I mentioned before that vampires heal exceptionally well, but as I'd begun to learn, all magic came with a cost. For us, it was blood. Just like a human burned calories for energy, we burned blood, and the more strenuous the activity, the more it consumed. After racing around town and healing several gunshot wounds, I was feeling more than a bit peckish. A few nips from Colin's neck and I'd be topped off, able to easily free myself and heal up.

"Neither of us is drinking from him." The words were a little more forceful than I'd meant them to be, and the female vampire regarded me more carefully. I quickly tried to explain myself.

"I mean, we need to wait for the authorities. The agents. He's obviously suffering from trauma or mental illness, and much as I might like to return the favor for this harpoon in my shoulder, I think it's for the best all-around if we let due process handle this."

She chuckled a little, a slightly higher pitch than I was expecting from her speaking voice. "Mind if I ask your name?"

"It's Fredrick Fletcher. But most people call me Fred."

"Fredrick, a classic name. I rather like those. I am Lillian." Without warning, she dipped her head and did a small formal bow. From the way her eyes went wide and she quickly sprang back up, I had a feeling it was more out of habit than deference.

"Well, Fred," Lillian continued. "This is the due process. This man, this human, tried to kill you. Have you committed any crime against him or his kin?"

"I . . . I don't think so. Not that I'm at all aware of."

"That doesn't surprise me; I've heard tales of a lone hunter going after our ilk lately. It was on my to-do list, some ways after tonight's meeting with the therians. At any rate, he tried to take your life, and as an Undead American, that means his life is yours to end. No muss, no fuss, no need for any *agents*."

Lillian spat that last word out, which didn't come as much of a surprise. Since I'd come to the parahuman world as an outsider, and my first friend in it was an agent, I hadn't been given the indoctrination of fear that a lot of others had. Truthfully, at first, I hadn't understood why everyone was so afraid of someone like Krystal. Then I saw Quinn, my maker, try to kill her. That sole experience had taught me that, if anything, people weren't afraid enough of agents.

"So, Colin's life is mine to take, right?" I asked, making sure I understood the minutia of what was happening. That's the thing about living in a country partly founded by parahumans: we do have rules about how things go, and arbitrary as they often felt, I knew that they mattered. Because agents existed specifically to deal with those who broke those rules.

"Correct," Lillian assured me.

"Then I choose not to take it. I spare him. And since he never even saw you, let alone fired a shot, I don't see that you have any similar claim. If you kill him, it's murder."

Bathed in the glow from the taxi's headlights, swaddled in the sounds of its still barely running engine, Lillian and I stared at each other for a long while. If she made this violent, I was done for. Even if I was normally a match for other vampires, which I wasn't, an evening of getting the utter crap kicked out of me had left me battered and weary. Unless Lillian was somehow more averse to violence than myself, a notion which Colin's bleeding head easily dispelled, she'd take me down in seconds. Hell, she was still holding the lighter, which meant she didn't even really need to get her hands dirty.

"You surprise me," Lillian said, speaking at last. "Not with your softness—you are far from the first doe someone has tried to turn into a wolf—but that you noticed that detail. I'm impressed. Most in your state wouldn't be capable of keeping such a calm head. Unfortunately for you, and this hunter, there is one flaw in your argument. I am a vampire, and he is a criminal. That much I heard him confess myself. By the law, that means he is fair game for me to feed upon, and while I'll certainly try not to kill him, accidents do happen. So tell me, how will you save the hunter this time, Fredrick?"

I'm not proud of how long it took, but that was when it finally dawned on me that Lillian didn't actually care if Colin died or not. Somewhere in the discussion, he'd become inconsequential. What she was interested in was me, or rather, if I could stop her from killing him. This was a game to her. Brains or brawn, she wanted to see what I was made of. Knowing that, I realized I only had one move left. I needed to go for a high stakes gambit.

"I guess I can't stop you," I told her, but even as I spoke, I began to back away. "Just, give me a few seconds to get clear first. I really don't want to be close enough to see what happens to you."

Her brow creased. This was not a method she'd been anticipating, because why on earth would she? It didn't really make sense, but if I shuffled the facts around fast enough, she might not notice that.

"What do you expect to happen? The hunter is down. I would easily sense if he'd awakened."

"Oh yeah, Colin looks down for the count. In fact, I think he needs some serious medical attention. But see, nuts as that hunter is, he's also shown himself to be really smart. He found out what I was by staking out my blood supply. He took away my car and communication before anything else. When I ran, he kept finding me, and I still have no idea how he pulled that off. Not to mention his weapons. Silver, fire, all the classics, plus some ingenious stuff of his own." I tapped lightly on the hook sticking out of my chest to illustrate the point.

"I'm sure he was quite formidable, before I cracked him in the back of the head," Lillian said. Her brow was still creased, but she was starting to grow impatient. She thought I was stalling for time, instead of building up to something.

"Formidable, and suicidal," I corrected. "No concern for his own well-being what-so-ever. If I weren't . . . me . . . then there were several chances I could have used to kill him tonight. Tell me, someone like that—someone cunning and informed, with very little sense of self-preservation—doesn't that seem like the kind of man who would booby trap his own blood, just in case he lost? One last 'screw you' to the vampire that brought him down?"

That got her attention. She looked from me to Colin, to the blood slowly streaming from his forehead. "Silver is poisonous to humans as well."

"Not right away. They can have a lot of it in their system before it does them in. There would be long-term side effects, but that only matters for someone who expects to live through the year. And it wouldn't take much to hurt a vampire, especially from the inside." It took everything I had not to fidget, or break our eye contact, or give any other indication of just how full of shit I was. I had no idea how long a human could last with silver in their body, or what amount of it would get to the blood, or how it would impact a vampire who drank it. This was all speculation and conjecture, which is a nicer way of saying a complete wild guess. It was all I had, though.

My only hope—actually, Colin's only hope—was that Lillian didn't know any more about the subject than I did. She contemplated him again for a while, then walked over to me, moving slowly until she was only inches away.

"Fredrick Fletcher, you are an interesting one." Reaching out, she took the hook poking through my chest and snapped it clean off, almost effortlessly. I'd love to say the bend loosened it for her, but the implication was clear. She'd been partaking in more blood, probably even that of other parahumans, and was *much* stronger than I was. That's the most dangerous thing about vampires—when we drink the blood of other parahumans, we absorb part of their ability. The strength and regeneration of therians is apparently a popular favorite, and the exact reason why so many of Richard's staff look at me with distrust.

"Congratulations, Fredrick. You have saved this hunter's life. I have no claim to kill him unless I am feeding, and you make the proposition of ingesting his blood a bit more than I'd like to gamble. That said, this sort of behavior cannot go unpunished." Lillian walked back over to Colin, the hook of the harpoon clutched tightly in her hand. Her foot flipped him over, pointing his unconscious face toward the sky. Dragging the blade of the harpoon forcefully across her skin, she opened a small cut on her palm.

I realized what she was about to do only seconds before it happened, and by then, I was already too late. Lillian crouched down and pulled open Colin's mouth, letting a few drops of her blood fall into his throat. That done, she carefully lowered his head back to the ground and looked up at me.

"Did . . . did you just make him a vampire?"

Lillian snorted, and as soon as she did, her eyes widened again. It was a brief moment, but it helped dispel a lot of the tension in the air. She'd slipped for a moment, letting me see that at least some of this "creature of the night" routine was for show. But the snort was gone, her face solemn again, and I chose to let the incident pass without comment.

"Fredrick, you really need to learn more about your own people. A vampire must drink a human's blood, then give them some of their own in order for the change to occur. What I have offered is nothing more than a bit of magical booster, something to speed his healing along. Of course, if he does have silver in his system, that healing will be quite the painful experience. But he'll survive, and be none the worse for wear. Eventually."

Then she was up again, stepping over Colin and walking past me. From her pocket, she produced a small phone, one a bit sleeker than what I'd lost. Moving her thumb at exceptional speed, she clicked through several menus, tapped a few digital buttons, and offered the phone to me. "Something tells me you need this more than I do."

"Thanks. Let me just look up the number and make a quick call—"

Lillian was already walking off though, shaking her head as she did. "Keep it; I'm due for an upgrade anyway. Plus, I wiped all the personal information. It's yours now, for as long as you like." She stopped, partway out of the alley, and looked out at the city of Winslow.

"You know, Fred, there are some interesting tales coming out of this city. Stories about one of our kind who's like no other. They say he brokered a peace with the therians, courted an agent, and that even the King of the West calls him by name. Part of why my clan has come is to try and broker a meeting with him, if he even truly exists. Should we succeed, I'll text that phone, perhaps even make an introduction. Someone like you could learn a lot from that sort of vampire."

Then she was gone—well, from the alley at least—but her words lingered long after her, even as I looked up the number for Charlotte Manor and finally called my friends. People were telling stories about me? And not only that, they were getting all the details screwed up. My stomach twisted into a bundle of nerves, though I was technically out of harm's way, and it wasn't hard to figure out why.

After several years as a vampire, I was finally beginning to get a sense of when there was trouble on the horizon.

7.

"WELL, THE BAD NEWS IS THAT YOUR CAR is going to need some serious work. It looks like Colin punched out a window and shot the engine when you ran off, which isn't surprising given the rage issues. Good news is that Bubba knows more than a few trustworthy mechanics, and the Agency is going to create an accident report where you aren't at fault for your insurance company." Krystal walked into the room, classically decorated and far from her style, not even pausing to kick off her boots before she dropped into bed next to me.

It hadn't taken long after the call for Krystal to show up, along with Bubba, Richard, and Amy all packed into her truck. Arch drove his own car—a surprisingly well-maintained Cadillac that was easily older than anyone other than its driver. They'd managed to arrive quickly, but not quite before Colin had woken up screaming. As it turned out, my insane theory had actually panned out, and Colin had been putting silver in his bloodstream. Amy assured me that, with vampire blood in his system, he'd make a full recovery, but the next few hours would be tough. Not even she could lessen the pain, however, since silver would work against her magic as well.

After that, things sort of became a blur. Arch took Colin into custody, shoving him in the back of the Cadillac after cuffing him; though, with how much pain the hunter was in, the cuffs might have been unnecessary. The rest of the harpoon was yanked out of me, and I was brought back to Charlotte Manor, where Albert, Neil, and Sally were all waiting. Charlotte slipped a glass of wine into my hand the moment I entered, and I said a silent prayer of thanks for the hospitality of the possessed house. The rest of the gang went to my apartment, apparently sweeping it for traps, of which they found a few, and getting my car towed out of the street.

I don't know how much time passed before Krystal returned, giving me a packet of blood from my fridge—silver free, she assured me—and escorting me up to her new room. There hadn't even been time to unpack yet, so it felt oddly foreign. Part of me wished for the familiarity of my own home, or even Krystal's old apartment, but that sentiment faded as soon as I remembered that I was probably in the safest spot in all of Winslow. Once that hit home, I sucked down my blood and simply took the news as it rolled in. The car was the latest bit, the last of the truly pragmatic stuff, and as Krystal sank deeper into the cushy mattress, I turned over to meet her gaze.

"What's going to happen to Colin?"

"Depends on Colin," Krystal said. "From what we've been able to dig up so far, the guy lost his family to a vampire attack a few weeks back. Watched everyone die, but managed to drive a silver knife into the head of his attacker when it was his turn to go. His prints matched the ones at a scene we'd been trying to figure out for a while. Anyway, seeing that kind of shit will drive most people off the edge, and he's no exception."

She reached over, gently touching the part of my shoulder where the harpoon had burst through. There was no scar to mark it; in fact, if not for the torn shirt and sweater vest, it would have been impossible to tell that anything had ever happened.

"He's not bad, though. Got a natural talent for this sort of stuff. Never seen someone try to *carpoon* a vampire before."

"How long you been waiting to use that?" I asked.

"Hours. Had to make sure you were okay first, or it would have been in bad taste." She grinned, but we'd been together long enough that I could see the worry behind her smile. I'd been in trouble tonight, and she wasn't there to protect me. I imagined that was a hard pill to swallow, especially for an agent.

"Anyway, if Colin can be reformed, taught to understand that not all parahumans are bad, then maybe he could work off some of his time with the Agency. If he can't, then the cops are going to easily locate the dude who shot up a gas station, carjacked a taxi, and I'm sure pulled off a lot of other illegal stuff on other nights."

"What if he tells people about vampires?" I asked.

"Let him. He's not the first, and he won't be the last. Prisons have psych wards too these days." Krystal let go of my shoulder, wrapped her hand around my torso, and tapped me gently on the back. "Have to put him in a good one though. He's crafty. Did you know there was a GPS tracker on your back? Stuck right into your sweater vest."

My mind drifted back to when I was first running away, after the silver bullet failed to stop me. I remembered those next few shots. Loud, but not nearly as powerful. I'd taken them to be normal bullets at the time, but a small tracker made a lot more sense.

"Guess that's one mystery solved. I was wondering how he kept finding me." On the subject of being found, my brain lit up with a sudden rush of forgotten concern. "Oh crap, Dr. Huerta, is he okay?"

"He's alive, and Amy is already talking with a few other local mages to get him fixed all the way up. They can even take away the memory, along with the rest of today, but so far he's been refusing it. Also . . . I think Dr. Huerta is done with the blood trade," Krystal said.

"Yeah. I sort of expected as much." A white business card was suddenly a few inches from my nose, clutched in Krystal's slender fingers. "What's this?"

"You're not the only vampire that prefers take-out. The Agency set up vendors centuries ago, ones who only buy blood at a fair rate. I never mentioned it, since they're a bit pricier than what your guy was charging, but it seems pretty relevant as things stand. And they have a speedy delivery option." She shook the card in front of me several more times, until I finally reached up and pulled it from her hand.

"They're Agency-approved?"

"It's better to say we keep an eye on them, and they know it," Krystal replied. "They probably fudge a lot of paperwork here and there, but they're smart enough not to try any big stuff. That one has a particularly good reputation. I asked around, in case it ever came up."

"Thank you." I slipped the card into my wallet, making a note to call them tomorrow. After I'd gotten a new phone. Much as I appreciated the assistance, I wasn't sure I wanted to use a device that someone else had had such recent access to. It seemed senselessly dangerous. I put the wallet away and pulled out the phone, prompting a bit of throat-clearing from Krystal.

"So . . . about the vampire who helped you."

"Lillian," I said. "She said she was here for a meeting with the therians. I assume that means Richard."

"Right. Well, we ran it down, and that part is mostly true. She's part of a vampire clan that's petitioning to meet with Richard. They want to move into town, but since Winslow is home to a lot of powerful therians, their badass leader, and the King of the West, coming in without at least an introduction would be a dicey proposal."

"Let me guess, I only got away with it because I never hunted and kept my head down?"

"More or less," Krystal said. "These things matter more with people who make a lot of waves, of which you are not one. Plus, you're just one vampire. If therians see a whole clan suddenly appear without warning, they're likely to think that the vampires are up to something. Maybe even an invasion to wrest control of the city. They tend to deal with those threats fast and hard."

"Sort of encouraging that they want to go through proper channels, then," I told her.

"We'll see what we see." Krystal shrugged, as if we were talking about whether our pizza would come with the proper toppings. It was hard to blame Krystal, though. While it seemed like a very dangerous situation to me, for her it likely wasn't even a blip on the radar. I never dug too deep into what it was to be an agent, but the few glimpses I'd seen had left me with an appreciation for the scope of their duties, and their abilities.

"Lillian said there was another reason they wanted to talk with Richard." I spoke carefully, not quite sure how best to broach this subject. In truth, I was still wrapping my own head around it, trying to convince myself that there was something I'd misunderstood. "She said they'd heard tales about a vampire who lived here. One who was on good terms with the therians, and dating an agent. Who was even not hated by the King of the West. I'm . . . I'm not crazy, am I? They're talking about me."

She looked at me for a long moment, then leaned in and kissed me gently on the forehead. "Yes and no, Freddy. Yes, parahumans love to talk—actually, who I am kidding, they love to *gossip*. But you know how those things go. Someone tells the story of catching a big fish, they leave out the hours of failure and trying different baits before the final success and cut right to the triumph. People chop the stories down to the interesting bits, pulling out the context. And without that context, some of the friendships you've made and things you've accomplished can seem almost inexplicable. So yes, the stories are about you in the sense that you have done those things, but no, they're not about the Freddy that we all know and love. Did she even realize you were the one she wanted to meet?"

"Not in the slightest," I replied. "In fact, she said someone like me could learn a lot from a vampire like that."

"See, there you go. A few rumors flying around, but nothing to worry about. Kind of fun, in a way." She reached up and poked my glasses, an affectation of familiarity and comfort rather than necessity. "You're your own Clark Kent."

"Except that my Superman is made up of gossip and mis-told stories," I pointed out.

"And you don't have the cape," Krystal added.

"Whew, so you didn't search my closet that carefully." It was a joke, but Krystal's smile faded a bit.

"About that, Freddy. You can't go home for a few days," she said. "Amy and I found more than a couple of booby traps in your apartment. Now, we're both good, but given how resourceful Colin was, we decided it was safer to get the whole place professionally swept. Not to mention, anything we find might help us figure out who else Colin has attacked. Anyway, the long and short of it is that, for the next few days, your place is a crime scene."

"That's more than a little inconvenient." I flipped back over, looking at the wallpapered ceiling. "At least I can get a room from Charlotte."

"Oooooooor . . ." Krystal drew out the word as she laid her head on my shoulder, the one not stained with blood. "We could take a vacation. Sort of. Arch needs to borrow Albert and Neil for something, but I've got vacation time saved up. What do you say we tag along? Get out of town for a little bit, let everything get settled."

"I have a sneaking suspicion that this 'vacation' will just end with more peril, if Arch is taking Neil and Albert somewhere," I told her.

"It's not like that. This is networking. Arch thinks they'd do well to meet someone else who wields a Weapon of Destiny. No crimes need solving, no monsters need slaying. And if they did, the sheriff is more than capable of handling it."

"That's reassure—wait, sheriff? Where, exactly, are we going?"

Krystal looked up at me, a mischievous twinkle in her eye that I knew all too well meant things were about to get chaotic. "I'm going to take that as a 'yes.'"

A SHERIFF IN THE COUNTRY

1.

THE PLANE BOUNCED A BIT TOO ENTHUSI-
astically upon landing and I reflexively grabbed Krystal's hand. While I am nervous about many things, flying isn't one of them. At least, normal flying isn't. The tiny little mechanism we sat in, supported only by a set of twin propellers, had proven to be a different story, though. I'd thought it would be quaint when I first laid eyes on it, something a little more classic than the monstrous jets that carry people around like cattle. What I didn't realize is that having a jet that big lessens the impact of turbulence,

whereas in the small plane that brought me, Krystal, Arch, Albert, and Neil across the country, one could feel every single bump of turbulence along the way.

And there was a *lot* of turbulence between northern Colorado and east Texas. By the time the doors finally opened, showing me the beautiful freedom of a starlit night above, I nearly ripped my seatbelt in half vaulting out. Even if the sun had been shining, I might still have chanced it, preferring to burn to death in its deadly rays than risk another minute in those cramped, shaking quarters.

"Yeah, that's how most people react the first time they take this flight," Krystal noted, taking a much more sedate pace down the airplane's steep stairs, duffel bag slung over her shoulder. Albert was only a few steps behind, clad in his usual t-shirt and jeans, stringy hair pulled back tight. If not for the blade and gold hilt of a sword strapped to his back, there would be nothing to mark the passage of time since he first came to work for me. He was taking his time in the descent, helping Neil along. Of us all, the young mage was the only one without undead constitution or years of practice taking similar flights. He staggered down the stairs, still looking green in the face despite filling up no less than three "sanitation" bags during the flight. Though the two of us were rarely on good terms, my heart went out to him.

If vampires could vomit, I almost certainly would have matched his record.

Arch was the last to leave, pausing to say a few quick words to the pilot. No sooner had he gotten outside than he reached into the pocket of his dark, functional slacks and pulled out a pack of cigarettes. I'd never known anyone who smoked more than Arch, or took less joy in it. It was an especially curious affectation given how crisp and precise everything else about him was, from his close-cut hair to the carefully concealed weapons all over his body. My best bet was that it had something to do with his parahuman nature. As far I could tell, Arch looked human—a young human, at that—but given his reputation and status with the Agency, I knew there was something I was missing.

"Been too long," Arch said, making his way down the stairs. I wasn't sure if he was talking about the cigarette or our destination, though the former seemed far more likely.

As near as I could tell, we'd landed in an abandoned field. At the far edge, I could see a shack made of sheet metal, and the runway the plane had used was well-kept, but nothing about our surroundings marked this as an airport. Which was probably why we'd had to take a special plane from the Agency in the first place.

From the edge of the clearing, I picked up a pair of lights moving toward us. A car, or maybe a truck; hard to tell from so far off, even with my eyes. It would be a while before it arrived, so I wheeled around on Krystal.

"We're here."

"Very good, Freddy. That is what the landing means." She was being glib, knowing quite well what I was driving at and taking joy in stringing me along.

"I feel I've been a pretty good sport about this, especially when you told me that you wanted our vacation to take place in rural Texas, but we had a deal. Once we arrive, you're supposed to tell me what's so special about this place." I conjured my very best "I mean business" face, which only managed to draw a few giggles from her and a half-hearted snicker from Neil, who immediately had to cover his mouth.

"All they told me was that there was someone else with a weapon, and I should meet them," Albert offered. Unlike me, he didn't mind being kept in the dark. Of course, he'd also come here with a purpose. As someone who had drawn a Weapon of Destiny, Albert was trying to learn how to use it, as well as figure out what he wanted to do with it. Speaking to someone who was on the same path could offer him a lot of insight. He, Arch, and Neil all had good reason to come out to the boonies. I just couldn't fathom what was so special about this place that Krystal insisted I *had* to see it.

"My plan was to let you see the place for yourself, but fine, if you really want to be a spoilsport, I'll tell you." Krystal held up her hands and gestured to the empty fields. "Freddy, welcome to the edge of Boarback, Texas. One of only three openly parahuman settlements in all of the United States."

"Excuse me, open settlements?" While I had a hunch at what she was saying, it seemed more prudent to get confirmation.

"It's just what it sounds like," Arch jumped in. "Boarback is a town where parahumans live in the open. All of the inhabitants are either parahuman or regular humans that have been brought here intentionally. We keep it off maps, the roads to get in are almost impassable unless you know the secret routes, and everything around here is wiped from satellite imagery. No one accidentally discovers this town. And because of that, there's no hiding. Everyone can be exactly what they are."

"That's . . . incredible." While I wish I'd come up with something a bit more eloquent, at that moment my mind was simply reeling too much for me to state anything other than the most obvious prattle. A whole town, a civilization of parahumans who weren't trying to blend in with human society. Granted, I was a big fan of human society, and aside from the dietary restrictions and sunlight issues, considered myself very much a part of it. However, my time with Krystal had let me glimpse other sides of the parahuman world, beings who had to go to much greater extremes to blend in. I'd always assumed that was the only option presented to them, but now, I'd just taken a bumpy plane ride to one I'd never imagined.

"Incredible, and necessary," Krystal said. "Try as we might to make them, there are some parahumans who just refuse to keep a low profile. They aren't dangerous or anything; some do it by accident, others out of stubbornness. Point is, they don't deserve jail, but we can't let them wander around with humans, either. This was the compromise someone came up with in the early days. Boarback was the first, and when it worked, they added more."

"Many choose to live here, now. Prefer it to spending a life among a species that can only fear them." Arch finished his first cigarette, tucking it neatly into the box of ash and stubs he always carried, and immediately began another. In the distance, I could finally make out the shape of the approaching vehicle. Definitely a truck; though, given the terrain it was driving over, that seemed a practical choice.

"It's pretty incredible. Everything is parahuman friendly. All the buildings have enchanted glass, just for the sun allergic, and there are underground tunnels to get around during the day. The library is full of ancient tomes for mages to study—along with a healthy romance section, from the invoices I've seen—and all the different dietary needs are accounted for. The Agency makes monthly drops to ensure food sources are on hand." Krystal was actually rocking on her heels in excitement.

I'd initially thought she was dragging me along just for kicks, but the longer she spoke, the more I realized how much she genuinely loved this place.

"If there are that many parahumans, it seems like it would be hard to keep the peace." Neil slowly tried to let go of Albert and stand on his own. Despite a shaky start, he managed to stay on his feet. "Do you keep agents posted here all the time or something?"

Krystal shook her head, smiling so big I could almost see her back teeth. "No need. Boarback has its own police force; a sheriff and a couple of deputies. In fact, one of those deputies is who you're here to meet, Albert. Those two alone are more than enough to handle most of the trouble that crops up in a town this size. But if there's ever anything serious, the sheriff will step in and deal with it."

"Is he a former agent or something?" I asked.

"He's something, all right." Arch's words were muttered, not so soft that he was trying to conceal them, but soft enough to not be part of the conversation. Krystal reached over and punched her fellow agent in the shoulder before turning back to me.

"Don't mind Arch. He just doesn't like losing."

"It was hardly a fair fight," Arch said.

"When are any of your fights fair? Isn't that the first thing you teach rookies to expect?" Krystal leered at him willfully, until Arch turned away and silently took another drag from his second cigarette. "To answer your question, Freddy, no, I don't think Sheriff Thorgood was ever officially an agent, but he has a lot of ties to the Agency. We send our more problematic cases—people who've just turned and don't know how to control their power yet—out here for him to look after."

And with that, I finally realized why Krystal was so excited to show me this patch-of-nowhere town. "They sent you here, didn't they? This is where you first trained."

"Only until I got the hang of using my skills, and made peace with the whole 'devil living inside me' stuff. After that, they put me in the regular program. But I spent a while in Boarback, learning from the sheriff."

With near perfect timing, the truck finished its forward journey, coming to a halt approximately twenty feet away from us. The passenger door popped open, and a man stepped out. He was big, by normal standards; though, after meeting men like Richard, my scale was somewhat skewed. Visually, he wasn't terribly impressive, akin to a shorter, less muscular version of Bubba, and he wore a beige policeman's uniform, complete with matching cowboy hat. His stomach hadn't quite reached the point of lapping over his gun belt, but it was a battle that could be lost any day. Large hands spread out as he stretched his arms wide (revealing a gold sheriff's badge on his chest) and motioned to Krystal.

"Is that Agent Jenkins? Get over here and give your old teacher a hug."

That was all the prompting it took, as Krystal raced forward and the two embraced. It was surprisingly familial, a sentiment I didn't see in my girlfriend very often. Rather than a teacher, it looked like she was being bearhugged by an uncle. Finally, they released, and he began making his way around to the rest of us.

"Arch, you better finish that damn thing before you get in my truck, or I'll hitch you to back and let you run for it." He slapped Arch on the back as he spoke, nearly knocking the agent's cigarette from his hand. "And you must be Albert, the zombie who pulled out the Blade of the Unlikely Champion. Pleasure to meet you, son." He held out his big paw of a hand and Albert shook it, looking more like he was hanging on than participating.

"Which makes you Neil, the apprentice, sorry, journeyman learning from Mage Wells. That's some big shoes to fill; I hope you're working hard." He grabbed Neil's hand and gave it a shake as well, moving so fast that even the usually brooding necromancer didn't have a chance to come up with something glib to say.

I watched all these exchanges in sheer wonder, marveled by what a touch the sheriff had with people. Despite being in what could be argued was literally Nowhere, he lacked the same southern twang I'd gotten so accustomed to with Bubba. Instead, his accent was neutral, and hard to even grasp beneath the warmth and volume of his words. Hard as I tried to pin it down, there was just some sort of charisma about him that made the sheriff seem inherently likeable. Now *that* was an ability I wouldn't have minded getting when I went vampire.

"And that just leaves you, the vampire that I hear is dating one of my students." He turned toward me and closed the distance between us in only a few steps. For having such an ambling gait, he moved surprisingly fast. "Anyone Krystal trusts enough to bring around is good people in my book. Pleasure to meet you; I'm the sheriff of Boarback, Leeroy Thorgood."

"Fredrick Fletcher," I replied, reaching for his hand. "But most people call me Fred."

The moment Sheriff Thorgood took my hand, a whole new sensation washed over me. I've mentioned before about how a primal part of my vampire brain sees the world in terms of predators and prey, and how catatonic I went upon meeting Gideon, an apex predator, for the first time. This wasn't quite the same, in that I didn't start babbling or fall over. In fact, I don't think my instincts saw the sheriff as predator or prey. They didn't know what to make of him. He didn't fit anywhere into my base vampire understanding of the world. The one thing I did know about him, that I could feel rippling off the man in physical waves, was that he was *powerful*. And I say that having glimpsed the true capabilities of an ancient dragon.

"Glad to meet you." If Leeroy noticed my reaction, he didn't let it show. Instead, he gave my hand a few pumps, then released it and nodded to the truck. "Suns up in a few hours. Let's get your bags and head into town."

2.

DESPITE THE BLEAKNESS OF THEIR AIRPORT,
I was pleasantly surprised to find the town of Boarback to be more than ten houses and a general store that doubled as a church and gas station. If that sounds ridiculous, allow me to remind you that Krystal and I grew up in a rural farming town. While ours wasn't quite that bad, there were others not too far off that dearly wished they could get up to ten houses. Such was not the case with Boarback, however.

Instead, Sheriff Thorgood pulled his truck along dusty, nearly invisible roads, one after the other, until we broke through a tree line and into a scene that looked like it was stolen from the mid-1900s. We were staring down what appeared to be an old-fashioned main street, complete with a worn, brick-paved road. Shops lined the block on both sides, which was curiously absent of cars. A few were about, but nowhere near as many as I saw in Winslow on any given block.

Other roads, leading to businesses that were too large to fit on the central street, branched off at regular intervals. But what struck me immediately was a fact that I should have expected: nothing was a chain store. Every business I could see, from "Grixxle's Repair" to "Uros Massage and Spa" to a squat yellow building that just said "Diner" was obviously independent. It was sort of funny, to me at least, that there were thousands of people all over the nation who wanted to go back to the "good ole days," and here it was, exactly as described. Except for the fact that almost everyone who lived here was pulled straight from the myths and nightmares of humanity.

The second thing to strike me was how busy the town was, in spite of the late hour. Now, I know vampires and other undead are all mostly nocturnal by nature, but I hadn't expected that trait to apply to every parahuman. Yet here they were, walking up and down the street, waving at the truck as Sheriff Thorgood drove by. Many of them were humanesque, perhaps with an odd horn here or animal eyes there, but some were so far removed from human that I wondered how they would have ever gotten along in the normal world.

Four small creatures with green skin, batlike ears, and overalls were walking past a centaur who was scribbling furiously in a worn notebook. Near the edge of the road, a small blonde woman and her daughter were both holding hands with a furry brown parahuman who was at least ten feet tall. His hands were so big, in fact, that I realized they were holding his thick fingers. And I say "he" because a pair of gray slacks covered the lower part of his body, so I was assuming that was where modesty kicked in. Not too far off from the trio was something I could barely wrap my head around, a being who seemed to be formed entirely out of molding clay with its face pressed up against the window of a shop. And yes, I mean literally pressed, which was what gave away the malleable consistency of its brown body.

"Holy hell." For a rare change, Neil and I were in agreement, though he was the one who voiced the words. Albert seemed dumbstruck as well, all of us staring out the truck's open windows in what I would later realize was incredibly impolite gawking.

"I never realized there were so many types of parahumans," I said, finally marshalling some control of myself. "Even at CalcuCon, there wasn't this much variety."

"The cons are fun, but not everyone can travel easily." It might have been my imagination, but Arch seemed a bit grumpier than usual, probably because he'd been forbidden from smoking in the sheriff's truck. "Besides, those only attract parahumans looking to do business or meet up with others like them. They're little islands of community in a sea of pretending to be human. These people don't have that need. They're always connected to the parahuman world."

"Yeah, they are." Albert hadn't quite reached the point of hanging his head out the window, but I put a hand on his shoulder anyway, just in case. I understood the reaction. Even for beings like us, who could blend in with little effort, the strain of always pretending, always staying careful and aware, was like a weight we carried around.

As we drove up the road and pulled into the sheriff's office, I felt that weight lift for the first time in years. This wasn't a con where walls, tenuous and easily breached, had been erected to keep our secrets safe. Here, the world was truly kept at bay, and in this town, there was no need to pretend. We weren't the oddities. We were just . . . people.

Sheriff Thorgood killed the engine and hauled himself out of the car, the rest of us following his lead. The office was a brick building, larger than I'd initially expected. Then I remembered the size of the furry man in gray slacks, and suddenly I could see why space might be important here. We walked inside to find a large central room with three desks, and a row of five cells at the back of the building. None were occupied, though they all had fresh blankets and a pillow resting on them just in case. Near the rear of the room, a small television was tuned into a baseball game on mute. Evidently, we'd caught someone relaxing before we pulled up.

There were two, and only two, candidates for who might be the baseball fan. Standing in the center of the office area, like they'd been waiting for us, were a man and a woman, both dressed in the same beige uniform as Sheriff Thorgood. The man had dark, spiky hair with what appeared to be red highlights, along with a lean frame and a sharp stare. The woman seemed entirely human, save for her eyes, which were bright yellow and a little too big for her face. Leeroy stepped forward and clapped his hands on both of their shoulders as he made introductions.

"Folks, I'd like you to meet the rest of the Boarback Sherriff's Department. The fellow who puts too much mousse in his hair is Deputy Ixen, though you can just call him Nax. And this bright-eyed young woman is Deputy Saunders, though she just goes by Sable. For that matter, I don't want to hear anyone calling me sheriff. I'm just Leeroy to friends. Nax, I think you're the only one who has met Agent Jenkins."

"Just Krystal, I get enough of that 'Agent Jenkins' shit in the field." Krystal nodded at Nax, who met her gaze for only a brief moment. "Good to see you again, kid. Uniform suits you better than cuffs."

"Joining Krystal today is her fellow agent, Arch; her boyfriend Fred; and the pair that came to meet Sable, Neil and Albert." Leeroy pointed at each of us as he went down the list of names, making sure Nax and Sable knew who was who.

"So, you've got one too." Sable started forward, coming close to Albert and then walking a bit past him to check out the sword strapped to his back. The black-and-gold scabbard that matched the hilt of his blade rested there, fixed in a harness that Arch had designed himself. Since moving to Winslow, the agent had been training my assistant on proper sword-wielding three evenings a week, and every other weekend. While no one was asking Albert to go out and start picking fights with his blade, it was agreed all around that him being at least somewhat proficient was in everyone's best interest.

"Blade of the Unlikely Champion," Albert told her, slowly drawing his sword from its sheath. The weapon almost hummed as it moved through the air, more magic than steel, or so we'd been told. Given that I'd seen him cut through the very enchantment that held a chimera together, turning it back into its base animals, I had no reason to doubt the assessment of Albert's blade.

"That is a pretty one." Sable walked across the room and reached behind one of the desks, pulling out a large single-bladed axe. It, too, was strapped into a harness, and she effortlessly pulled the weapon free from the straps and cover concealing its blade. "Mine is the Axe of the Forsaken Child. Obviously, it doesn't have the gentlest of requirements to wield, but it packs a hell of a wallop."

She spun the weapon easily, her years of training visible in the fluid grace of her movements. Bringing it to a stop, the bone-white blade extended outward, she moved the head of her axe closer, bit by bit, to the humming steel of Albert's sword. Carefully, she tapped the edge of his blade against her own, and a soft, melodic tone echoed around us.

"Looks like these two get along." Sable pulled back her axe and slipped it into its harness once more. "Sometimes they can be finicky, if the destiny of each wielder is in conflict. Good news, Albert. Looks like you and I aren't meant to fight each other."

"I didn't even realize that was a possibility," Albert said.

"All of these things are trying to drag their owners somewhere," Sable replied. "How much we let them is on us, but there are many out there that are working toward different ends. When they touch, you don't get a pretty chime, trust me."

"Now that everyone, animated and otherwise, has been introduced, what's say we go get some grub?" Leeroy suggested.

"Actually, I wouldn't mind dropping off my bags and showering first," Krystal interrupted. "I was sitting a little closer to Neil than the rest of us on that flight."

The necromancer's face went flush and he lowered his head. "Sorry."

"Not a problem. I've gotten far worse on me in the line of duty. Still, wouldn't say no to a good scrubbing."

"All right, we'll go to the inn, let everyone unwind and unpack, and then off to the diner," Leeroy acquiesced. "Tonight's special is chicken fried steak, and I'd have to arrest myself for the crime of letting you folks miss it if they run out."

"It's a CFS night? Hot damn, I'll shower fast." Krystal grabbed my hand and dragged me back out into the street, where she began shoveling the bags at me so fast that I didn't get the chance to ask her why she was taking things *out* of the truck if we were about to leave the station.

3.

AS IT TURNED OUT, THE REASON KRYSTAL had dragged all our bags out of Leeroy's truck was that there was no need to get back in the vehicle to reach the inn. The Bristle Inn, Boarback's one and only place of lodging, was within walking distance of the station. In fact, everything within the town square was walkable. While cars were needed to reach some of the neighborhoods and single homes further away, once a traveler was on the main street—which I learned was actually called

Sunshine Lane—they needed only shoe leather to make it to any other destination.

The walk to the inn took around ten minutes, but it would have been five if Neil's slower gait hadn't caused everyone else to match his pace. Part of the comparative slowness was that he was one of the few humans in the group, magic-slinging skills notwithstanding, but it was also due to the fact that studying tomes of ancient magic wasn't an activity that did much for cardio.

I'd expected the Bristle Inn to be like Charlotte Manor, quaint and dated, but in fact, it turned out to be one of the more modern buildings in town. Once we got to our room, a spacious area with a king-sized bed and a flat-screen, Krystal had explained that since Boarback got more than a few visitors in the form of agents and general parahumans, they'd invested in a nice place for people to stay. That was all she could muster before slipping into the shower, the water running so hot I could see the edge of the mirror beginning to fog within minutes.

While she showered, I unpacked my own small suitcase and changed into what I considered my more outdoors-y attire: jeans, sneakers, and a short-sleeve button down paired with a robin's egg blue sweater-vest. My more formal clothes were quickly folded and carefully put away, which still left me with time to kill before Krystal finished her shower.

Pulling out my laptop, I was pleasantly surprised to find a Wi-Fi signal in our room, which I immediately jumped onto and began checking my e-mail. It had only been a day since the Colin incident, where I was hunted all over Winslow—a day which I'd spent hunkered down in Charlotte Manor with a laptop retrieved from my apartment, trying desperately to carve out a bit of breathing room in my work schedule. It helped that Krystal was busy setting up the trip, and that some of my parahuman clients understood that being hunted by an insane human can throw off a schedule. Still, I was barely treading water, so anything I could get done in the small bits of spare time I had would be a big help. Things were reaching a tipping point though, there was no getting around that. Either Fletcher Accounting Services would have to expand, or I'd have to start turning down work, a prospect which utterly galled me.

It's impossible to say how long I was working before I heard Krystal's voice making a "tsk" sound and saw a polished red fingernail begin to tip my screen forward, closing the laptop even as I hurriedly tried to save my progress.

"I did not book us this place so you could work."

"You booked it because it's the only hotel in town," I countered, mercifully clicking the outdated icon of a floppy disk and shutting the laptop myself. "Good internet, too."

"This place isn't as podunk as you might expect." Krystal grinned at me, and I noticed for the first time what outfit she'd changed into. A red flannel shirt tied off at the stomach, jean shorts that were far from Daisy-dukes but still quite higher than her usual sweats or slacks, all topped off with a beat-up straw hat perched atop her blonde head.

"You're making such a clear case for that," I replied.

"What, you're the only one who gets to dress more comfortably?" Krystal asked.

"I was actually just wondering where you were going to hide your gun." I nodded to the black belt and attached holster lying on the bed where she'd left them. Inside was her firearm, the one accessory Krystal never left home without. Earlier in the relationship, I'd considered the practice paranoid. After a few months, I wondered why she didn't carry two.

"That thing will totally throw off my outfit. It can stay in the room. I'll hang a 'Do Not Disturb' so no one will come in and fuck with it." Krystal turned, picked up her firearm, and set it to the side, completely missing the look of shock on my face. Fortunately, it was still there by the time she turned back, or at least, I assume it was, because she gave me a world-class roll of the eyes. "What?"

"You *never* leave your gun behind. Bubba took us night fishing, and you wore that gun belt over a bikini.

I've seen you take it with you when you run downstairs to get mail. Can you blame me for being a little surprised?"

"I suppose I do have a bit of an attachment," Krystal admitted. "That's just prudence in my line of work. But it's not necessary here."

"Why not?" There was something in her eyes, something she was hiding. When it came to her job, Krystal was probably a master deceiver, but in her personal life, she so rarely said anything other than the blunt truth that it became obvious when she was trying to choose her words.

"Because in this town, we're safe." Krystal walked back into the bathroom, pulling out her toiletries kit and grabbing a stick of deodorant. "Aside from the petty bullshit that any place has, there's no real crime here. No outside threats, either. You probably got a hint of how strong Leeroy is, and his deputies are no joke. Boarback is peaceful. Fun, too. After the diner, if there's time before sunrise, we'll hike up to Cervain's Lake. It's so clear you can see the moon's reflection like you're looking into the sky."

Nice as that sounded, I still couldn't help but feel like she was changing the subject, though from what, I had no idea. There was just something defensive about her excitement, like she was trying extra hard to sell me on how much she loved this place.

"And during the day, we can take the tunnels around to check out the shops. They've got all kinds of unique items here, handmade, the stuff you'd have to special order in the outside world. Some of the craftsmen out here are incredible; we hire them as independent contractors for the Agency sometimes. Of course, given our reputation, not many take us up on it, even with all the perks doing contract work provides. Oh, and everything is parahuman owned, obviously. They get a pretty good deal on land and lodging out here, so it's a big sell for starting local businesses."

At last, it all fell into place. There were many things about which Krystal would happily talk with neither prompting nor explanation, but the viability of starting a small business was not one of them. That was for my benefit, and I could only see one reason why she would bother to give me such information.

"Krystal," I said, walking over so that she could see me from the bathroom. "I do run my own company, you know. I'm perfectly aware of what a sales pitch sounds like."

The deodorant paused, all the confirmation I needed, then she let out a sigh and finished applying. Putting the cap back on the white chalky stick, she faced me, a rare solemn expression on her face. "This is a good town, Fred. Lots of parahumans with businesses who could use a talented accountant. Internet to let you work with your old clients. Nice, quiet people who want what you've always wanted: a normal, peaceful life."

"And no hunters suddenly showing up to try and kill me," I added.

"You think that's why I'm trying to sell you on Boarback? Fred, that guy was a chump. If you'd had to, you could have taken him apart. He's not—" Her words halted, and she looked away from me, just for a few seconds. "You know the vampire who made you, Quinn, was a real rat bastard, right?"

"Seeing as he tried to kill all of us and successfully ripped your throat out, I won't be jumping to his aid anytime soon," I said.

"Well, it turns out that he was also a real, territorial rat bastard. The reason we've seen so little vampire activity in Winslow is because it was considered Quinn's, and he didn't like to share. But word got out that he finally went too far and stepped against the Agency, so now he's on the run. That means other vampires have begun moving back in, retaking the territory that Quinn used to hold. Places like Winslow." Krystal walked over to the pants she'd traveled in and began digging through the pockets.

"I don't understand, is that why you want me to relocate? Fear of other vampires? You've gone out of your way to tell me that we're not all bad, that you work with several who are good people. Why does more vampires coming to town automatically make you want to hide me away?"

"Plenty of vampires *are* decent people," Krystal replied, finally locating her phone and yanking it out from the pocket it was lodged in. "But you know who usually aren't? The ones who go around seizing another vampire's territory after he goes on the lamb. Those are the ambitious types, and they play by the belief that if you aren't with them, you're against them. The rumor mill worked its magic, and now lots of people know there's another vampire in Winslow, Colorado, one who has pulled off a whole lot of impressive stuff. That's the sort of situation where the new vamps either have to make you join, or get you out of the picture."

"Wait, you think they'll kill me just for living in my own town?" My voice may have leapt up a few degrees on that one. I'd gotten used to the idea that the parahuman world was a less restrained one than what humans dealt with, but offing someone just because they lived in a town you were moving to seemed a bit extreme.

"Most likely, they'd compel you to join, but you're a smart guy. You can probably beat them at the strategy game. So then, they'll wait for an opportunity to use a loophole in the treaties, one that lets them take offense with you. After that, they can challenge you for honor, and if you happen to die in the process, then so be it." Krystal held her phone tightly, the edges of her fingers beginning to turn white from force. "I've seen it happen before. And if they do it, Freddy, then I can't protect you. I'm an agent, and that means I have to work within the laws and treaties. I'll have to stand there and just . . . watch."

Moving slowly, I wrapped my arms around her and gave her a small kiss on the top of her head. Tough as Krystal was, powerful as the monster inside made her, I knew she'd said early goodbyes to too many loved ones in her life.

"That's a lot of 'ifs' and 'maybes,'" I told her. "While I'm not exactly thrilled about new vampires moving to town, we don't know that I'll be a target. What the vampire people are gossiping about might be something, but I'm just an accountant. There's a good chance they won't even care about me."

"Not as good as you think." Krystal turned on her phone, the glow lighting her face from below, and made a few swipes before finding what she was looking for. Stepping back from my embrace, she handed me the phone, which I picked up slowly. "That request was put in the night you met Lillian. Came less than an hour after we'd picked you up."

Before me was an e-mail, from an address that was unrecognizable, alerting Agent Jenkins that her romantic partner, Fredrick Fletcher, had been named in a formal information request between the House of Turva and Richard Alderson. It mentioned a lot of things I didn't understand, negotiation dates and reference numbers, but those details were irrelevant. What mattered was my name, and the people who wanted to know more about me.

"You're on their radar," Krystal said, likely reading the comprehension on my face. "And sooner or later, that's a thing that will require dealing with. Richard's a friend, and he's not going to tell them anything you wouldn't want known, but you run a public business, Freddy. It won't take much to learn who you are and where you live. Maybe it's idle curiosity, maybe they want some taxes done, but not everyone is as kind-hearted as you. I've seen these things turn before, and if they're handled carefully enough, then we agents don't have any recourse."

I sat down on the bed, my own body suddenly feeling very heavy. "I can't just leave town, though. What about our friends?"

"Albert and Neil can come with us." Krystal sat down next to me, gently taking her phone out of my hands. "This is where Arch wanted to bring them in the first place. Plenty of space and time to train, plus a fellow weapon-wielder to spar with. Bubba and Amy would stay in Winslow—he's been climbing the ladder with Richard, and she's too deeply rooted to just up and leave—but they'd still be able to visit us. Amy's wares alone could sell enough to justify the trip."

"Us?" I stopped staring at my empty hand and faced Krystal, who was only a few inches away. "You said us. Does that mean you'd come, too?"

"You know how my job works; it doesn't matter much where I call home. And I'm already packed up anyway. Plus, I love Boarback. I wouldn't mind coming home to it at the end of my missions, especially if my boyfriend was already here waiting for me." Krystal leaned in closer, wrapping her arms around my shoulders. "I was going to ease you into this, Freddy, not come on right away with the hard sell. We've got a day and a half left here, so just think it over. Take the town in; imagine what it would be like to live here. That's all I'm asking."

"I'll keep an open mind." I kissed her, partly out of affection, partly because I genuinely had no idea what else to say. Krystal made good points, and if she thought there was reason to worry, then I had no doubt there was. Still, Winslow was my home, and while I've never been ashamed to admit that I am a coward by nature, the idea of being forced out of my town left a hard pit in my stomach.

But that feeling was nothing compared to the wave of nerves that washed over me when I imagined an entire clan of vampires, all of them Quinn in my head, discussing exactly how to deal with a vampire already operating on their turf.

4.

BY THE TIME WE'D COMPOSED OURSELVES and made it downstairs, the others were already waiting, so we cut a quick pace to the diner. Though I asked, and everyone agreed it had once had a more formal name, the moniker had been lost somewhere in the sands of time. For as long as anyone could remember, it was just "the diner," and when we arrived, I found those simple words written at the top of the laminated menus. With the yellow-painted walls and over-stuffed red booths, it could have easily fit in off any highway exit in America, save for the staff and clientele.

Since arriving at the sheriff's office, I'd somewhat forgotten the spectacle of driving down Sunshine Lane and seeing all the different parahumans out and about. But the realization of just how far out of normal bounds we were came rushing back the moment our waitress slithered over to us. That was not creative language, by the way. Our waitress, Yenny (as she introduced herself), was a fairly normal-looking woman with brown hair and eyes a pale shade of orange. She wore a yellow shirt with white trim that matched the restaurant's walls, and nothing else. I don't mean to imply anything lude, it's simply that Yenny's bottom half was that of a bright orange snake's tail.

Mercifully, I wasn't the only one who was a bit surprised, as Neil wouldn't quit staring and Albert dropped his menu to the floor as soon as he saw her. Yenny took it surprisingly well, glossing over their shock with warm greetings, and then getting down to the business of what we'd be eating.

Ordering was a quick affair. Leeroy declared that the chicken fried steak was the best thing to be had, and he was seconded by Krystal, Nax, and Sable. With no point of reference for anything else, and a keen eye that noticed some of the menu items were clearly designed for parahumans rather than mundane palettes (unless raw sparrow eggs and powdered coal were delicacies I'd some-how missed), it made sense to trust the group consensus.

In spite of the heavy burden weighing on my mind, dinner was an enjoyable affair. Periodically, new parahu-mans would get up from their seats or walk in, which gave us peeks at the creatures we'd never laid eyes on before. Leeroy entertained the whole table with stories of the town's history and the various incidents he'd been called on to help with over the years. I'd never consid-ered the possibility that a troll could hibernate, grow, and end up stuck under a bridge, but as Leeroy recount-ed having to borrow farm equipment to get the fellow unstuck, it seemed like the most natural thing in the world. Even Arch chuckled a few times, when he wasn't outside taking his cigarettes.

I would also be remiss if I glossed over the food, which was incredible. Chicken fried steak was hardly a new cuisine for me—nor most anyone, I'd imagine—but sometimes the simplest dishes are the best when every element is handled perfectly. From the first bite of spiced meat, crisp crust, and decadent gravy, I understood why Leeroy had insisted we not miss this special. I would have bitten through a hundred dirty tires for a meal like that, and once again, I was grateful I had retained my taste buds despite being undead.

The experience as a whole was oddly serene, at least for me. Ever since reconnecting with Krystal at our high school reunion, I'd been drawn progressively deeper and deeper into the parahuman world. And while many of those experiences helped me meet important people in my life, they also all tended to be fraught with chaos, if not outright peril. So somewhere in my brain, I suppose I had made the connection that the more parahumans one was around, the more hectic and dangerous things would be. But here we were, eating chicken fried steak an hour before dawn, in a town filled almost exclusively with other parahumans, and it was one of the more peaceful moments of my last few years. It didn't even feel like we were all vampires and zombies and other inhuman species. It just felt like sitting around with a bunch of friends.

By the time the food was eaten and we were heading back to the inn to beat the sun, I'd begun to consider the possibility that living in Boarback could have its merits. True, one meal did not a happy life make, but I'd promised to keep an open mind, and it was hard to deny that the town did have a charm all its own. I was so lost in thought, and in observation of the people walking up and down Sunshine Lane, that I didn't even hear Arch speak. Krystal nudged me in the ribs, and I turned to find the vertically challenged agent staring at me, clearly waiting for a response.

"Sorry, what was that?"

Arch didn't roll his eyes, yet somehow, he still gave off the same feeling as if he had. "I was letting you know that I'm going to be borrowing Albert and Sable for a training session while those who need it grab a nap. Since you don't need sleep, I offered to let you come along and watch. Though, at the moment, I'm rethinking the wisdom of that decision."

"I'd love to, but . . ." I glanced up at the sky, which was already growing gray as the stars faded, declaring retreat against the overwhelming forces of daytime.

"This place is underground," Arch assured me. "Sunlight restrictions aside, it's more prudent to have a training facility away from prying eyes. Despite how Mayberry this place might look, it was founded as a sanctuary, and nobody knows the importance of a place to hide like parahumans."

Arch's reference to Mayberry caught me off guard, although it shouldn't have. I often forgot that though he looked comparable in age to Neil and Albert, he'd been alive for at least a century, or so I guessed from what I'd gotten through context. He never discussed his exact age, and I made a point not to pry where agents were concerned.

"I like to think of it more as a place to shelter while problems are handled," Leeroy added. "But it works just fine for sparring grounds and a gym these days."

After a moment's consideration, I nodded. "Sure, I'll tag along. I'd like to see as much of Boarback as possible. That's what I'm here for." I gave Krystal a quick kiss, which she used as an opportunity to show approval of my choice by squeezing my, um, rear, and then bid farewell as she and Neil began heading up to the Bristle Inn.

"I'll show you all down there." Leeroy headed toward the police station, while I marveled at the fact that he hadn't said "y'all," despite the rustic surroundings. The sheriff of Boarback might live here, but he definitely didn't hail from this region of the world. Then again, with how long some parahumans lived, it was entirely possible that the place he'd called home didn't exist anymore. Countries fell all the time, back in the older days of history.

Nax walked with us to the station, then peeled off as he proclaimed that "someone had to be on duty," and that, by process of elimination, that was him. Duty didn't seem that bad, though, as he immediately went to his desk in the middle of the room and kicked up his feet, eyes on the old television in the corner.

We were taken through one of the doors near the back of the station, which led to a staircase. This wasn't a small set that took us a basement, however. These were slick, worn, and went on for so long that not even I could see the bottom, which was not a common occurrence. All us of proceeded down, Leeroy in the lead, followed by Sable, then Albert, then me, with Arch bringing up the rear. While some neurotic part of me wondered if he was taking the back position in case we were threatened from behind, the more logical part of me had a hunch that it was because these steps were a little slippery, and if anyone went tumbling, they'd take his smaller frame down with them.

It was impossible to gauge how far down we'd gone by the time we reached the bottom. I only knew that I wasn't too worried about stray beams of sunlight getting in anymore. Leeroy yanked a lever near the bottom of the stairs, and a new set of bulbs flickered on, hung at irregular intervals through the rough corridors sprawled out before us. They seemed to twist and turn in all directions, but Leeroy didn't hesitate as he continued on, taking us through one turn after another until we arrived at our destination.

The cavern was vast—by underground measures, at any rate. It was roughly half the size of a football field, with a domed ceiling that rose twenty feet in the air. A small rack of weaponry—swords and maces and the like—was set up at the end furthest from the entrance. Halfway between the rack and the way in were what looked an awful lot like benches etched into the very stone of the cavern.

"No way this is natural." I didn't mean to say the words out loud, but the sound of Leeroy's chuckle informed me of my slip-up.

"You hit the nail on the head," he said, grabbing me by the shoulder and leading me over to the benches while

Arch took Albert and Sable toward the middle of the cavern. "Artificially carved, save for a few of the tunnels near the entrances that were used as a starting point."

"Was this made for the town?"

Leeroy gave his large head a mighty shake. "Other way around. Part of why we picked this spot was because these tunnels were here. They were originally home to . . . well, maybe you're happier not knowing. Something that had to be rooted out. Anyway, the Agency doesn't forget about useful assets, especially when all they need is a few light bulbs and minor remodeling to be made livable."

"Prudent, and cost-efficient," I noted.

"Doesn't matter where you go in the world, governments are always looking to pinch their pennies as hard as possible," Leeroy said. We arrived at the stone bench and took our seats while Arch continued instructing Albert and Sable. I didn't entirely grasp what he was telling them; all I could discern was that he kept moving their arms and legs to slightly different angles than where they'd been. My best guess was that this was some sort of stance advice, though I confess that even that assumption was predicated on watching a cornucopia of action movies.

"This will be interesting." Leeroy was watching the same spectacle I was, but he didn't seem nearly as befuddled by what was going on. "Not even I've gotten to watch a sparring match between weapons of destiny in a long while. They always put on a good show."

I was going to ask what he meant, but before the words could form in my mouth, Arch had backed up and the match had commenced. After that moment, the question was no longer necessary. I understood exactly what made their tussle interesting.

5.

NEITHER ALBERT NOR SABLE WERE ATTEMPTING to injure the other. Their movements were slow and deliberate. This seemed to be about control more than anything else, as their respective weapons would draw near to the other's flesh without ever touching it. The sword and axe did clash, however, as each used their respective tool to block the incoming strikes. It was those moments that made this different from any battle I'd ever seen, in cinema or reality.

When the blades of two weapons of destiny collided, they sent ripples out through the world. I realize that sounds as though I'm saying there were flashes of light and waves of sound, which there were, but please understand that there was also something more. At every clash, the very world around them seemed to warp and distort. It was for less than a second, and if not for my vampire eyes, I doubt I would have even seen it. Yet it was undeniably there. Like stones across a lake, these two weapons would ripple through everything around them as they made contact.

"As much as I would like to trust Arch not to put anyone in danger . . . is that safe?"

"Safe is a relative term in our world," Leeroy replied. "If you mean, 'are they guaranteed that nothing will go wrong,' then the answer is no. One of them could slip and lop the other's head off, or they could cause a tear that turns them into slugs. Neither is likely, mind you, just possible. But if you mean, 'is this safer than them never having the experience until they fight an unfriendly weapon and get caught off guard,' then I'd have to say yes. Education is always safer than ignorance."

He had me there, although I did scoot further back in my seat at the word "slug." We sat in silence for some while after that, watching his deputy and my assistant trade blows, halted occasionally by Arch scurrying in and moving someone's foot or elbow. It was strange to see

Albert wielding a blade, all the more so because he actually seemed competent with it. If there was anyone less inclined to violence in the world than me, it was Albert. His avoidance wasn't from cowardice, however. The young man just genuinely seemed too soft-hearted to hurt anyone. I'd only seen him swing that sword one time with intent, and it was when Neil's life was on the line.

"Krystal tells me you two might be hunting for a house around here soon." I started at the voice, having grown so engrossed in the fight that I forgot Leeroy was sitting next to me. His eyes had turned away from the match. Now, they were taking me in with careful observation, which made my slight jump all the more embarrassing.

"It's in discussion," I told him. "She clearly loves it here, and my current home may not be as safe as it once was. Plus, your town does seem quite idyllic."

"Don't let her rose-colored glasses fool you. We get our share of problems same as anyone else," Leeroy replied. "The Agency likes to dump the more problematic potential recruits here for training. Sometimes it works out fine, like with Krystal and Nax, but not every parahuman with power and attitude problems ends up on the straight and narrow. I've got two deputies for a reason."

"Still seems safer than a town where hostile, territorial vampires are moving in." I hadn't actually intended to spill my problems to the sheriff, but if Krystal had told him that we might be moving, it seemed a fair bet she'd also let him know why. Since he didn't seem at all surprised by my statement, my hunch appeared to be right on the money.

"That does look a little worrying," Leeroy agreed. "But let me ask you this, Fred. As a businessman, if you were to move to Boarback, what is one of the very first things you'd do?"

While there was a laundry list of answers to that question, it was clear Leeroy was angling for something specific. I took my time, thinking through every step in moving my business, and almost immediately, I realized what he was trying to say. "I'd look into any other accounting firms in Boarback."

"Because you were planning to kill them?" Leeroy squinted at me in a way that only police seem to be capable of, like they're joking, but don't want to let on that they're joking in case you're willing to accidentally incriminate yourself. If you've ever been pulled over for speeding, then you know the exact look I'm talking about.

"Of course not. Because they would be my competition, and the more I understand about them, the better prepared I'll be. I'd need to know what services they offer, and more importantly, what they don't offer, as well as what failings they have that might entice their customers to look my way. It's the basics of business." His point was obvious; however, there was one glaring flaw in the comparison. "I don't think these vampires are trying to start their own accounting firms, though."

"No, they're trying to move into a territory with a strong therian presence, an ancient dragon, two agents, and a fellow vampire who's allegedly made alliances with all those powerful people. That sound like a hospitable place to you? It's a big country, you know. Plenty of spots with easier pickings. Why do you think these vampires are coming to your town, fully aware that they'll be under the scrutiny of much more dangerous beings?" Leeroy turned back to the watch the fight; evidently, he didn't expect me to come up with an answer anytime soon.

"Because it's safe." I caught a bit of surprise in his eyes as Leeroy glanced at me, but kept on going. Now that the pieces were starting to line up in my head, I couldn't keep them from tumbling out. "Yes, Winslow is very dangerous if you're the sort of parahuman who breaks the law, but the flip side is that all those therians, and agents, and Gideon mean that if you keep to the treaties, then you don't have a lot to fear. A few months ago, a therian tribe tried to overthrow Richard, and they were crushed in a single night." Actually, they'd been wiped out completely, but I preferred not to think about that part. Not that I, or anyone else, could have saved them. They attacked the King of the West directly, and no one stops Gideon when he's moved to anger.

"A tribe tried to take over Richard's spot, huh? Because they just wanted it so bad?"

"No, they were driven . . . out . . . of their home." I'd forgotten about that detail, amidst all the kidnappings and overthrow attempts. "Are you saying these vampires are refugees fleeing from something?"

Leeroy leaned back, pressing his bulk against the stone wall. "I'm saying there are a lot of ways for a territory to get taken. Maybe you cut off a food source, or drive the locals into a frenzy, or compromise people's safety at home. And if you're smart, you can do it just legal enough to keep the law off you, be they agents or cops. Wouldn't be the first time one group of parahumans has tried to expand their holdings by pushing all the others out. Course, shit like that won't fly in a well-organized town like the one watched over by Gideon. Dragons are damn fine negotiators; the rules they play by are different than everyone else's. He doesn't need to wait for the law."

It made sense, looking at it from that angle. But there was still one glaring flaw in the hypothesis that I couldn't get past. "Krystal would know about that, if it were the case. She wouldn't feel the need to worry about me."

"Because every fear is always rooted in rational thought and logic?" Leeroy lifted an eyebrow at me and shook his head. "Krystal Jenkins is a good person, a tough lady, and one of the better agents I've gotten to train in a long time. That said, she is absolutely terrified of losing people once she lets them in. Can't blame her, given her history, but it clouds her judgment sometimes. I'm not going to say these vampires have pure-hearted intentions; they might very well want to put you under the boot or leave your head out to meet the sun. But then again, they may just be trying to make sure you won't have them all slaughtered by your therian friends for stepping on your turf."

"I highly doubt Richard would kill a clan of vampires for me, no matter how much I saved him on his taxes," I said.

"But *they* don't know that," Leeroy countered. "All they know is that this is a town with a lot of powerful people, and some vampire is allegedly connected to most of them. It would be bad business for them not to try and figure out who that is before they get in too deep. Whether it's to kill him or ask him for help is up for discussion; either way, asking about every vampire they know of is the prudent move."

"Well, this certainly made the situation more complicated." I let my head fall back, feeling the impact against the hard stone even though there was no accompanying sense of pain. "I expected you to try and sell me on moving here, since it's what Krystal wants."

"Don't get me wrong, Boarback could use someone with your skills to help audit the books, and I'm sure you'd save my citizens a pretty penny come tax time. Not to mention, I'd love to have Krystal around again. But there's a reason she didn't settle down here before. The lady likes chaos, even on her downtime, and we've only got that in spurts around here. If she comes back, I'd rather it be because she's reached a point where this is the right town for her."

A loud clang filled the air, dragging our attention to the sparring match. Albert was on a knee with his sword held high, Sable's axe pressed against it. Apparently, he'd just stopped a strong blow, as evidenced both by their position on the ground and the fact that a small portion of the rock around them had suddenly turned to glass. Arch let out a whistle and they backed away from each other, seeming to notice for the first time the effect their attack had had on their surroundings.

"If you don't mind me asking, what would you do in my shoes?" I realized that Leeroy and I were in totally different leagues as far as our power went—just shaking his hand had driven that message home loud and clear—but he'd shown an adept mind and offered good perspective, so I was genuinely curious to get his opinion.

"Guess it depends," he said. "The old me would just crush them before they even got a foothold, kill off all the leaders and put the rest to work under my rule. New me would probably just let them be until they stepped out of line, at which point, I'd try to make an example of a few and hope the rest took the message. You're not me, though, even aside from the undead thing. You've got to figure out what the right move for you is."

It was sound, true advice, and I was about to thank Leeroy for it when he continued.

"I will say this, though: running away is almost always an option. It doesn't vanish the moment you decide to stick around for a little while longer. There's no shame in retreating from a bigger, stronger threat, but only you know if you'll be okay with running from just the idea of danger." Leeroy hefted himself off the bench then, and began to clap as he walked over to Albert and Sable. I didn't know what he would say to them—probably encouragement, since Arch had combat advice on lockdown.

As for me, I stayed put, the sheriff's words echoing through my head. I'd never had any issue with fleeing, as a human or a vampire. But he was right; there was a big difference in running away from a real, tangible threat, and just bolting from the possibility of danger. Whichever one I did, I needed to be sure about my choice, because being undead meant that I would have to live with it for a very long time.

6.

AFTER A FEW HOURS OF TRAINING, SABLE headed back to the station and Leeroy led us through the underground tunnels to another set of stairs, this one emerging inside the Bristle Inn. By then, the others were awake, and we began touring the various shops accessible through the interwoven tunnel system. I had no idea how Leeroy, or the occasional other parahumans we encountered below the surface, navigated such a winding structure. Evidently they did, though, as we would take turn after turn, seemingly doubling back on ourselves, yet always arriving at the exact destination we'd set out for. The tunnels were nearly deserted, as going above ground was far more convenient unless one suffered a sunlight allergy, but the shops were always filled with at least a few patrons. Given the wares they had, I could hardly blame them, as each store was fascinating just to window-shop through.

Neil purchased a few crystals and a bag of powder from a one-eyed woman in a store full of books, scales, and bowls of ingredients that I couldn't identify. They were labeled, but it was a language I wasn't familiar with. In fact, Neil seemed to be the only one among us who could tell what was what, which led me to suspect that perhaps the signs were more magical than linguistic.

At a store with homemade flasks and barrels, I picked up a bottle of Boarback Merlot, along with a six-pack of local mead for Bubba. Krystal also bought some beers, though we'd barely made it out of the store before she cracked one open and guzzled it halfway down. I wasn't sure what the law was as far as open containers went, but seeing as we were walking with the sheriff, it seemed to be okay. Along with the wine and beer, I'd also picked up a new faux-silver flask, this one boasting exceptional thermal insulation and an equally exceptional storage capacity. The clerk made a lot of claims, at least some of which I hoped were true. There were few things worse than room-temperature blood.

Albert picked up a pair of wrist guards at Arch's suggestion—one of the more harmless purchases possible at a store full of armor and weaponry. It was disconcerting to walk into, actually, nestled as it was amidst the small-town craft stores. This one looked like it would be more at home in a renaissance fair, except that the weaponry there is dull and not suited for real battle. And before you wonder, no, I do not want to go into why I happen to have that knowledge.

No one else seemed bothered by the existence of an armory in the middle of town, so I just chalked it up to "one of those parahuman things" and busied myself examining shields while Albert found a set of wrist guards that fit his arms properly. Thankfully, they didn't take too long, or else I might have ended up buying one of the bucklers to hang over my mantle. Purely for the aesthetic, of course.

We spent the rest of the day browsing the shops, picking up knick-knacks and gifts for those back home. As we made our way through town, I kept my word to Krystal, surveying everything with a critical eye. If we made the move, these would be my only shopping options, and as much fun as they were to visit, I had to try and wrap my mind around not being able to buy anything from outside them. I also kept an eye on the stores we saw through the enchanted windows, making note of the services Boarback offered. There were plenty to be found, but no matter how much I looked, I didn't see so much as even a flyer for any accounting practices in the area. Whether that was good or bad, I still hadn't quite yet determined.

In the evening, Sable and Albert went down for more sparring, with Neil tagging along behind Arch this time. Krystal and I borrowed Leeroy's truck to take a drive into the nearby hills, eventually switching to foot and hiking our way up to a large lake that rested at the top of a steep path. There were no signs or boats to be seen; only a lone gazebo with a golden bell that Krystal informed me I was not to ring under any circumstances. Her promise of the lake's reflectivity had been spot on, as I could see the quarter moon hanging in the sky just by glancing at the smooth surface.

"I wouldn't have expected a place like this when we landed," I said, transfixed by how undisturbed this natural body of water was. It was unsettling somehow. All the more because I realized the reflectivity meant I couldn't see what dwelled below the surface. Beautiful and still wasn't the same as peaceful; I'd learned that lesson long ago.

"There are plenty more like it." Krystal leaned over, pressing her head to my shoulder like a cat trying to scratch its ear. "Boarback is bigger than just the town central. Lots of places and parahumans you'd never get a chance to see in the outside world. Most of them friendly, too, or at least not outright hostile. Pretty much the same thing."

"You love this town quite a bit. If I can ask, why didn't you settle here? It's obvious that you get to pick where you call home between missions, and seeing how fond you are of Boarback, I'm shocked you didn't build a life here." Perhaps it was overstepping my bounds somewhat to ask such a question, but given what Krystal had asked of me, I felt the question was warranted. Something had kept her from this town before, and if we were considering making the move, then I wanted to know what it was, and why it was no longer an issue. *If* it was no longer an issue.

"Lots of reasons," she said, not even flinching at the query. "Travel, for one. I don't hate that plane as much as you, but I don't want to fly on it that often, and it's the fastest way in and out of here. Timing was also a factor. The missions I was getting back then were almost all time sensitive, so being somewhere central made it easier to respond. But the sad truth of the matter is that those were just things I used to convince myself that it was the right call. The real reason I didn't come back was my fiancé, Tem. When training ended, we'd already become an item, so I decided to settle down where he was and see how things played out."

As we were currently cuddling in front of a romantic lake, I knew quite well how that relationship had turned out, though I was fuzzy on the details of how and why. Krystal rarely talked about her ex-fiancé; in fact, this very well might have been the first time I'd ever heard his name. It certainly seemed like one that would have stuck in my memory. The experience had been a painful one for her, so I didn't press the issue. What had come before didn't matter to me; I only cared for our future.

"Once that went to shit, I threw myself into my work. There were stretches where I didn't see my apartment for months on end. I just stopped caring where I hung my hat, and even after I eased off the gas at the Agency, where I lived didn't matter much. Not until I had people worth coming back to, anyway."

I'd always wondered why it was so easy for her to move to Winslow from wherever she'd been before, but the reasoning made sense. Even aside from our budding relationship, she'd had Albert to watch over, and then her old friend Bubba to visit with. Since then, the number of reasons to come home had only grown. And if we moved to Boarback, we'd lose almost all of them.

"Krystal, this town is beautiful, and I'm still struck with wonder at the idea of getting to live openly as a vampire instead of worrying every day about being discovered. We could be content here, I think." Her head rose from my shoulder, affection evident in her eyes; however, I leaned back before she could make contact. I needed to finish this, while I still had the courage to do so.

"But I'm not okay with content. I would have been, a few years ago. If you'd promised me a town where I could be safe and have a reliable income stream, I'd have jumped at it, no questions asked. Things have changed, though. As appealing as contentment is, the price is simply too high. Being with you, having all our friends, it makes me happy. Happier than I ever thought I could be. That's not something I'm inclined to give up easily. Maybe if this threat becomes real, if we learn the new vampires definitely want me out of the picture, then it will be a different story. I just can't run yet. Winslow, and more importantly the people in it, are my home. I don't want to lose that unless it's absolutely necessary."

"This from the guy who ran away from a few were-wolves at a high school reunion," Krystal said.

"To be fair, they were also total assholes," I replied. "Werewolves or no."

"That they were." She leaned in closer to me, and I didn't pull back this time. My piece was said. How she chose to respond was up to her. "I had a feeling it wouldn't be that easy of a sell. You're more willful than you think you are. We can go back and see where things lead, as long as you're willing to promise me one thing. If it comes time to run, you *run*."

"I can assure you that will not be a problem in the slightest," I told her.

"Yeah, you say that, but sometimes . . . never mind. Let's just enjoy the vacation while we can."

The gap between our faces disappeared as she leaned in, kissing me with more fury and need than her usual playful affection. It is neither possible nor prudent to say how long we stayed like that; I will simply say that when we parted, we turned our eyes skyward to the true moon and stars rather than their watery reflections.

"Fred," Krystal whispered, possibly in the softest tone I'd ever heard from her.

"Yes?"

"If you die on me, I'm going to kick the shit out of you. Fair warning."

I pulled her closer and ran my pale hand through her golden hair. "I am suitably intimidated, and will do my best to avoid the ass-kicking."

"See, that's why I like the smart ones. They know how to take a good threat."

We lay under the stars for several more hours before finally making our way back down the trail and driving to town. It was the most serene evening we'd had in a long time, even if unknown danger did lurk beneath the surface.

7.

AFTER ANOTHER DAY OF SHOPPING, delectable food from the diner, and training for Albert, Neil, and Sable, the time had come to head back out to the field and catch our plane home. Packing our bags was a quick affair, and after a brief hike from the Bristle Inn to the police station, we piled back into the sheriff's truck to head out. This time, however, Nax and Sable were coming along to see us off, so that put two of us riding in the truck's bed. I was almost entirely certain that such an act was technically illegal, but given everyone's respective hardiness, it didn't make sense to fret about being thrown from the rear.

To no one's surprise, Arch immediately volunteered to take a position in the bed, hand already on the cigarettes in his pocket. But before he could move, Sheriff Leeroy had grabbed me by the shoulder and started moving us both to the back.

"None of that, Arch. You've only got a little time left with my deputy. I want you imparting every bit of knowledge that you can before the plane arrives. Fred and I will ride in the bed." Leeroy caught the annoyed, frustrated look on Arch's face and met it with a wide grin. "Unless you'd like to tussle for it. I've told you before, I'm always up for a rematch."

There was a long moment where I genuinely thought Arch and Leeroy were going to have a sparring match over who had to ride on the hard, bouncy surface of a beat-up truck bed. After a lengthy stare, however, Arch slowly made his way back to the front of the vehicle, pausing before entering to throw one last line Leeroy's way.

"The next time we fight, it will be when I *know* I am going to beat you."

"Looking forward to it!" There was so much enthusiasm in Leeroy's voice that what was almost certainly a taunt came off sounding sincere. I still didn't know what Leeroy was—or Arch, for that matter—but I did know Arch's reputation according to Krystal, and he was considered one of the Agency's top people. For Leeroy to have beaten him, well, let's just say that the sheriff of Boarback was apparently packing more than just an aura of power.

I leapt into the back—literally, in my case—while Leeroy pulled himself up through the tailgate. His large hands smacked the side of the truck twice, and Nax started it up, pulling out of the driveway and onto Sunshine Lane.

Due to the speed with which everything had happened, and the interaction with Arch, it wasn't until we were driving away from town that I realized Leeroy had purposely pulled me away from the group so that it was just the two of us. Otherwise, he'd have just let Arch take the other side of the truck bed. Sure enough, Leeroy was watching me, his cheerful eyes peering out from under his beige hat. I waited for him to say something, to start the conversation, but the seconds ticked by into minutes and there was only silence. Finally, my own nerves got the best of me and I blurted out the first thing that came to mind.

"Am I about to get the 'don't hurt her' speech?"

"Beg pardon?" He tilted his head back a couple of inches, removing the hat's shadow from his face.

"You know, the speech where you tell me that I should make sure not to hurt Krystal, or you'll hurt me. It's a cliché classic, and when you pulled me back here, I sort of assumed . . . ." My voice trailed off as Leeroy began to loudly chuckle, small waves of laughter washing over him.

"Fred, I don't need to tell you not to hurt Krystal. For one thing, it's plain as day that you two are in love. And that means you're going to hurt each other; it's unavoidable. You'll make mistakes, say the wrong thing, pick the wrong action, and her feelings will get hurt. Same thing she'll do to you. The ones we love can hurt us the most easily, but we can also forgive them just as freely. Long as the hurt stays unintentional, I think you two will be fine for a while yet."

His laughter finally subsided, and he looked out at the woods the truck was winding through on a narrow path. "Besides, if you ever screwed up really bad, what could I do to you that's worse than what Krystal would? By now, you've probably figured out that she doesn't need anyone to fight her battles for her, especially not an old sheriff half a country away."

"I suppose you have me there," I admitted. "Then, what did you want to talk about?"

"Who said I wanted to talk about anything?" Leeroy replied.

"You pulled me into the back of the truck, and didn't let Arch take my place. I assumed there was a reason for that."

Leeroy nodded. "There was. I like riding in the back, and I'm not a fan of cigarette smoke. Ruins the scent of the outdoors. Arch is a good agent, but that habit of his drives me nuts. You don't smoke, and you seemed pleasant enough, so I decided to drag you along to keep him from joining. Sometimes a ride in a truck is just that."

If that wasn't a cue to shut up and enjoy the ride, I didn't know what was, so I let the subject drop and looked out at the trees. The path we were driving on was so small that the vehicle barely fit. Branches stuck out from both sides, coming within inches of scratching me. Leeroy, with his wider frame, got smacked occasionally, though he didn't seem bothered by it. I wasn't entirely sure he even noticed. As the trees struck, he simply sat there with the same placid expression he'd been wearing since we met. I'd met several parahumans who were considered to be incredibly powerful, but none of them had been as relaxed and cheery as Sheriff Thorgood. In an odd way, that made me even more afraid of him than the others.

"You do remote work?" Leeroy's voice stood out like a horn in the hypnotic rhythm of the truck's engine. It caught me so off guard that I took a few moments to process the question, and several more to work out what exactly he was asking.

"Depends," I told him. "I've learned that most para-humans keep paper records, so I have to be on-site to process those. If they've gone digital, then it's another story. Those jobs, I can do anywhere. At a cheaper rate, too, since it doesn't take me nearly as long."

"Yeah, we're still on paper," Leeroy admitted. "Krystal says your company does a good job, though. Might be worth it to fly one of you out here come April. Dealing with the city finances is my least favorite part of this job."

"Wouldn't that be a job for the town mayor, or treasurer?" Even as I spoke, I realized that I'd never actually seen a city hall anywhere in Boarback, nor had there been any mention of a governmental system. It was just the sheriff and his deputies.

"It's all on my plate," Leeroy said, confirming my suspicion. "You make something, be it a kid or a town, it's on you to look after it."

"Wait, are you saying you founded Boarback?" It was more surprising than shocking. After all, the town couldn't be more than a few centuries old, and there were certainly parahumans that measured their lives in millennia. With how powerful Leeroy seemed, it made sense that he'd been around for a long while. I just hadn't expected the town's founder to still be working as its sheriff.

"Seems like yesterday," he told me. "Except for the paperwork. I'd swear I've done lifetimes' worth of that. Makes me miss the old days, before there were so many forms and boxes. Someone showed up with a bill, and you either paid it or drove them off. Of course, that was before I held a respectable office, like sheriff."

Despite not completely understanding what he was talking about, I did my best to conjure a sympathetic nod. "April is a tight time for me, and all other accountants, but since you're a friend of Krystal's, I can carve out a few days to come lend a hand."

Leeroy waved me off. "We don't need the boss down here; things aren't that tough. One of your people will be fine."

"The company is just me and Albert, and he isn't properly trained to do a full accounting service on his own."

"Oh." For the first time, Leeroy looked a touch surprised. It didn't last long, though. In seconds, he'd faded back to the warm, relaxed grin that was usually there. "Well then, sure, we'd gladly accept your help. I can even pay some in advance."

I began to protest that it wasn't necessary, but before I'd gotten more than a few syllables out, Leeroy had produced a small glass vial. Inside were a few drops of red liquid that my base instincts immediately recognized as blood. There was something off about it, though. A curious rainbow sheen seemed to shimmer on the edges, like gasoline spilled on a lake. He tossed it to me and I caught it on reflex, my arm moving without even bothering to check with my brain.

"Had a feeling that would come in handy," he said. "Takes a hell of a lot to make me bleed, not even I can manage it without a proper weapon, but a few decades back, there was a rough dragon that tried to settle down in the hills. Sucker managed to get a few drops from me, so I put them away for a rainy day."

"This is your blood?" Even through the glass, I could smell what was inside. It smelled delicious, and savory, and *strong*. Much as I loathe to admit it, my mouth had begun to salivate, acting completely on its own, with no regard for propriety.

"Sure is. Few drops will give you quite the pick-me-up. Might come in handy if those new vampires decide to cause trouble." There was something in Leeroy's eyes that I couldn't quite place. Not aggression, and not judgment. Curiosity? Regardless, the vial had most of my attention. The few drops inside were so powerful I could feel them before they even hit my tongue. If I drank it, would I be safe? It was hard to imagine any other vampire being a threat, not unless they were feeding off a dragon.

With a last long, lingering look at the blood, I tossed it back to Leeroy, who easily snatched it from the air. "Thank you, but Fletcher Accounting Services only accepts payment by check, credit card, or direct deposit, and we don't take advances for services not yet rendered."

Slowly, he put the blood back in his shirt pocket, eyes never leaving me. "You have any idea what you just threw away?"

"Power, strength, the ability to live without fear of any who might do me harm. Like I said, thank you, but no, thank you. I got a taste of that last year when an ancient dragon gave me his blood. It was more inconvenience than anything. I'm fine with what I've got. Maybe it falls short for a conquering vampire, but for an accountant, it's more than enough." My fingers were still tingling from where I'd been holding the vial, though the feeling was finally fading.

The truck made a few more turns and had just burst into the clearing when Leeroy spoke again. The cheer had faded from his voice, and something else was there in its place. Experience, wisdom, some indefinable quality that only one who has lived far beyond mortal years is able to conjure.

"I've seen many things, long as I've been alive. The rise and fall of countries, the very earth shift beneath our feet, the birth and death of waves of human generations, gone so quickly it's like the flash of a firefly. Yet, in all that time, I've only encountered a handful of people, human or para, who had what it took to turn down power when it was before them. I think I might see what Krystal loves in you, Fredrick Fletcher."

Something shivered down my spine as he said my name, but by the time the willies had passed, so too had Leeroy's shift in mood. He was smiling again as the truck began to slow, our plane already in sight.

"Don't you go dying on me before April, now. If I have to deal with all those finances myself, I am going to be quite annoyed. Push comes to shove, I'll even lend a hand to keep you alive if needed. Just make sure it's really necessary. Like one of my favorite humans said: 'If you must hit, do not hit softly.' I don't pull my punches."

I nodded my understanding as the truck finally came to a stop and everyone began to hop out. All of a sudden, the vampires waiting back in Winslow didn't seem quite so scary; at least, not when compared to the man who watched over the town of Boarback. The weight of his offer slowed me even as we loaded our bags back into the plane's small cargo hold. Did he mean that I could call him in if things got too dangerous? This wasn't a quick trip. How would he get there in time? And if he did come, how much of Winslow would be left standing when he was finished?

Goodbyes were said, and hands were shaken. Albert and Sable exchanged e-mail addresses, while Neil stood awkwardly nearby. Leeroy pulled Krystal in for a long hug before finally releasing her, then slapped Arch heartily on the back as he snuck in one pre-flight smoke. Nax also gave Krystal an embrace, though his was more tentative than the bear hug Sheriff Thorgood had used.

Eventually, all the pleasantries were exchanged and we boarded the plane. Neil took a window seat, downed a glowing green potion he'd mixed up in a water bottle, and promptly passed out. I wasn't sure if he'd tried to make something to suppress nausea or to force him into sleep, but either way, given who Neil's instructor was, I knew that what he'd taken was bound to be potent. And possibly illegal, though I never quite understood where alchemical potions fell in terms of drug use. Albert took the seat next to Neil, three air-sick bags already in hand, just in case, and Arch sat down across the aisle from his pupil. They'd probably spend the flight reviewing Albert's matches with Sable and which techniques to polish, none of which interested me in the slightest. Listening to Arch talk about fighting made me understand how most people felt when I tried to explain the difference between an IRA and a Roth IRA.

I ended up with a window seat as well, since Krystal liked to stretch her legs into the aisle while she napped. This afforded me a view of Boarback as the plane began its wobbling rise upward. We started out so low that I could see the sheriff's truck's headlights in flashes as they moved through the woods. Further out, the lights of Boarback's town center glowed, a small oasis of light in a sea of dark trees. It looked peaceful, even from so far up. Maybe, one day, I would come back to this place for more than an accounting job. Maybe Krystal and I would move here when things were too dangerous, or we just wanted a more peaceful daily life.

This was not that day, though. As the plane rose higher and Boarback faded from sight, I felt an unexpected sense of relief in my stomach. Even after only a few days away, I'd gotten homesick for Winslow, Colorado, and the people who lived there. It had been a nice vacation, but I was glad that it was coming to an end.

Waiting vampire clans be damned, it was time for us to go home.

A LAWYER IN THE MANSION

1.

DESPITE THE WORRY WITH WHICH WE returned to Winslow, relatively little happened in the weeks to follow. My home was released, having been officially cleaned and cleared of all the traps Colin, the rogue hunter, had left behind. I was also relatively certain that roughly half the beers I kept in my fridge for guests had vanished as well, but since Krystal was the largest consumer of those, that was her battle to fight. Apparently, none of the Agency's trap-detectors had much of a taste for red wine.

For the first few days, every time my new phone rang, I was sure it would be Krystal calling to let me know that more inquiries had come down and she thought I was in danger. Eventually, though, the fear subsided, and I fell back into my regular routine. This process was helped along by the fact that I was positively swamped, fighting my way back to being on schedule after the short trip to Boarback. I even had to ask Albert to skip a few lessons, so great was my need for assistance. In the hectic rush of working overtime to hit my deadlines with every client, there was little room in my mind for the more abstract fears, like what a new vampire clan in town was up to.

Perhaps that was why I didn't bristle with suspicion when Amy and Bubba showed up at my apartment one evening, announcing themselves with a quick phone call five minutes prior to let me know they were on their way. My instincts finally whispered that something might be up when Amy walked through the door holding a fine bottle of pinot noir, with the cork still intact. While Amy Wells was a good friend and a talented mage, she wasn't the type to bring a bottle of wine just for a drop-in, and if she did, then she would almost always try to . . . augment it with some of her concoctions.

"This looks lovely," I told her, accepting the bottle because, suspicious or not, there are certain rules one is supposed to observe when playing host. "May I ask what the occasion is?"

"We need a favor." Bubba, at least, was a man I could always count on to cut to the quick of things. Towering over both me and Amy, he wore his usual arrangement of flannel, denim, and a beat-up trucker's hat. Compared to an alpha therian like Richard, Bubba wasn't much, but outside of that anomalous group, he was easily one of the biggest people I'd ever met. Also one of the most loyal and kindest, which was perhaps why Richard had been tasking Bubba with more and more assignments in recent months. Loyalty was worth its weight in gold, even in the parahuman world.

"Way to ease him in," Amy muttered, tossing an elbow to his ribs that I doubt he even registered. "But yeah, Bubba's right. We need a favor. Well, actually, I need it. Well, actually, some friends of mine need it. Well, actually—"

"If possible, can we jump ahead to the details?" I asked. Amy had small green orbs rotating around her irises, which meant she, as usual, had tried one of her own potions. Without knowing how this one impacted her mind and thought pattern, it was best to try and corral the conversation toward productive ends.

"A mage died last week," Bubba said. "Herbram Clover."

"Oh, I'm sorry for your loss. Was he a friend?" I asked Amy.

"Met him a few times at the swap meets for spell-casters. Decent guy, but after a few beers, he could talk the ears off a sphynx." Amy didn't seem particularly broken up about it, though whether that was due to her own feelings or the magical concoction coursing through her blood was anyone's guess.

"Herbram did some work for Richard at times, along with a lot of other folks. He was a talented enchanter, very respected, very pricey." Bubba walked over to my fridge and pulled out one of the recently restocked silver beer cans. At this point, everyone knew they were there for guests, so there was little need for formality. "Thing is, he had two children, Ainsley and Zane. He also left behind a damned hefty estate, and he actually drafted somethin' of a will."

"The problem is that he didn't get nearly specific enough," Amy added. "All he said was that the estate was to be split evenly between his children. That's it; that was the whole will."

A year prior, I might not have grasped what she was saying, but after becoming a Certified Public Parahuman Accountant and working with all my new clients, I'd learned a great deal about how parahumans regarded paperwork. Turns out that, much like regular humans, they despised it. And since they had so many ways to avoid it, very little was ever actually done. Putting all that together, I could instantly see the issue with Herbram Clover's estate.

"He never had any of it appraised or insured, did he? It was just a note saying to split things evenly, trusting his children to work the rest out themselves." I knew I'd hit the nail on the head by the long draw Bubba took from his beer.

"Right between the eyes," Bubba replied. "It's been a fine mess ever since. They're bickerin' over who gets what, what's worth what, and meanwhile, Herbram's business is falling apart."

Amy took a seat at my dining room table, although I noticed the chair seemed to move when she reached for it, rather than when contact was made. "Herbram was a friend of Richard's, and I've worked with Ainsley a few times, so we got them to agree to use a lawyer who would settle the matter fairly. Problem is, she doesn't have the numbers background to properly work through Herbram's books, and said it would take weeks longer unless we got an accountant. Well, actually, she said it would take an extra four weeks. Well—"

"Got it. Estate in trouble, accountant needed, and I'm one of the few in town who actually knows how to do parahuman books." My mind raced as I tried to do some hurried guesswork. The fact that Herbram had kept books and made a will were both quite promising facts. They'd be terrible, of course—I'd yet to meet a single parahuman aside from myself who kept fastidious records—but it was still more than I was accustomed to starting with. With a lawyer to help and a confined estate to work with, there was a good chance I could get the job done in only a few days. It would be a tight squeeze, schedule-wise, but I couldn't turn down a request from friends. Especially Richard, who I suspected might be the only reason there had yet to be any unfamiliar vampires knocking on my door.

"If I pull a lot of overtime this weekend, I should be able to clear some space out for early next week. Assuming things are remotely in order, I'd require roughly three to six days," I told them. "However, you'll need to take on the job of explaining to Krystal why I'm canceling our weekend plans. That task is non-negotiable."

I'd expected some sort of relief or happiness at my willingness to help. Instead, Bubba and Amy exchanged a long glance between themselves. While not the most astute reader of body language in the world, even I could tell that meant something was wrong.

"What? Is six days too long? If the books are somewhat in order, I might be able to do it faster, but I can't make any promises yet."

"No, that's not the problem. Well, actually, it is, since they need it done soon. Well, actually, we need it done soon. Well—"

This time, it was Bubba who cut Amy off, which I was grateful for. "Ainsley and Zane ain't exactly the most chummy of siblings. Things are gettin' heated the longer it goes on, and when mages get heated, that can cause trouble all around."

"I see. So, how soon were you hoping I'd be able to get started?"

Bubba's eyes darted down to the half-cracked watch on his wrist, which told me all I needed to know before he even spoke. "The lawyer was hopin' to meet us in about an hour."

"An hour?" While I'd technically finished all my work for the day, having stayed at my computer through the sunlight hours to keep at it, that didn't mean I relished the idea of zipping off into the night for a sudden job. There were still things that needed doing, and if the job took half as long as I was expecting, it would cause me to miss deadlines, something I considered an unforgivable sin for a fledgling business. "Look, you know I'm always happy to help out, but this is just too little notice. I can't abandon everything else at the drop of a hat."

"Lawyer said you might feel that way, so she got the Clover children to authorize an extra fee on top of what you usually charge, for the short notice," Bubba said.

"I can't imagine there's a number that would justify me tossing my entire schedule out the window for one unexpected client."

That sentiment lasted exactly as long as it took for Bubba to tell me the number.

"Then again, I suppose it couldn't hurt to at least take a look at the books," I said, backpedaling quickly. It wasn't greed that motivated me so much as pragmatism. With a sudden income influx that high, I might be able to lure in some other parahuman as an employee, whether they liked the work or not. Besides, I could always forgo my daily sleep for another week or so to rebuild the lost time. I didn't usually get loopy until it had been at least ten days without nodding off. Seriously loopy, anyway.

"Great, I'll drive," Amy said. A jolt of fear raced through me, but Bubba shook his head before she'd even gotten out of her chair.

"We took my truck, remember? I'll drive. Fred, get whatever you need." Bubba finished off his beer and tossed the can in the recycling. He didn't go the fridge for another, which I appreciated. Therian constitution or not, I preferred my guests limit their drinking to one an hour if they were getting behind the wheel. Given that he could probably polish off a keg on his own and not pass out, Bubba was a surprisingly good sport about it, and Amy always preferred her own work anyway. In fact, the resistance most parahumans had to mortal vices like alcohol was what fueled her business. Those who wanted a buzz needed something stronger, products that only a talented alchemist could provide.

As I stuffed my laptop into the bag already filled with other supplies, hefting my remote scanner under my arm, I heard Amy's voice from the kitchen. "Maybe we should warn him."

"Warn me about what?" Despite my reluctance to admit accidental eavesdropping, I'd long ago learned that if there was a warning to be had, then it was something I wanted.

"Nothin' dangerous," Bubba said, a hair too quickly. "She just means we should let you know what to expect before we get there."

"Is this place hidden in a dark forest that's only accessible through magical means, or something?" I asked.

Bubba shook his head. "Pretty much the opposite. Just try to keep in mind, everybody mourns in their own way."

2.

AS IT TURNED OUT, WHAT BUBBA MEANT was that some people mourned by surrounding themselves with people. While most of us might go the route of having loved ones nearby, evidently Zane Clover was one to prefer quantity over quality. I could see the people milling about on his yard even as we made our way up the long driveway, Bubba's truck an anomaly amidst the more ostentatious luxury vehicles already parked on the side of the drive. The valet booth at the front explained how so many cars were so neatly arranged, and we watched as a sleek black automobile pulled up, a pair of stunning people tossing over their keys without a second thought. If you're wondering how there was room for so many vehicles—and who could blame you?—it turned out that there was a reason Bubba and Amy had referred to the inheritance as an "estate."

Herbram Clover's mansion was in the Cloudy Meadows community—easily the most expensive, exclusive area of Winslow, Colorado. Just to get in, Bubba had been forced to drive past two guard gates, where they checked his name and ID, along with another guard in front of Herbram's actual driveway. The grounds were sprawling, with large trees separating the property from their neighbors—not that the next house was in earshot, anyway. As for the house, it seemed more akin to a castle than a home, albeit one with modern lighting and a DJ booth set up out on the lawn. At least a hundred people were milling about in front of elegant tables with fine food and expensive liquor that had been set up at careful intervals. White-shirted wait staff made their way around, blending into the background as they cleared off finished plates and made sure drinks never got below half-empty.

"The good news is that if this is the rate they're blowing through the inheritance, I doubt it will take much time at all to figure out how much to split."

"You'd think that, but the parties are all out of Zane's trust," Amy said. Since leaving, she'd drunk a test tube of purple liquid that changed the orbs around her irises to long, shapeless blobs. It had also lifted the tone of her voice by several octaves, but since she'd stopped with the "well, actually" stuff, I considered it a more than fair trade.

"*Parties*? As in, he's done this more than once?" With just a cursory glance, I could see thousands upon thousands of dollars spent in every corner of the lawn. What it cost as a whole boggled the mind, let alone multiplied into multiple events. Part of me wondered if I'd gotten low-balled on the extra fee.

"Done one just about every night since his dad passed." Bubba pulled behind a bright yellow sports car and killed the truck, popping the door open and tossing his key to the approaching valet. The red-vested man seemed a touch confused by the beat-up truck amidst a sea of luxury, but he didn't let it stop him from doing his job.

"He took the loss hard," Amy added.

"So I can see. What exactly did Herbram Clover do, again, that afforded such a lifestyle?"

"Enchanter," Amy told me. "Brilliant work, passed down through the family for generations. The Clover name is synonymous with power and craftsmanship. And that's the sort of thing you pay a premium for."

There was no debating that part, as Amy and Bubba led me into a front hall filled with more staff, offering drinks and to take coats, along with a fresh wave of partiers. All around me, I saw designer labels and surgically perfected faces. The scent of plastic was practically overwhelming, at least for my vampiric nose. We got a few strange looks as Bubba politely cleared a way through the crowd, Amy's flowing, simple dress and my professional attire likely costing less than anyone's individual shoe. Thankfully, they did move, as a man Bubba's size commands an instinctual respect, regardless of how much his clothes are worth.

Finally, we made it to a stairway with only a few partiers drifting about, climbing quickly past a velvet rope with a guard who'd have seemed intimidating if Bubba didn't have at least half a foot on him. To my surprise, the guard greeted us with a genuine smile, pulling the rope aside and letting us pass as he and Bubba exchanged a few words. My best guess said that he was a fellow therian, as they were renowned for being good muscle, though he didn't look at me with as much disdain as I'd have expected. Perhaps he was just a muscular human who appreciated dealing with regular folks instead of an endless stream of the wealthy.

After navigating several long hallways, we at last arrived in front of a pair of double doors, blocked by two more guards who nodded at Bubba and Amy on sight. They looked at me suspiciously, but Amy whispered a few words and they stepped aside without comment.

"We got Ainsley to hire the guards after the first few drunks wandered in and bothered the lawyer," Bubba whispered as one of the guards unlocked the door. "Moved the work to a secure room, too. Used to be Herbram's study; supposed to be warded six ways to Sunday."

It occurred to me that I'd never asked for more information about this lawyer of theirs. Everything else had been so overwhelming it was a detail that slipped through the cracks. I was about to inquire when the door opened, and I saw a figure flipping through files, free hand dancing along the nearby notepad as it jotted down the bits deemed worth remembering.

"Asha?"

Sure enough, a familiar face looked up from the notepad, and there was Asha Patel. She looked a little different since I'd last seen her—hair cut shorter, clothes less formal. She also didn't look half-terrified, most likely because this time, we weren't trapped in Charlotte Manor under threat of death. In Charlotte's defense, it had been an issue of self-preservation, and she'd apologized for the incident several times since.

"When they said they knew an accountant, I had a feeling it would be you." She rose from her seat as I walked in the room, followed by Bubba and Amy. We exchanged a brief hug, more familiar than I'd be with most colleagues, but there's nothing like a near-death experience to create a bond.

"Well, I had no idea I'd find you here. What happened? Last time we talked, you were heading home to try and drink until the previous few hours were nothing but a blurry memory." Behind us, the doors shut once again, and I heard the lock being slid back into place.

"Damnedest thing, I was out of wine. Can you believe it?" Asha said. "That, and once I got away, I couldn't stop thinking about everything you told me, and that I'd seen. I ended up going back to the site with the parahuman law books. I thought if I understood it all, maybe it wouldn't be so scary."

A sound idea, and one easily executed. Parahuman laws are hidden in plain sight in the form of a role-playing game. It allows them to be easily accessible by anyone, without humans realizing what they're actually seeing. Most people think it's just a very dry, boring game, though I've heard there are a few diehard fans scattered about the country.

"It sort of worked," Asha continued. "After a few hours of reading, I was able to fall asleep. Then I did the same thing the next night, and the next, and eventually, I realized that I was forcing myself to learn. There was this whole other world of law and precedent I'd never seen before, and I wanted to know everything about it. You can probably fill in the details from there."

"Once you had the knowledge, you wanted to use it, which you couldn't do at Torvald & Torvald," I surmised. "So you started freelancing in your off time."

"Close, but not quite," Asha replied. "I got a few certifications while still at the company, but once I was cleared to go, I made the jump whole hog. Turned in my resignation and started up my own company. Been going around two months now, and business is booming."

"Glad to hear it. Though, honestly, I didn't even know normal people could work with parahumans in such a capacity," I said.

"It's not exactly smiled upon, but there's no law against it." Amy's voice came from my left; she had wandered over, running her hands along the files as she did. "While we're not supposed to go around telling humans that we're here, a few find out anyway. If someone knows, and they decide to fill a need in the parahuman market, there's not any real reason to stop them. Long as they exercise discretion and don't go blabbing, it's okay."

"Long story short, I had to fill out so many confidentiality agreements and secrecy clauses that I had a two-day long hand cramp." Asha shook her fingers, as if the ghost of the pain still lingered in her digits. "But I pushed through, and now I'm certified to work with parahumans. Good thing, too. For a culture that has real vampires as a part of it, there are shockingly few lawyers."

"Low blow," I told her.

"My job, I get to make the jokes." She patted the table, drawing my attention the large stack of files and ledgers spread out across it. "I assume Bubba and Amy filled you in on our situation?"

"They understated the scope, but I got the gist of things. Huge inheritance, the only directive is an even split, and our clients can't agree on a fair division. Did I miss anything?"

"Just the most problematic point." Asha sat back down, grabbing a nearby file, and I pulled up a chair next to her. Bubba and Amy also took seats, though they kept well away from where the paperwork was being discussed.

"The liquid assets, cash and gold, were kept mostly in bank accounts and treasure chests," Asha began, running her hand along a line of numbers so large I thought I might actually swoon. "Those, along with the house, were relatively easy to calculate a value for. Same for a lot of the antiques and collectibles. It'll take time, but I can get some appraisers in to assess a value. What's kept this procedure from moving forward is the tools."

"I have a suspicion you don't mean a belt sander," I muttered.

"What I wouldn't give," Asha replied. "No, these are enchanter's tools, passed down along the Clover line for centuries. Part of what makes their products so valuable. Very powerful stuff, or so I'm told. Apparently, it's a complete set, and it can't be split up without reducing the usefulness to a point where they might as well be generics. That's our biggest issue: whichever child gets the tools is essentially being handed the Clover business. The other can trade on the name, but without those tools, the odds of producing the same quality of goods are almost null."

"Interesting. So, in fair division of assets, we have to calculate the value of the tools in terms of potential income for an expected mage's life span, and offset the gain for one client by giving the other an equivalent amount of the other assets." Hesitant as I'd been to come along, I'd be lying if I said the challenge didn't intrigue me. The calculations needed to put everything together were going to be uniquely complex, and that was without planning for the usual hiccups one always encountered in this kind of work.

"They have weird ideas of interesting," I heard Bubba tell Amy from across the table.

"Do either of the children have a better claim to the business than the other?" I asked, ignoring my friend's words of boredom. "If one lacks the talent to actually keep the business afloat, then that would give the tools a diminished value in their hands."

Asha shook her head, flipping a few pages ahead to a small summary showing a pair of striking similar people. "Both were educated by their father, and are considered top-notch mages. Ainsley has a bit more technical know-how; some people think she's already passed her father's level of skill. Zane is a much better people-person, though; in case the party downstairs didn't tip you off. He's been handling a lot of the new client acquisition for several years."

"I suppose that's easier then. The tools are equal in value regardless of who gets them." I looked at the mound of ledgers and papers lying on the table, most of which were of the same style as the one Asha was holding. "Did you do all of this?"

"Transcribed a lot of it; kept the original for some, though," Asha replied. "I like to keep things organized."

"On that point, we definitely agree. Do you have the records for what Clover earned off his tools for the past decade or so? I'll need that as a starting point."

"Way ahead of you." Asha grabbed a particularly thick file and plopped it down in front of me as I pulled out my laptop.

"Then let's get to work." Looking back, perhaps it would have been more prudent to downplay my excitement, but in that moment, all I could see was the intriguing prospect of the challenge set before me.

3.

IT'S IMPOSSIBLE TO SAY HOW LONG WE'D been working before the doors burst open. I was so absorbed in combing through the numbers that I'd completely lost all sense of time. The only thing that really betrayed the ticking of minutes was Bubba, who'd fallen asleep in his chair and was snoring softly. Amy had downed another potion not long after he nodded off, and every time I glanced at her, she was staring up at the ceiling. Truthfully, I had no idea if she was conscious or not, especially since her reaction to the doors slamming open was a quiet, bird-like *cheep*.

"Enough is enough!" The woman who came striding through, unhindered by either of the bulky guards standing at the door, was quite striking. Emerald robes hung from her body, complementing her dark skin while simultaneously giving her an air of wisdom and mystique. Clutched in her hand was a large wooden staff, intricate symbols carved up and down its length. As I looked at them, I thought I caught a few shifting, ever so slightly slithering about along the staff's surface. Her eyes took the whole room in with a glance, locking on Asha and promptly ignoring the rest of us.

"We brought you here to put an end to this impasse," she declared, crossing the room in several quick-stepped strides. Despite the aura of power she threw off, I realized that she was actually rather diminutive, no more than a couple of inches over five feet tall. "But still the matter remains unsettled, and meanwhile, my brother fills this house with revelry night after night. I just caught sight of someone . . . *relieving* themselves in my herb garden. Do you know what that does to nightshade?"

"Depends on what the person has eaten today," Amy said, her voice so soft and detached that I think I was the only one who heard it. In spite of the commotion, Bubba still snored in his chair. That, at least, wasn't much of surprise. As a former trucker, he'd gotten used to taking rest wherever he could, and it would take more than a little shouting to rouse him.

"Ainsley, please calm down. I promise, we're making progress." Asha motioned for me to come over, so I slowly made my forward, catching Ainsley Clover's attention for the first time. "This is Fredrick Fletcher, of Fletcher Accounting Services. He's here to help me calculate the fair distribution of assets for you and Zane."

Ainsley scrutinized me, slowly moving her eyes up and down, as if she were trying to a pick apart every aspect of my being. "A vampire? Are you sure he isn't one of my brother's guests who wandered up from downstairs? I've never known a vampire to be good for more than decadence and betrayal."

"With all due respect, Ms. Clover, Asha called me in to help with this case as a favor. If you don't want me here, then I can take my leave. And if you're going to continue to make those kinds of comments, I think I'd rather go, regardless." Ainsley wasn't the first client I'd met who had certain ideas about vampires, and honestly, it was hard to debate those people on many points. Since vampires could take the abilities of other parahumans by drinking their blood, my species had earned a reputation for feeding by any means necessary. However, that didn't mean I had to work with people who couldn't manage basic civility. Swamped as I was, there were plenty of clients out there who could at least mind their manners; I no longer bothered with the ones that lacked that skill.

Asha's eyes went wide at my words, though I'm not sure if she was afraid for my safety or the fact she'd have to try and find another CPPA on such short notice. Ainsley just kept staring at me for another few seconds, then finally dipped her head.

"Forgive me, Mr. Fletcher. I've never been quite adept at interacting with others, and this business with my father's estate has me out of sorts. You're right. I've no place to judge you by your fangs, and if Asha has brought you in, then I trust that you have the skill to do the job."

"It's all right. This happens more than you'd think," I assured her. "And please, call me Fred. Everyone else already does."

"Then you may refer to me by my first name, as well." Ainsley turned from me back to Asha, her tone much calmer than when she'd come bursting in the door. "I appreciate that this is not an easy task, but please tell me that we're nearing completion. The sooner this is all settled, the sooner I can get back to work. Zane has his parties, but without the tools, all I can do is plan and research."

"We're making headway," Asha said. "Fred coming on board is a big step in cutting down on our timetables. With a little luck and a lot of coffee, we might be able to get it down in a few days. Maybe a week more, at most."

Ainsley didn't exactly seem thrilled with the news, but she accepted it with a stalwart sigh. "Very well. I know that no delicate work is helped along by hurrying. If you'll excuse me, I'm going to go have a word with my brother about his 'guests' and their understanding of where the bathrooms are."

With a graceful twirl that sent her robes spinning, Ainsley strode back out of the room. Though no one touched them, the doors gently closed behind her, and I could hear the lock sliding back into place.

"Well, that was certainly something." I sank back down into my chair and set about the task of finding the spot where I'd been interrupted in my work.

"Ainsley's got a good heart. She's just a little brash," Asha told me. "It doesn't help that her method of dealing with stress seems to be work, and enchanting is off the table until we finish dividing the estate."

"Why is that, exactly? Are you trying to stop any new goods from being produced that might impact the figures?" I asked.

In response, Asha dug through a few files and pulled out a thick stack of papers. Unlike the pages all around us, these were yellow and weathered, the script scrawled across them a handwritten cursive. "This is Herbram's will. The actual instructions are just the top page, the rest is all spellcraft and enchantments that I can't make heads or tails of. As Ainsley and Zane explained it, the tools and the other really valuable stuff is being held in a sort of magical escrow. Not even they can get to those items, not until the estate is divided. Only when they're both satisfied will they sign the back page, and that's what undoes the spell."

Now *that* was an impressive escrow system. Carefully, I took the pages from Asha and read through them. The first one was indeed a will, or as little instruction as could be given and still constitute one, but the rest appeared to be nothing more than gibberish and runes. This time, I was certain the runes were moving, as I flipped a page and caught one in mid-slither. Amy might have been able to make sense of what everything was, but seeing as she'd mentally checked out and it didn't actually impact my job, I decided to just trust Asha.

"It's a smart system," I said, handing her back the stack of pages. "Though a bit inconvenient for his kids. Did he really think they were going to snatch everything up before it could be divided?"

"From the way Ainsley and Zane describe it, I get the feeling it was more concern about external threats," Asha replied. "In case the house didn't give it away, the Clovers are worth a lot of money. Keeping everything locked up until it has a rightful owner was Herbram's way of making sure nothing got lost, or taken, in the handover. You can add magic and vampires, but good old corporate espionage is still the same all over."

"Well, the old clients didn't challenge for blood when they got robbed," I pointed out.

"See, that statement is how I know you were in the office too much. If you'd been out schmoozing, you'd know just how many blood oaths people were swearing." Asha tucked the will back under her file of financial records and pulled a ledger forward. "I've actually been surprised by how mundane a lot of my work is. Aside from almost every parahuman species having their own treaties, laws, and exceptions, there's really no difference from working with humans."

"Except for the occasional outburst of chaos and danger," I said.

"Do you get a lot of that? My closest call was in Charlotte Manor, and once when I mixed up my dates for a meeting with a weretiger. She thought I was a trespasser, until she noticed the briefcase."

"Give it time; soon, you'll build up quite the stock of stories. Seems to come with the territory," I told her.

Asha's mouth was open to reply, but her words were lost as the sound of a thunderclap tore through the room, shaking everything around us like a three-second earthquake. It was so loud that it woke Bubba, who tried to sit up, got confused, and tumbled to the floor. Even Amy seemed to shake off her lingering stupor, turning her vacant gaze from the ceiling to a nearby window. I followed her eyes, looking out to see a red glow flickering through the glass.

Moving carefully, lest another blast shake the room, I carefully peered out to see what was causing the light show. I thought maybe one of the drunken guests had found a propane tank to set off, creating the explosion and setting the yard on fire. What met my eyes was not panicking guests and a blazing yard, however. The red glow was actually coming from the sky, which seemed too close for comfort, slicing down and parting the driveway less than a quarter of the way out, forming an opaque red wall that carried on in every visible direction.

What was more worrying was that everyone seemed to have vanished. No wait staff, no partygoers, no valets. Just empty buffet tables and glasses of fizzing champagne slowly going flat. Bubba, Asha, and Amy crowded around me as we took in the scene, trying to figure out exactly what had happened. From a few inches away, I heard Asha mutter darkly under her breath.

"You just had to go and tempt fate, didn't you, Fred?"

4.

AMY PULLED OUT A SMALL BOTTLE WITH several symbols etched on the side, popped the top, and took a long gulp. When she finished, the shapeless blobs around her eyes dissolved, although she had grown a small set of horns just below her hairline. I honestly couldn't have cared less about the new forehead accessories; all that mattered to me was that our resident alchemist was visibly more focused than before. As the only one of us who even remotely understood magic, we were all waiting for her to shed some light on what had just happened.

"Well, I'll be damned," Amy said, after looking at the scene with fresh focus. "I have no idea what the hell that is."

"I thought you were a mage." Asha's tone was strained; she was understandably a bit on edge given the circumstances.

"I'm an alchemist. That's like asking a dermatologist to fill in for an advanced brain surgeon. Sure, they're both doctors, but they've got specialties that the other wouldn't be as educated in, and this is some of high-level enchanter shit." Amy pointed to the red wall, as if we weren't already staring at it. "Best guess, this thing is a giant bubble that split us off into a pocket dimension."

"Seems like a big ass pocket," Bubba rumbled, having finally wiped the last of the sleep from his eyes.

"Just a phrase. It means we're not quite in the real world at the moment, sort of compacted into a magical space that's adjacent to it. I can explain if you really want me to, but the basic theory takes five heavy books and half a day to cover," Amy offered.

"We'll take your word for it." I scanned the area outside, still searching for any signs of life. "The bigger questions are: how did we get here, where is everyone, and what do we do to get home?"

"Look!" Asha grabbed my arm and pulled me a few inches over, shifting my perspective so that I caught sight of a suit-wearing figure just barely visible from our vantage point. Whoever they were, I could see them making broad gestures with their hands, either talking in an animated manner or perhaps casting a spell.

"Seems like we've got someone to question," Bubba said.

There was no discussion of the issue. He was right, and there was no getting around that. We needed to figure out what was happening, and there was at least a chance that the person down there might know. Amy fiddled with the lock, flinging the doors open to reveal an empty hallway. No guards, no sounds of guests from downstairs; just a whole lot more nothing, exactly like the lawn. Moving swiftly, but with our eyes peeled for any potential danger, we made our way down the stairs.

"Holy crap." Asha's voice was a whisper as she veered away from the group. We'd just hit the bottom floor, and while the rest of us were occupied with getting outside, something else had caught the lawyer's eye. It didn't take long to notice what, either. Directly before her, hovering in mid-air, was a glass filled halfway with scotch. A few feet away was a dish piled high with large shrimp, right next to a floating glass of wine.

All around us, bits of dishware and cutlery hung about, supported by some invisible force. Bubba stuck a finger in a flute of champagne and gave it a quick swirl, watching the bubbles fizz in reaction to his touch. Then he took hold of the glass and tried to move it. Not so much as even a budge, and I knew well that Bubba's strength was nothing to turn a nose up at.

"Are these what the guests were holding?" Asha asked, picking up a shrimp and turning it around in her hand before dropping it to the floor. The crustacean tumbled unimpeded, hitting the fine marble below us with a moist squish.

"Must be," I agreed. "But why just the glasses and dishes? If it's what they were holding, there was bound to be other stuff."

"These are part of the mansion." Amy's head was tilted backward, staring up at the underside of a plate. "They all bear the Clover crest. Whatever happened, it kept the mansion, and every piece of property inside, intact."

"Somehow, I think that's even creepier." Asha shuddered and walked back over to us. With the mystery of the floating dishware solved, or as solved as it was likely to be, we continued on, heading down the long hallway and out into the night air.

The four of us stepped into an argument, but it took me several seconds to realize that a fight was even happening, I was so distracted by the feeling of the air around me. It was completely still, unnaturally so, and a part of my more primal mind reeled at the incongruity.

Outside was meant to be alive, the air always moving, slight currents bringing in new smells and feelings. None of that was here, though. This air was flat. Empty.

Dead.

"Oh, fuck you, it's my fault! Was I supposed to just let you hex me?" The voice snapped me out of my fixation with the air, turning my attention to the pair of people bickering nearby. One I knew right away—the large staff and green robes made Ainsley unmistakable, even if her back was turned to us. The other person was the one wearing the suit that I'd seen from the window. Without introduction, I instantly knew that this would be Zane, the other Clover sibling. He and Ainsley were nearly identical, only a few small facial differences between them, despite being of different genders. If that weren't enough, though, I likely could have pieced it together from the foot-long wooden wand glowing a soft blue in his hand, runes just like the ones in Ainsley's staff scrawled across it.

"If you were half-decent, you'd have taken the spell. Stars know you deserve worse. Do you have any idea what I walked in on your *guests* doing in the restroom?" Ainsley yelled, waving her staff around as though she were debating taking it to her brother's head, which actually seemed quite in the realm of possibility from how heated things were.

"No, and I don't care. It's a party! That's why I pay people to clean up when these things are over."

"This is our home, you bastard, the Clover estate. Do you have no regard for the generations of our family that spent their lives in this mansion? What I am even asking, we both know the answer is no," Ainsley spat.

"Kiss my ass with the Clover estate shit. It's just a house! Quit trying to memorialize everything like it's so damned precious. Dad's gone; turning the home into a shrine won't bring him back!" Zane threw his hands about as he talked, which explained the erratic gestures I'd noticed from the window.

Ainsley opened and closed her mouth several times, but no words were coming out. I did notice that her grip on the staff had grown tighter, though, and suddenly, the inadvertent silence seemed like a good place to announce ourselves, before there was only one conscious mage to talk to.

"Excuse us, but I'm hoping you two have some idea of what's going on?" I tried to keep my voice calm and easygoing, but both of the Clover siblings easily jumped half a foot off the ground at the sound of my words. They spun around, staff and wand leveled at our group, before Ainsley finally seemed to recognize us.

"What . . . Fred? How did you four get here?" She threw a look to Zane, who merely shrugged, their feud momentarily forgotten amidst the mystery of our appearance.

"Sort of what we were hoping you could tell us," Asha replied. "We were up in the study, working on the will, when there was a loud boom and suddenly, this red bubble is everywhere and we're in some sort of purse dimension."

"Pocket dimension," Amy, Zane, and Ainsley all corrected simultaneously.

"*Whatever*," Asha snapped. "Point is, we're here, there are plates and glasses floating around, and it's not a great work environment. Can you fix this?"

While I didn't know much about the history between Ainsley and Zane, or their personalities, I easily recognized the sheepish, guilty look that flashed between them at Asha's question. We weren't going to like the answer, and they were probably going to be embarrassed by it.

"Here's the issue," Zane said, taking over the conversation with a smooth delicacy that I immediately envied. "This whole thing was our doing, sort of, but in a much bigger way, it's the work of our father. Raising a pair of mages in the city can be troublesome, especially twins, since, like all kids, we would quarrel. And since he was the one who enchanted our staff and wand respectively, he added a little something extra. Every time spells from our tools clashed, the magical implements would trigger a spell that stuck us in our own pocket dimension. He did it partly to make sure we couldn't go around using our magic in front of humans before we understood the consequences, but also as a punishment.

This is the equivalent of our time-out room, and my dear sister activated it when she came storming downstairs in a tizzy and tried to launch a hex at me."

"That ain't much of an explanation on why we got dragged along," Bubba said.

"Yeah, that I don't know about," Zane admitted. "Usually, the only things that come with us are our tools and possessions. Dad could walk in and out, since he created it, but he was the only one."

"I've got a theory." Ainsley stepped forward, though I noticed she kept several feet between herself and Zane at all times. "They were locked in the study when you callously blocked a spell you deserved and trapped us here. Father placed more than a tome's worth of enchantments and wards on that room, so it's possible that one of those spells tethered everything in it to our location, people included."

"It's as good a bet as any," Zane agreed. "Dad loved to test new spells around the house. I wouldn't put it past him to have thrown a pointless one on the study and forget about it."

"He did *not* cast pointless spells." Ainsley whirled around on Zane, a new head of steam already building for a fresh fight. But it was Amy, thankfully, who stepped forward and retook control of the situation.

"Look, we get that you two have shit to work out, and that's great, but maybe we could focus on how to get out of your time-out space? I'm pretty sure the party guests have noticed that all their plates vanished, and eventually, someone will realize that the homeowner is gone, too."

"No, Dad made this place to keep us from exposing our magic," Zane said. "Just like space, the time is compressed. We'd have to spend months here before any measurable time slipped by on the outside."

"He'd leave us in the bubble for weeks sometimes," Ainsley added. "Bringing by food and water if needed, but otherwise, we'd be on our own."

"Wow, and I thought my dad was strict," Asha muttered.

"To the old man's credit, we could get out anytime we wanted to." Zane tilted his head toward Ainsley and rolled his eyes. "All we ever had to do was apologize to each other. Since we always went in here for fighting, he didn't let us out until we made up. But someone never learned to lie well enough to sell him on the fake ones, so it took much longer than needed."

"Excuse me for not wanting to deceive our father," Ainsley shot back.

"Okay, look, your dad's not here to judge the authenticity of an apology, so why don't you both just say you're sorry and get us out of here," Amy suggested.

Another look flashed between them. It wasn't much, but it was enough that I knew, even before Zane spoke, that things wouldn't be quite so simple.

"Yeah, see, the apology was what he demanded before letting us out, but it didn't end the spell on its own," Zane admitted. "For that, we need the chime of a clearing bell; the same one he used when creating the enchantment."

"So, where's the damn bell?" Bubba asked. Now it was my and Asha's turn to exchange looks, as we both had the exact same hunch on what the answer would be. And unfortunately, we were dead-on right.

"We don't have the exact location." Ainsley's eyes were suddenly very preoccupied with the grass down by her feet. "All we know is that it's with the rest of his enchanting tools, locked away in magical escrow."

5.

FIERCE AS MY OWN INITIAL RISING PANIC was, I was far more concerned with how Asha would take the news. Bubba, Amy, and I were all accustomed to a certain level of chaos popping up at unexpected times. Asha, however, was new to the parahuman world, only being acquainted with it for a few months. There was a very real chance that the terror of such an impossible magical predicament could overwhelm her, and we needed everyone functional if we hoped to break out of this pocket bubble.

To my shock, Asha looked cheerier than she had in the foyer of floating plates. If anything, she seemed relieved by the news, which only served to make me wonder if I'd misheard Ainsley's explanation.

"Asha, are you okay?"

"Huh?" She looked over at me, more perplexed by the question than the issue of how we were going to escape. "Sure. I mean, I was worried for a while there, but it looks like this will be an easy fix, after all."

Zane and Ainsley were shooting expressions at Asha that perfectly mirrored my own. "Perhaps being locked in the study made you forget, but escrow means there's no getting at the tools until we've decided who the owner is," Zane told her.

"Right, which is exactly what Fred is here to help me do," Asha agreed, still unbothered by our dour dispositions. "And this is better in a lot of ways. We've got however long we need to do the work, since time doesn't matter, and according to you, no one will even notice that we're gone. All we have to do is iron out the will, and whoever gets the tools can pop us out of here."

"Don't mean to be a party pooper, but there's the issue of food and water to think about." Bubba spoke between bites of shrimp; evidently, he'd taken a handful from the plates in the foyer. I'd have been worried about someone noticing the absent crustaceans when the time bubble vanished, but with the amount of alcohol I'd seen flowing, I sincerely doubted anyone would assume missing shrimp were stolen by a giant therian.

Ainsley lifted her head slightly higher. Now that the situation wasn't so hopeless, it seemed she didn't feel quite as ashamed for getting us into it. "We've got enough bottled water and food in the pantry to last for months. Father always used to say that a mage's home should be a fortress unto itself, impregnable and self-sufficient."

It seemed Herbram Clover shared the same thoughts on home-safety as the mages who had built Charlotte Manor. I could only wonder what his children would think of my friend, the animated house.

"And do you also have a stock of blood on hand?" In the silence that fell after Amy's words, every eye slowly turned to me. Asha was scared, and trying not to show it, having no doubt only just remembered that, as a vampire, I needed blood to survive. Ainsley and Zane both looked more concerned than fearful, regarding me as a potential threat that might need dealing with. Bubba and Amy were worried, but there was no terror in their anxiety. They knew the situation from my vantage point, and understood that the biggest potential issue was me starving myself, as I had no desire to take anyone's blood, especially unwillingly.

"Never let it be said that I am unprepared." Reaching into my back pocket, I pulled out the enchanted flask I'd purchased in Boarback. "Had a run-in with an unfriendly fellow several weeks ago, and ever since, I've made a point of always keeping some emergency blood on hand. Just in case."

A wave of relief washed over the rest of the room. With my own meals handled, there was nothing to stop us from buckling down and pushing through the paperwork. If anything, this might be a blessing in disguise. Instead of having to carve days out of my schedule to work in, Asha and I could handle the whole thing in one marathon of number crunching.

"Seems as though you've got work to do," Zane said, nicely summing up the situation. It might have been that easy, too, if only he hadn't kept talking. "But after tonight's attack, it can no longer be denied that my sister lacks the temperament to run this business. Divide the resources fairly, just make sure that I get the enchanting tools, regardless of how much else you have to give her."

"*You?* Your skills aren't even up to what Father could do, yet you want to take over his business?" Ainsley whirled on her brother, staff trembling in her angry grip.

"My work won't be as good as what you can manage." There was no bitterness or bite in Zane's voice; it was like he'd accepted the truth of the statement so long ago that it no longer hurt him to utter it. "But all the skillful enchanting in the world doesn't matter if you yell at the clients and scare them away. I can build the Clover business beyond where Dad left it. Meanwhile, you'd be lucky to still get any jobs after a year."

"The Clover name is about quality. Our enchanting is some of the highest caliber on the market!" Ainsley yelled. "People pay for *that*, not because you buy them a few rounds of champagne and tell them what they want to hear."

"We're not the only high-level enchanters out there. Without that champagne and ass-kissing, they'll take their business elsewhere." Zane was a curious contrast to Ainsley. As she was getting more worked up, he seemed to be getting calmer and more detached. It was like watching an ocean smash against a boulder; there was plenty of movement and action, but ultimately, nothing was changed in the end.

"That's why our work has to get better, so there's no one out there who can compete with what we do." Ainsley turned from her brother to Asha, though she needn't have bothered. All of us, even Bubba and Amy, already knew what Ainsley was going to say.

"Unless I get the tools in the split, I'm not going to sign."

"For once, my sister and I see eye-to-eye on something," Zane said. "I, too, am going to have to hold firm on the condition that I be the one to carry on Dad's business. It's the enchanter tools, or no signature."

"Oh, *come on*." Asha threw her hands up in the air, a motion I'd thought existed only in expressions, until I actually saw her get so frustrated she didn't know how else to show it. "You realize how impossible that is, don't you? We can't give you both the tools, and we need the damn things to get out of here. You're literally holding us all hostage by being too petty to compromise."

"You have my sincere apologies," Zane said, and admittedly, he did sound pretty darn sincere. "I don't take any joy in dragging you into this; however, I can't let my sister undo generations of family achievement by driving off all of our customers. Maybe this seems petty to you, and you might not be wrong, but this business was Dad's pride and joy. I have to protect it, and if that means inconveniencing you, then so be it. There's plenty of food and water to live on, and I'll pay your respective rates until we break free. Consider it a working sabbatical."

"Do we have rates?" Bubba whispered to Amy, who shrugged her shoulders. It was unlikely either of them had thought about billing, since they were just pitching in as a favor to Richard, but I'd make sure to calculate one for each of them before the matter was settled. I'd be damned if I'd see my friends get nothing for the trouble of living in a pocket dimension.

"Zane's right," Ainsley added. "This is more than just a business. It's the Clover legacy. I'll do whatever it takes to make sure it's carried on properly, by me."

"Again, you're handing us an impossible task." Asha looked between the stone-faced twins, trying to appeal to their sense of reason. "We can't give you both the tools. One of you has to cave on this."

"Then I suggest you make a compelling proposal," Zane said. "Convince one of us that what you're offering in the split is a better deal. Otherwise, it's a matter of seeing who breaks first."

"Oh, I think we already know who that will be. You love your precious parties too much to be away from them for long. All I need is a workspace and a library to be happy. In fact, I've got some experiments to check on. Let me know when the papers are ready to be signed." With that, Ainsley stomped off into the mansion, nearly knocking over several champagne flutes with the wide swings of her wooden staff.

As she vanished, Zane seemed to deflate, the confidence and surety he'd used to hold back her anger falling away. It wasn't that he seemed less charismatic, just more weary. He watched his sister go before turning to the rest of us.

"Again, I am genuinely sorry for all of this. How about, for now, you focus on getting the assets fairly divided, like you already were. I'll try and think of a way to make Ainsley come around by then. For now, though, I think I need a little time to recuperate." Zane slipped into the foyer then as well, moving carefully between the plates so that nothing would be disturbed. He didn't climb the stairs, however. Instead, he grabbed an unopened bottle of champagne off the table and headed to the left, toward a part of mansion I'd yet to lay eyes on.

"Might as well make myself useful," Bubba declared. "I'm gonna go take stock of the pantry, see what we've got in terms of food. Got a hunch that neither of those two is much for cookin', so I'll earn my keep by makin' sure we all stay fed."

"I'll try and see if anything I've got can break us out of here." Amy swung her bag around and began to rummage through it. While it only looked large enough to hold a few books and perhaps a water bottle, I'd seen, more than once, just how much bigger it was on the inside. "Don't think I have any potions that can break dimensional walls, but there's nothing like necessity to spur innovation."

"Let's call that Plan Z." Bubba tilted his head toward me and Asha. "Best case is these two gettin' the twins to settle their differences."

Asha threw a look of hope in my direction, but the best I could muster was a weak grin that was supposed to be reassuring. This was a family matter, and I'd done enough estate work to know those were always more complicated. As much as they claimed it was about the business, there were also decades of fighting, disagreements, and other troubles to contend with, all compacted by the sense of loss at their father's passing. I wasn't sure anything we said or did was going to move them before they were ready.

But even if that was the case, we still had to get the estate division done. Until that part was handled, it was impossible to proceed. So, with no other options, I motioned to Asha, and we headed back to the study.

6.

TIME WAS FUNCTIONALLY MEANINGLESS inside the bubble. Sure, the clocks moved, but with no day or night cycle, only the ever-present red glow of the wall cutting us off from reality, it all just blurred together. The moment we'd been trapped in was nighttime, though, which mattered only in that I never felt the familiar wave of weariness crash over me, signaling that the sun had risen. I wasn't sure if that was a good thing or not, as I'd already gone far longer than usual without the cathartic release of a long day's rest. Still, I didn't feel too loopy or out of it yet, so I pushed on. It wasn't as if I could change the situation, even if I wanted to. My best bet would be asking Amy for a potion, and there was no way something that specific wouldn't be experimental. As I've said before, Amy's alchemy skills are highly praised and impressive, but even she has to break a few eggs in the process of creation.

Instead of fretting about how long a vampire could retain their sanity without sleep, I focused on getting the work done. Asha and I holed up in the study with her files, working tirelessly to account for every asset, owning, and piece of property in the Clover estate. When she slept, I worked on calculating the value for the tools, poring through old receipts for work done, trying to quantify what the trends in the enchanting market were and extrapolating how much they could earn over the next several decades. It's not my place to speak about a client's finances, but suffice to it say that when I finally finished assigning those items a value, there were a *lot* of zeroes behind it. More impressively, though, there was enough of the estate to make up for the split, assuring each of the siblings an even cut of the inheritance.

Of course, the real problem was that neither of them would accept the half without tools, and that didn't seem to be changing anytime soon. Bubba gave us reports when he came in with meals for Asha. Ainsley only let him in to deliver food, having locked herself away in her workshop, and Zane was in the wine cellar, slowly carving his way through the offerings of every region in France. Neither was talking, except to say that they weren't going to budge.

"We have to do something." The words came out of nowhere, Asha and I having fallen into what had become our usual silence as we worked on organizing the assets. She broke that silence, looking up from her work with a pinched, tired expression on her face. "Judging by how often I've slept, it's been three days in here, and I'm going to lose it pretty soon." Evidently, I was wrong about time being meaningless, at least for those who still had mortal bodies to keep track of.

"We're almost done," I said. It was meant to be a hopeful statement, but the words only highlighted the larger issue at hand. We'd been focusing on the work because it was what we could do. Once that was over, we'd have nothing else. It became a waiting game to see which of the twins would break first.

"That's the problem." Asha laid her hand on the thick stack of parchment that was Herbram's enchanted will. "A few more hours of ironing out the detail work, tops, and we're finished. Unless we can think of a way to find another set of enchanting tools passed through their family, we're going to be stuck here."

"Is that an option? Not inherited tools, I mean, but this set has a value. Could we get a set that's comparable in terms of power?"

"Doesn't seem likely," Asha replied. "You've seen how important these are to the family; my understanding is that most mages treat the really potent stuff the same way. Even if there was an open market for them, it doesn't help us in here. That's the sort of deal we'd have to have in place before one of them was willing to sign."

"And splitting the items up is off the table?" I'd gone through the history of every piece in Herbram's enchanting tool kit as I assessed their cumulative value; there were six, in total. If only the twins were willing to divvy them up, then perhaps we could get out of here.

"Doing that would mean they either both get a weakened set, or have to agree to work together." Asha jerked a thumb toward the window, where that familiar red glow still lingered in place. "These really seem like the kind of people who are willing to work together?"

"Sadly, no," I admitted. "Though they'd clearly be better off if they were willing to do so. I can't imagine what's stirred up so much animosity between them."

"I've got a guess," Asha said. "We both know this stuff is newer to me than it is to you, but I did a little research when I got offered the job. From what I can tell, Herbram telling his kids to split the inheritance however they saw fit is an oddity in the mage world. Normally, Herbram would have bequeathed the tools specifically to one of his children, essentially choosing which of them he trusted to continue his work. When he didn't do that, he left them both out of sorts. Neither knows who he wanted to have take over, which makes it all the more important to prove themselves by doing so."

"Huh. I am beginning to suspect that Herbram Clover might have been something of an asshole."

"Or just didn't understand how things are between siblings." Asha stood from the desk, taking a long stretch that produced audible pops from her back. "I think I'm going to ask Ainsley for a shower to use. Living in these clothes for the past three days hasn't been my idea of fun, and I'm sure it's no treat for you either."

I hadn't mentioned it, for obvious reasons, but there are precious few humans that can go unwashed for three days and not be picked up by vampiric nostrils. Thankfully, my selective attention was excellent, so I'd put the inevitable scent of sweat and time out of mind, right up until she mentioned it.

"While I'm up there, I'll see if I can make any headway with her, competitive sister to competitive sister. Maybe you can drum up a conversation with Zane," Asha suggested.

"I'm afraid I don't have any siblings to use as common ground," I said.

"No, but if memory serves, you know your way around a bottle of wine. Seems like common enough ground to start with." She finished her stretch, laid a pen between the pages of a ledger to mark her spot, and made her way out into the hall.

I worked for a while longer, both to find a good stopping point and to try to plan out what on earth I could say to Zane that would move things forward. Not surprisingly, nothing sprang to mind. Aside from us being trapped in a dimension cut off from the real world, it was hard to argue with either his or Ainsley's points. Alone, either of them would falter, Ainsley's temper driving off customers while Zane's skill lowered their reputation for quality. With enough work and training, one of them might be able to grow and overcome the limitation, but there would still be lost ground to recover.

Eventually, I faced the fact that no brilliant bolt of insight was going to strike me and rose from the desk to head downstairs. Brooding wasn't productive, and if I talked to Zane, there was a chance I might uncover something that could get us free. The trip down was quick, though I got a bit turned around near the kitchen, as I'd only seen bits of the massive estate. Fortunately, I finally remembered that people who spend their days in wine cellars don't tend to take shower breaks, so I sniffed around until I located Zane's pungent scent. From there, it was just a matter of tracking it through an empty house and down into a wine cellar bigger than my apartment.

I'll admit, for as much as I like to think myself wise enough to be content with my own earnings, I was filled with jealousy at the sight of their cellar. Climate-controlled, gently lit, and filled with rows upon rows of gleaming bottles. The ones I recognized, which were fewer than I'd expected, were the sort of vintage that sat near the top of wine lists in fancy restaurants, serving as conversation fodder for what kind of person would spend so much money on a single bottle of alcohol. Red, white, even the odd rosé, all lined up in rows upon rows of carefully sorted bottles. It was like walking into a wine library, or museum, and I idly wondered how big my business would have to grow to justify this level of extravagance.

The sound of clinking glass drew my attention to one of the rows at the far end of the room, where I discovered Zane leaning against a wall, a bottle of merlot in one hand and a burrito in the other. At least Bubba had been making sure the mage didn't wallow on an empty stomach. Slowly, I made my way over, though it wasn't until I was less than a few feet away that Zane bothered looking up.

"Ah, there's my undead worker. How's the will coming?" His voice was a little slurred, though not nearly as bad as I'd expected from the number of empty bottles rolling around near him. Perhaps he'd been going slower than the rest of us realized, or maybe mages had a higher tolerance than I knew. Neil was too young to drink, and Amy tended to prefer her own work, so I didn't have a great example to work from.

"It's almost done," I told him. "We've found a way to split it all up evenly. The last part is determining which of you gets the tools."

"Those damned things." Zane lifted the bottle to his lips and found it nearly empty, so he set it aside and began to search for another.

"Here." I grabbed one of the few wines I recognized from the shelf, a cabernet sauvignon that I'd always wanted to try, and handed it to him. "You may as well stick to red, since you've made the commitment."

"An excellent idea." Instead of reaching for a wine opener, he pulled out his wand and mumbled what sounded like gibberish under his breath before tapping it to the top of the bottle. To my surprise, the cork began to worm its way upward, eventually dislodging and falling to the ground with a small *pop*. He took a long draw from the bottle, then offered it to me. "Care for a sip?"

"You should really decant something like this first." I took the bottle anyway and slid down to the ground next to him, taking a deep whiff of the wine before allowing it to actually hit my tongue.

"It's just the cheap stuff." He leaned back, letting his head rest on the cool stone wall behind us. "Always assumed they'd go to Ainsley, you know." It was a bit of a topic jump, but with how little we'd both talked, I had no problem sussing out his meaning.

"The tools?"

"Of course, the tools. She's a better enchanter than me. Better than Dad, too, and he had over a century of experience on her."

It was a good thing I'd yet to sip the wine, because I would have snorted it out at his words. I knew that mages lived longer than most people, though I'd never thought to ask why, but over a century . . . that was more than I'd been expecting.

"It just seemed like a lock, you know," Zane continued, either unaware or unbothered by the surprise in my face. "Ainsley was the one who could do the best enchanting, so she would be the one who got the tools. I was just the guy who did the talking, worked the deals, and got us a few extra percents on the bottom line."

"That's nothing to undersell," I told him. "Businesses live and die by their profit margins." Now that the wine's scent had fully been appreciated, I allowed myself to take a small swallow from the bottle. It was so heavenly that for a moment I actually forgot the situation and just allowed myself to revel in the joy dancing along my tongue.

"Do we particularly look like we need the extra margins?" Zane gestured to the cellar, but he just as easily could have been pointing to the house, the estate, as a whole. "No one cared that I brought in more money; there was always so much of it. At least, that's what I thought."

I handed him back the bottle, which he took a glugging drink from, spilling more than a few drops down his neck to an already stained shirt. "What changed your mind?"

"Well, he didn't leave the tools to Ainsley, did he? He left it up to us to figure out who should get them. Sort of felt like Dad was giving me a chance. Saying that I could get them, if I proved myself worthy." He sighed and took another drink, then handed me back the bottle. "Instead, I've gotten into a pissing match with my sister just like when we were kids, dragged a lot of innocent people along for the ride, and hid away in the cellar. Truly, a son to be proud of."

"In all fairness, Ainsley is being just as stubborn, and she's locked herself in her workshop." I'm not sure why I felt bad for Zane. He was part of the reason we were stuck, and none of things he just said were untrue. Even more, he seemed like the kind of person I should have despised. Wealthy, charismatic, and handsome, he'd been handed all the advantages in life that I hadn't, yet I couldn't bring myself to hold that against him. I guess I just knew a little too well what it was like to not be what your parents were hoping for.

"For her, this probably feels like a robbery. The tools were supposed to be hers, and now she's scared of losing them to her screw-up of a brother. Can't say I blame her for digging in. Truth is, Ainsley should get the tools. I understand it, you know, deep in my gut, but I just can't bring myself to let go." He pulled out his wand once more, rolling it gently between his fingers. "I'm a lot of things, and I've made peace with most of them. I just don't want to be a quitter. I want to fight. I want to prove that I can make the old man proud, too."

It was hard to think of a way to fault him, or to argue with that sentiment, so, instead, I just took another sip from the bottle of wine. Somehow, it wasn't quite as magical as the first time around. Maybe I'd already gotten used to it, or, more likely, Zane's sadness just made it impossible to find such joy in a fermented liquid.

I could see that he was nearing the breaking point, guilt slowly gaining on pride and determination. He'd break in a day or so on his own, and if I pushed him carefully, we might be free in the next few hours. Yet, to my own surprise, now that the key to our escape was within reach, part of me didn't want it. Not like this. Zane was right; he deserved the chance to prove himself, just as Ainsley did.

And I was beginning to have an inkling of an idea of how to give them just that.

7.

BASED ON BUBBA'S MEALS AND ASHA'S NEED for rest, it took another day to do the fresh contracts. We probably could have pounded them out in half the time if we'd raced through it, but the one good thing about being trapped in a timeless pocket dimension is that there's no compulsion to rush. Instead, Asha and I took our time, crossing every "t" and dotting every "i" to make sure our work was airtight. Given that we were dealing with mages and an enchanted will, it seemed prudent to leave no wiggle room anywhere in our documents.

That was the sort of thing that would just open up more trouble down the line.

Finally, when we were sure the language was word-perfect, we waited until Bubba made a food delivery, and then asked him to bring everyone to the study. Less than ten minutes later, Ainsley, Bubba, Amy, and Zane entered the room, in that order. No words passed between the siblings as everyone took their seats, though Amy filled the silence by asking Bubba about his recipe for the omelets he'd made that "morning." When everyone was seated, I looked to Asha to start things off. She was the lawyer and main employee, after all. I was just the numbers guy.

"Before we get going, let me double check. Are either of you willing to let the other have the enchanting tools in exchange for the lion's share of the rest of the estate?" Asha's eyes darted between Zane and Ainsley, neither of whom spoke, though both looked far less stalwart than they had when first making their ultimatums. I had a hunch that, now that they had both cooled down, it was as much a matter of pride as it was actually wanting the inheritance.

"About what we expected," Asha continued. "Fine, then. You've forced Fred and me to really think outside the box on this one, since none of us want to spend the next forty years stuck in here. So, here is what we're proposing as a compromise."

That was my cue. I rose from the desk, contracts in hand, and made my way around the large table, now almost completely cleared off of all the clutter we'd needed to work with. I laid a stack of documents in front of Ainsley, then Zane, before returning to my seat, where an identical packet was already waiting. They began flipping through the pages the moment they got them, and before I was even settled, I heard Ainsley's voice echo through the room.

"Joint custody?"

"*Temporary* joint custody," Asha corrected. "Since neither of you is willing to give up your claim on the tools, it seemed like this was the best way to determine who should get them. For the next year, you'll alternate days where the enchanting tools are yours to use. In that time, you will both work to build the Clover business as best you can. You'll find and book your own clients, do your own work, and make your own money. After a year's time, Fred and I will sit down to look at the numbers. Whoever does the best business will get the tools. Couldn't be more fair."

"Why should I have to compete for my rightful inheritance?" Ainsley demanded.

"Because it's not yours yet." I actually hadn't planned on speaking, but sometimes poor social skills means blurting out the things you didn't want to say as much as losing the chance to say the ones you did. Still, I'd stepped in it, so it seemed the best course of action was to press on. "Your father's will left you both equal claim to these tools. Maybe he did want you to have them; everyone seems to agree you're the better enchanter. But maybe he wanted you to earn them, rather than just be given them. This way, neither of you ever has to wonder if Herbram chose the right person to carry on the legacy. The winner will be the one who proves themselves most worthy."

My eyes may have flicked to Zane at that, and I caught sight of a small grin on the corner of his lips. To my surprise, Ainsley actually seemed to calm down as well. Maybe she and Zane weren't so different, after all; they both wanted the chance to show that they were the rightful heir.

"Now, obviously, there is always the chance that in the coming year you might need to work together on something," Asha said, bringing us back to the technical arrangements she and I had planned out. "The Clover name is a prestigious one, and Zane might find a client who needs an enchantment that even Herbram would have struggled with. In those cases, rather than doing a slipshod job or turning the client down altogether, there is a provision allowing him to work with Ainsley. You both get equal credit for the job, and the payment is split evenly into both your ledgers. Much as we want to see who the best is, I think we can all agree that preserving the Clover reputation is equally important."

Zane and Ainsley both nodded, almost in unison. It was possibly the first thing I'd seen them agree on since arriving at the mansion. Asha was visibly relieved; getting this far along meant that they weren't dismissing the idea outright. Truth be told, we didn't have a Plan B if this failed, aside from waiting for one of them to crack. For their sakes, I hoped they went along with our idea. It seemed a good bet that either one actually winning sole ownership of the tools would drive a wedge between them that would not be easily broken. And nothing, not even a generations-long legacy, was worth losing their family over.

"There is one more provision to discuss." Asha turned a page in her own packet, a signal for them to do the same, which neither twin picked up on. "Should the year end and you decide that more time is needed, perhaps because there are joint projects to finish or business to wrap up, you can elect to not call us back for the review. In which case, the agreement rolls over for another year. However, and I cannot stress this enough, should that happen, then the rules change slightly."

Zane and Ainsley leaned in closer, as did Bubba and Amy for some reason. I guess after being cooped up for so long, even contract discussion was exciting for them to watch.

"The first year is an impartial timeframe. You both start from the same place and get the same amount of time to work in," Asha explained. "After that, it's a little different. One of you could backend your business, destroy in the second year, and then call us in to review what looks like a successful business when it is really an emptied out pipeline. So, in the interest of fairness, if you collectively choose not to call us in at the end of the first year, the contract stays in effect until you both agree to have us make the determination. Neither of you gets to pull a fast one on the other. Any objections?"

"My sister and I sometimes have . . . issues . . . seeing eye-to-eye," Zane said. "It might take a while before we can agree on a year when we both feel like we've got a shot at winning."

Which, in truth, was exactly what Asha and I were counting on. These two were skillful in their own right, but neither would be as strong alone as they were together. If they could never agree on a year to bring us back, then they'd be stuck with each other, building the family business bigger and more respected than it ever was before. And, more importantly, neither had to lose or resent the other over their father's legacy.

"Then just have us come in at the end of the first year," Asha replied, keeping a far better poker face than I would have managed. "We added that stipulation for your benefit, not ours, in case you decide one year isn't long enough. Either of you can call us to make the determination at the end of that first year. Of course, since this is a competition, I'd have to advise you to keep your books secret from one another. But honestly, they're your records, do what you want with them."

"About that . . . ." Ainsley's voice had cooled; quick as she was to anger, she was just as fast at letting it go—at least when not being continually provoked. "Zane and I aren't really the best record keepers, and this seems like it requires a lot of that."

"I'd recommend you both hire personal assistants, then," Asha suggested. "You've got the cash for it, and I'm sure there are countless younger mages that would jump at the chance to work for the Clover family. Just to ensure accuracy though, Fred has agreed to do a quarter-ly review of both sets of books. For a fair rate, of course."

Neither had an immediate argument for that; I was about as independent a party as they were going to get. Instead, they looked at each other across the table, for what might very well have been the first time they'd made eye contact since their initial fight.

"I'm okay with this if you are," Zane said, breaking the silence first. "We both get a fair shot at Dad's tools, and it's not the best enchanter or schmoozer that wins. It's whoever does the best business."

"My quality versus your quantity." Ainsley actually smiled as she spoke, nodding her head just a bit. "At least we can put the argument to bed. And I want you to know that, when I win, there will still be a place for you in the company. Those valets need supervising."

"I was about to say the same to you, though I was going to let you know that your new office will be in the corner of the basement," Zane teased back.

Just like that, the tension that had been filling the mansion since that red bubble first appeared began to dissipate. Asha pulled out several pens and slid them down to where the twins were sitting.

"Let's get you to sign those documents, and when you're happy with that, we can have you autograph Herbram's will and get the hell out of here."

"Sounds good to me," Zane agreed, reaching for a pen. "And, Ainsley, I'm sorry. Not just about this fight, but about all the partying lately. It's just that the mansion feels kind of . . . empty since Dad passed. I guess I was trying to avoid that as much as possible."

"I know," Ainsley said, picking up her own pen as well. "I always knew that was why you were doing it, but instead of leaving my workshop, I just shut the doors tighter. That's where he and I used to do most of our work, and if I got deep enough in a project, I could sort of forget that he was gone for a little while. But I should have come out to check on how you were doing, instead of leaving you alone. So, I'm sorry, too."

The loud pop that filled the air rattled the table, along with everything else in the room that was not bolted down. Right on the heels of the burst was the screech of music that I'd managed to forget was playing, along with the chatter of hundreds of people out on the lawn, moving about like nothing had happened. Which, for them, it hadn't.

We all stared at each other, momentarily shocked by the sudden change. All save for Amy, whose now glowing orange eyes merely swept the room before she gave a half-hearted shrug.

"Guess you just needed to apologize, after all."

8.

TO MY INCREDIBLE RELIEF, NO LONGER
being trapped inside a pocket dimension didn't dampen
Ainsley and Zane's enthusiasm for the agreement. Asha
and I walked them through the contracts, while Bubba
and Amy helped the rest of the guards shut down the
party. This was done half because we wanted less noise
while working, and half because he and Amy had done
a lot of cooking and alchemy experiments downstairs,
which meant that the longer people were down there, the
greater the chance of them noticing the sudden changes.

Thankfully, the fight had come after the party was in full swing, which meant most of the guests were too liquored up to notice anything more than a few inches in front of them. Cars were pulled up, drivers taken off break, and one by one, the wealthy and well-dressed guests were hustled off the Clover property.

Meanwhile, we spent an hour and a half walking the twins through every page before they signed, making certain they understood what they were agreeing to. Anyone could see their eyes glaze over after the first fifteen minutes, but Asha and I were professionals, and as such, we were accustomed to that, just as we knew it didn't change our duty to explain it all anyway. Better bored for an hour than feeling swindled for a lifetime.

Finally, the guests were gone and the last signatures on our contracts were drying. Each got an equal share of the estate—which had been a much easier task after we'd pulled the tools out of the equation—and now, there was only one document left to sign, but it was by far the most important.

Herbram's will was as thick and largely illegible as ever. Asha set it down at the far end of the table, forcing both Zane and Ainsley to walk over to it. I'll confess that, up to this point, I'd been worried that there was some other aspect to signing that we weren't privy to. A magical quill, ink from their own blood, really anything along those lines. As it turned out, a cheap plastic pen and regular ink did the job, as each of the twins leaned over and scratched their signatures onto the bottom of the page. Unimpressive as the signing was, what came next was a sight to behold.

Just as Zane finished scrawling out his name, the pages began to glow a faint red, not unlike the bubble that had held us prisoner for so long. They began to twitch before he'd even fully backed away, quickly escalating to a full flutter, like the wind was rustling only the pages and nothing else in the room. The movements grew more and more violent, until the pages flew up from the table, swirling around the room in an intangible tornado. They danced all around us, always coming close but never quite making contact, before they began to head back to the end of the table. Rather than landing in a pile, however, each page seemed to fold as it drew closer, pressing into the others that had already taken shapes of their own. In less than a minute, they'd all landed, folding and connecting to form a large red box. Slowly, the glow began to fade, and I could see that the object was no longer made of paper. No, now it was a smooth metal covered in rapidly fading runes, zero seams or signs that it had ever been formed from dozens of separate pages.

Ainsley and Zane both reached forward, touching the front of the box. The moment they made contact, a door formed, swinging open to reveal several gems, a pile of scrolls, and one black bag with a single silver buckle in the center. Stylized on the front of the buckle's shiny surface was an ornate "C." The Clover family enchanting tools had finally been recovered, it seemed.

"Smaller than I expected," Asha said, tilting her head to get a good view into the box.

"Trust me, there's more to it than meets the eye." Ainsley reached forward and tenderly picked up the bag, cradling it like one would an infant. "The bag alone is enchanted with the work of countless ancestors, and it's easily the least magical part of the set." Slowly, she extended her arms, holding out the black bag to her brother. "It's past midnight, so today is the fourteenth. You get the tools on even days. Part of the contract."

"I guess it was." Zane accepted the handoff, though he was visibly uncomfortable pulling them from his sister's hands. For several long seconds, there was silence as he held the prize they'd dragged us through time and space to claim for themselves. "You know, we're pretty backed up on orders that came in before Dad died. Maybe we should work together to clear those out before the competition officially begins. Keep the clients happy and give ourselves an even start."

"Is that allowed?" Ainsley looked at Asha, who managed little more than a shrug.

"Your business. Run it how you want. We just get called in to check the results."

"Then I think that's a good idea," Ainsley told Zane. He offered her back the bag, which she accepted. "Let's go move everything somewhere safe, first."

Zane nodded, reaching into the box that was once a will and scooping up the remainder of the contents. The two of them left the study then, discussing which project to start with, not that I really understood the minutia of what they were talking about. Numbers, I got. Magic was a whole other animal.

As the sound of their voices faded up the stairs, Asha and I looked at each other as we finally gave in to the sense of relief. The job was done, we were out of the pocket dimension, and we'd managed to make both our clients happy. Plus, we were going to be able to bill for several days of working hours at an overtime rate, which always made a hard job more palatable.

"Are you thinking what I'm thinking?" Asha asked.

"Get out of here as quickly as possible, before they get into another fight and we're stuck in the bubble again?" I ventured.

"Damn, I was going to say a stiff glass of scotch, but that idea makes a lot more sense. Let's pack it up." Asha headed back over to the table, unplugging her laptop and stuffing the copies of the contracts into her bag. "You did good work, by the way, Fred. I'll keep you in mind if I ever need an accounting consult again."

"In this town, there aren't many other options," I warned her. "But I'd still appreciate the call. Hopefully, I'll be able to take whatever you throw my way. Though, to be honest, my schedule is uncomfortably full these days."

"Lot of demand and very little supply. Part of why I made the jump over to parahuman work," Asha said. "But you know how business works, if you're in that high of demand, just increase your rates. The smaller clients will fall away and you'll be able to get more for your time."

"I guess." Asha was right, that was how any introductory business class would advise me to handle being so overworked. Then again, those classes hadn't gotten to meet and interact with all the parahumans I'd helped. Most of them didn't have money like the Clovers or Richard. They were just working-class people trying to get by, and I was able to help them do that. I wasn't cheap, by any means, but I also didn't price myself out of affordability. If I upped my rates significantly, I'd have more money and free time. All it would mean was turning my back on the less-wealthy parahumans.

"I remember that look." Asha's voice pulled me out of the reverie I didn't know I'd fallen into. She was staring at me, an unexpected expression of concern on her face. "You used to get that way when word came down from the Torvalds to drop a client so we could move resources to someone more profitable. I think that's why I remembered you even after you quit. A whole department of accountants, and you were one of the few who saw the clients as more than numbers."

"More of us do than you'd think," I told her. "Torvald & Torvald just had a knack for recruiting the more ruthless among my profession."

"Sort of missed the mark with you, didn't they?"

"Well, I'm not ruthless, but my accuracy rates certainly looked like I was trying to shame everyone." I tucked away my laptop and the few papers needed to log the hours I'd put in. "And if I can, I'd rather expand the client-base than shrink it. That's also good business sense."

"Good luck with that." Asha zipped up her bag and threw it over her shoulder. "I'll keep an ear to the ground, just in case I run across a therian looking to do an internship."

"With my luck, they'll think my company is a front for something more impressive and get bored as soon as they realize it really is just accounting." We headed out of the study and began walking down the stairs. Asha and I were in the foyer when I heard Zane calling our names.

We turned to see him rushing over with a bottle in each hand. "Glad I caught you two. Ainsley and I wanted to say thank you for all your help. And, obviously, apologize for the inconvenience. We'll process your bills as soon as they come, but for now, this is a token of our gratitude."

He held out each bottle, one of scotch for Asha and a merlot for me. I didn't even remotely recognize the label or brand, but from the way Asha's eyes went wide, I had a feeling she knew what hers was, and my wine was probably just as rare and valuable.

"This is a bit much as a thank you," Asha protested.

"Agreed, the rates cover our work," I added.

"Sorry, I think you'll find these bonuses non-negotiable." Zane held up his hands and backed away, cutting off all attempts to return the bottles. "You two went above and beyond what anyone could ask of you. Here in the Clover family, we believe in saying thanks for that kind of dedication. And if either of you ever need any enchanting done, I think we can manage a sharp discount. Friends and family price, if you will."

Asha merely nodded, but I responded. "Thank you very much. I may take you up on that one day." Having glimpsed the tip of what magic could do, I wasn't going to turn down such an offer out of hand. One never knew what sort of needs might arise in the future.

"I hope you do, because I really mean it." Zane snapped his fingers and pointed at me, nearly causing me to drop the bottle of probably priceless wine. "Speaking of, Fred, are you associated with the House of Turva? I checked over the pending orders, and we've got a large request for sunlight-proof glass from them. I don't want to haggle too hard if they're your people."

"N-no," I stammered out, trying to keep my cool as best as possible. "No relation. They're new in town, from what I hear."

"Guess they're planning on staying awhile; they've ordered enough glass to retrofit a whole building. But if they're not your clan, then they'll be paying full price for it." Zane wandered off, seemingly unaware of the sudden cloud of worry that had formed over my head. Perhaps it was because, as a vampire, the blood didn't rush from my face in times of terror.

"You okay?" Asha asked as we began exiting once again, now with bottles in hand. "You seemed to go pretty stiff when he mentioned the other vampires."

"I'll be all right," I said, probably with more hope than I felt. It had been so long since the Turvas came up that I'd managed to forget about them, but one mention from Zane brought it all rushing back. What's worse, they were apparently setting up shop, so the moving-in process was going smoothly.

"Let me know if you need a lawyer," Asha offered. "But maybe wait a few days first. After this, I'm taking a long weekend."

"Not a bad idea," I agreed. We parted at the door, she heading to her sedan and me to the truck where Bubba and Amy were already waiting.

I climbed in and rested my head against the window, watching the moon sink slowly from the sky. How long had it been stuck there, while we scrambled about inside the mansion to try and broker a peace between two siblings? I could feel the familiar fuzziness at the edge of my thoughts that came when I'd stayed awake for too long. Maybe Asha was on the right track. I couldn't afford to take a whole vacation, but this time when the sun rose, perhaps I'd let sleep claim me. One day of solid, uninterrupted rest.

It wasn't much of a splurge, but by God, I'd earned it.

A LAWYER IN THE MANOR

1.

"THEY WANT A MEETING."

Those words had hung heavy in my mind since Richard uttered them, not three seconds into a phone call with me. While details had followed, I'd barely listened, as such words weren't truly necessary. There was only one "they" who would seek a meeting with me through Richard, only one group that would put such gravity in his voice. The House of Turva, Winslow's newest vampire clan, was finally beginning to move. What that meant for me was anyone's guess, as they'd done little interacting beyond the basics of making peace. My only way to find out if they were friend, foe, or apathetic neighbor was to take the meeting.

Of course, that didn't mean I had to be stupid about how I did it. My car eased into the parking lot in front of Charlotte Manor, a new night's stars twinkling overhead. A massive Jeep that looked like it had been driven over straight from war was already parked nearby, and was obviously Richard's ride. I couldn't begrudge him the extra room; there was no sedan on the market that had the space to comfortably contain a man of his size. Pausing to lock my doors and double check that I had, in fact, remembered my briefcase, I headed up the front steps, where Charlotte was already waiting for me.

I realize that this can be a bit confusing, so allow me a moment to clarify the difference between Charlotte and Charlotte Manor. Charlotte Manor is the proper, given name of the structure that served as half B&B, half rented-out home to a pair of agents. Charlotte, on the other hand, was the house's personality, its physical representation that usually took the form of a young woman who favored dresses so large and complex it was rare to see them outside of a period play. Neil had once said it best: Charlotte was the house's avatar, the way it interacted with us.

That was who was waiting for me as I stepped onto the porch. She offered me a glass of wine—materializing food and drink was one of her less spectacular but more useful abilities—which I had to refuse.

"Working tonight," I informed her. "Wouldn't be appropriate."

"Really? Because the big guy inside has already downed five glasses of ale. And my mugs are well above normal pint size." There was a touch of pride in Charlotte's voice; she took great satisfaction in her hospitality skills.

"Richard isn't the one who needs to worry."

"You wouldn't know that from the way he's pacing about," Charlotte replied. "When are the other guests arriving?"

I headed for the door, and she followed along beside me, matching my steps perfectly. "Soon. We set it for two hours after sunset, but there's no guarantee they won't be early. Richard briefed you on what to do?"

"He's been here for hours; he won't shut up about it." Charlotte made a small gesture with her hand and the front door opened to reveal another, identical Charlotte waiting patiently. "I'm supposed to look like the little old lady and wait staff, do nothing to draw attention, and keep up the normal appearances. Unless they try anything."

This was why I'd chosen Charlotte Manor as the meeting spot between myself and the Turva clan. If things took a turn for the aggressive, Charlotte could easily keep them captive long enough for me to escape. She was technically built to keep people out more than in, so holding a pair of vampires indefinitely would be a tall order even for her, but she could buy me time. That would be enough.

"Yes, but wait for my signal," I reminded her. "Let's not make a move unless it's necessary."

Whatever Charlotte would have said next was drowned out by the stampeding footsteps of Richard Alderson barreling down the front hall. No matter how times I met the man, it was impossible not to be taken aback by his size. He was enormous, tall enough to make NBA players feel threatened, and his wide body was completely packed with muscle. Add in the shaggy blond hair and teeth that were just a little too white and sharp, and I considered it one of my greatest personal accomplishments not to have collapsed in fear the first time we met. Then again, he'd been in leader mode then, which was far more outwardly intimidating than the man behind the curtain.

"Fred, I'm sorry. I tried to stall this for as long as I could."

The apology didn't surprise me; Richard had been giving them ever since he dropped the bomb that a meeting was formally requested. Evidently, he'd kept a lot of people between himself and the new vampires, ducking them at every chance for a lot of reasons. However, the thing about parahumans is that, while they might have little respect for the rules of humanity, they would, at least publicly, adhere to the letter of their own laws and treaties. A formal request sent through the proper channels was impossible to ignore without causing trouble, even for someone of Richard's status.

"I've told you, it's fine. If they wanted to talk with me, it was going to happen sooner or later. At least this way, we control the terms," I assured him. "Maybe they just want me to go over their books."

"Seems like the sort of thing an e-mail could convey. You're never shy about handing out those business cards." This voice belonged to neither me, Richard, nor Charlotte. Instead, it came from the blonde woman currently descending the stairs. For a moment, I almost didn't recognize my own girlfriend.

Krystal's usually free-flowing hair was pulled tight into a ponytail, a set of ill-fitting glasses perched on the bridge of her nose and an oversized sweatshirt swallowing up her torso. While her jeans were the same as usual, she'd traded her standard boots for a set of sensible sneakers. There was also something off about her face, though I had to really stare to realize that, while she seemed to be wearing less makeup than usual, she was actually wearing more. She'd used it to contour her features and somehow appear less striking than normal. All of this was enhanced by the way she moved, meticulously, with a slight slouch in her spine and her head always tilted a touch downward. Normal Krystal barreled through a room like a panther with the excitement of a Labrador. This version inched along as though she wasn't even sure she wanted to be there.

"That's a . . . new look." I racked my mind for something positive to say. It was obvious she was trying to dull herself down, but not even I was so inexperienced at love that I would say such a thing without prompting. There's being willing to meet with potentially aggressive vampires, and then there's just plain suicidal.

"You like? I saw the latest fashions from Milan and just had to get my hands on it." She stuck her tongue out and made a sound not unlike someone passing gas, and, for a moment, I could see the real Krystal shining through, clothes and makeup be damned. "There's no way I'm letting you take this meeting without me nearby, but I didn't want to raise too much suspicion."

"Do you think they'd assume you were an agent just from your normal style of dress?" I asked.

"Doubtful, but the more I blend into the background, the better," she replied. "And plus, if it comes out that I'm your lady, no one will bat an eye."

"You think they would normally?" I looked to Richard and Charlotte, both of whom had suddenly found things on the wall and ceiling to stare at with unwavering interest.

Krystal released her false walk, bounding the rest of the way down the stairs and over to me. "Freddy, I love you dearly, you know that. But the people who don't know you as well as we do might think you come off a little . . . dull. I just thought this version of me might be easier to swallow for those who make the wrong assumptions about you."

"Well then, I have to say you've failed." Before she could reply, I leaned forward and kissed her, a very rare show of public affection spurred on by a combination of gratitude and fear. "You're still much too lovely for the likes of me. I'm afraid there is just no amount of makeup or frumpy clothing that will ever conceal how beautiful you are."

It was one of the precious few times in our relationship that I'd managed to be the one to take her by surprise, and I savored the slight blush in her cheeks as she hurriedly recovered.

"After a line like that, I'm damn sure not letting you get killed," Krystal said at last. "Richard, tell me you've got a plan."

Having finished staring at the wall, Richard swung back around and led us to the dining room. "The Turvas contacted me, saying they wanted to discuss business with Fred. I told them to call him themselves, he's not hard to find, and they countered by saying it was business outside the normal spectrum and that they'd greatly appreciate an introduction. A gesture of friendship, they called it."

The nerves faded from Richard's voice, replaced by something far heavier. The man had an entire clan that depended on him, and he took that job seriously. While many would have seen it as a license to do as they pleased, Richard understood it was a duty, a burden, one he had to be strong enough to bear.

"Present company excluded, vampires can be a real pain in the ass to deal with. Their treaties give them a lot of freedom when it comes to hunting, as long they don't kill their victims, and since therians in human form are allegedly hard to distinguish from regular mortals, it's hard to go after them for taking blood from my people. So far, the Turvas have been playing very nice, keeping a wide berth from any parahumans and being discreet in their feeding. If I can, I'd prefer to have them keep that up. Violence would come with costs to both our sides, ones I don't want to pay."

"Again, Richard, it's fine. You couldn't very well refuse such a simple request without reason," I reminded him. "And it might be all around better that you didn't. That could have betrayed that we're friends. As far as the Turvas know, I'm just someone you hired to save you money on your taxes. The more mundanely they see me, the less reason they have to show fear or be interested."

"Still doesn't sit right in my gut." Richard opened the door to the dining room, where Charlotte was already waiting. She was surrounded by waiters—all of them also her, just in another form—that were holding serving dishes waiting to be opened. The table was currently cleared off, except for two pairs of place settings on opposite sides.

"As requested, a fine meal is waiting to be served at your leisure," Charlotte informed us.

"Wait, what?" This wasn't part of the plan; it was supposed to be a quick meeting. I certainly didn't want to spend a whole dinner with these people.

"My idea, Freddy," Krystal said, walking calmly over to one of the place settings. "Give me your briefcase."

I complied, and she set the case down in a chair before one of the settings. Wordlessly, she picked up the utensils and handed them to a waiter, where they vanished into thin air. Reaching into a compartment on her sweatshirt, Krystal pulled out identical utensils, setting them down carefully in the same spots the original ones had been.

"A little bit of insurance, just in case," she explained. "Having dinner justifies the place settings, and no vampire is afraid of a butter knife. But you aren't going to be eating with the same tools as everyone else, Freddy. You're going to have silver utensils. Specially made too, just like agent-issue tools, so that they won't be easily detectable by scent."

It was an odd kind of brilliant; silver was the ultimate double-edged sword in the parahuman world. The material hurt almost all of us, which made it both effective to use and dangerous to handle. As a result, very few parahumans messed with the stuff, and certainly none would think to suspect that a vampire's utensils were made of it. Silver immunity was nigh unheard of among the undead.

"When, exactly, did you have silver duplicates of Charlotte's utensils made?" Richard asked, bringing up an excellent point that I was a little ashamed about not noticing.

Krystal shrugged, barely visible through her oversized shirt. "Around the same time I moved in. Always pays to be prepared. I told her I was doing it, though she's the one who gave me the molds."

"Just be sure to pick those up when this is done." Charlotte had moved several feet away from the table. As a being composed almost entirely of magic, silver was more painful for her than most parahumans. It meant a lot to me that she was tolerating it on her table.

"Agent's honor," Krystal promised. "And Freddy, I know I don't really need to tell *you* this, but these are for defensive purposes only. Try to resist the urge to pretend you're an action hero."

"Somehow, I think I'll find the self-control." I hadn't realized how on edge I was until I heard the squeal of tires from the parking lot. Evidently, I'd let my usual shutting out of the vampire senses lapse, because that noise was far too quiet to be heard with human ears. Still, I did appreciate the warning.

"Looks like our guests have arrived," I told them. "Everybody into position."

2.

I WASN'T SURPRISED TO SEE LILLIAN AS one of the vampires who'd come out to meet me, though I was taken a bit back by her choice of wearing a pantsuit, as I'd assumed the last time she'd worn one was solely out of deference to their meeting with therians. She hadn't really seemed like the type to embrace professional attire as habit, but I suppose I, of anyone, should have known better than to judge a book by its cover.

The man with her wore a lovely pinstriped number that I knew on sight had been hand-tailored. He was also one of the oldest-looking vampires I'd encountered, which, admittedly, was a sample size of three before him. A few wrinkles hung around his eyes, and his dark hair had gone silver in streaks along the side. His face was handsome, but approachable, the sort you'd find as a department head or neighbor that ran the HOA.

"Mr. Alderson, thank you for making the time to meet with us." He bowed to Richard, not very deeply, but enough to show respect. For his part, Richard had his game face on, which consisted of being stiff, detached, and more than a bit terrifying. Unless these two had been drinking some incredibly potent blood, Richard could probably take them apart by himself. Unfortunately, that would also cause quite the incident between vampires and therians, which is why he was around more for show and friendship than backup.

"And you must be Mr. Fletcher." The man turned to me, giving another bow. I rose from my seat and stuck out a hand. Bowing might be the way vampires did it, but accountants were taught the art of the handshake to show our respect.

"Yes, sir, Fredrick Fletcher of Fletcher Accounting Services."

He looked at my hand for a few moments before taking it and offering a firm shake. "I am Petre, of the House of Turva." The shake continued; he was waiting for something, though I had no idea what. It might have gone on forever if Lillian hadn't stepped forward.

"Fredrick, it is common courtesy to announce the name of your clan in meetings such as this."

"It is?" This time, I did bow, a little. I'd made the mistake, so it seemed like meeting him halfway on tradition was a good form of apology. "I'm terribly sorry. I don't have a clan, as far as I know."

"Your clan is your sire's clan, unless you've been cast out," Petre told me.

"My sire never taught me anything about that. He turned me and left me on my own. The only other time I saw him was when he beat me senseless and threatened to kill me." Both Petre and Lillian seemed to shrink back at that news, the former finally allowing our handshake to come to an end.

"Then it is I who am sorry," Petre said, quickly recovering himself. "The bond between a sire and their child is meant to be a sacred one. For you to have survived on your own, learning the way of the night without an instructor, is no small feat."

"Well, movies helped a lot." I appreciated the praise, but I really didn't want them thinking more of me than was strictly necessary. "I knew to avoid silver and sunlight right off the bat, and since I didn't plan on driving any stakes through my heart, that was already off the table."

Petre regarded me with a long stare. There was a lot going on in those cool, pale blue eyes, most of which I was probably happier not knowing. "I suppose that is one benefit to our culture being absorbed and spread throughout the humans' consciousness."

"It's nice to see you again, Fredrick," Lillian butted in, offering a much needed respite from the intensity of Petre's gaze. "And you're not even hooked to a taxi this time. Makes you look more composed."

"I appreciate your help that night," I replied, choosing my words carefully. Anything that signified a debt between us could be dangerous, especially if this turned to negotiations. "You look well, yourself."

"It's only proper." Lillian smiled like she knew something I didn't, which was completely unnecessary. We were all keenly aware that she and Petre had things hidden up their sleeves, just as they no doubt assumed I had a few tricks, as well.

"If you're done with introductions, can we get this moving? I have other tasks to see to tonight." Richard's voice was edging on an animal's growl, his inner lion poking through. Rough as his tone was, I was glad for it, since it helped to keep things speeding along.

We all took our seats at the table as the kitchen door opened and a waiter breezed in, carrying a tray of crab cakes. Petre and Lillian both looked momentarily distressed by the appearance of staff, so I spat my words out as quickly as I could.

"It's fine, this whole place is parahuman friendly," I told them. "There's a presence in the house, so everyone here is already in on the secret. We can speak freely."

"What an intriguing establishment." Petre watched the waiters closely, but Charlotte was doubling down on her avatar. Every step they made squeaked, each motion was clumsy enough to be human, and she was even replicating the sound of blood pumping through a heart. Unless either of the vampires tried to take a bite, they'd have no idea their waiter wasn't real. "How ever did you find such a place?"

"I was called in to help settle some ownership issues and account discrepancies. Things went well, so they put my services on retainer." Now that the conversation was finally steering toward business, I jumped on the opportunity to pop open my briefcase and pull out two identical sheets of paper.

"Since Richard called me here for a meeting, I took the liberty of putting together some information about exactly which services I offer, and the general estimations of hours needed for each task. As you'll note, I have different projections for digital records versus physical ones, since that adds a lot of time, but the hourly rate stays consistent throughout."

Petre and Lillian both examined their documents, looking them over dutifully despite the fact that I doubted either of them had needed such services in a very long time. As I've said before, parahumans are not the best at record-keeping in any capacity. Finally, Petre lowered his back to the table.

"You have quite the list of services, Mr. Fletcher. It's not often one sees a member of our species take on such . . . thankless tasks. Those who are turned tend to lean toward grander spectacles, using their new abilities to reach heights unattainable by mortality."

"I like to think I did the same. After all, becoming a vampire was what gave me the push to start my own company." My smile was placid, as though I hadn't even noticed that he'd tried to tactfully call me boring. If Petre thought I was going to take offense to something like that, he clearly hadn't done much homework.

"Indeed." His fingers ran along the edge of the page, crinkling it ever so slightly as it rested on the wooden surface of the table. "May I ask why you wished to share this with us? Perhaps you were looking for insight on what options need to be added?"

"A generous offer, but I've got it well in hand. I was showing you the price list because I have a policy of being upfront on cost with all potential clients. You called the meeting, so there's obviously something you're looking to book an accountant for, but it's important to me that you have a fair sense of the price going in. All part of running an upstanding business."

While that truly was my philosophy when meeting new clients, the odds of that being applicable here were slim. I'd decided that my best bet for making it through this encounter was to play it dumb. As an abandoned vampire with no clan and minimal knowledge of vampire society, it took very little acting to pull off. My hope was that if I could convince them I was a non-threat, that I was just an undead guy who was good with numbers, they'd see there was nothing to gain from dealing with me. Except maybe a reliable person to call during tax season.

"The honesty is appreciated," Petre replied. "However, we did not call this meeting to request your accounting services. Rather, I requested it to get to know you on a more informal level. There are very few vampires in the area; Quinn, the traitor, made it quite inhospitable for any that tried to make a home here. I was surprised to learn that he'd tolerated the presence of another. Tell me, was he kept at bay by the need for your services?"

"No." The word came out with an edge I was only mildly aware of, prickling my tongue as it fell away. "No, it's safe to say Quinn did anything but leave me alone. But I already told you that my sire abandoned me."

Now *that* got a reaction. Petre's lip twitched for the barest of moments, a snarl he forcibly kept from forming.

"I wish I could say I was surprised that even he would do such a thing, but the truth is that among Quinn's crimes, such an action is hardly notable. It is still awful, though, and I'm sorry you had to endure it. Trust me when I say there is no love lost between the House of Turva and Quinn, the traitor."

"Nor do I hold any affection for my sire." That part required no fudging whatsoever. Quinn had tried to kill me, along with my friends. I never considered myself a hateful person, but I wished all the ill the world could muster on the man who turned me.

"Quinn is a real dick," Lillian chimed in. "And I don't think anyone is sad that he's gone into hiding. But tell us, Fredrick, how did you survive? You mentioned he threatened to kill you, and Quinn had a reputation for making good on such promises."

"I was lucky," I told her, no shame in my voice at the admittance. "Before he could get to me, Quinn picked a fight with someone else. An agent. That went about the way you'd expect it to, and as far as I know, he's been running ever since."

Petre made a noise halfway between a harrumph and snort. "*Agents.* They do have their uses, I suppose. Quinn was always more ambitious than smart. I can't say I'm shocked that his brashness finally caught up with him."

I couldn't think of anything to say that would close the topic without inviting further questions, so instead,

I picked up my silver fork and scooped out a piece of the crab cake cooling before me. Like everything Charlotte made, it was scrumptious. It took me three more bites before I noticed that Lillian and Petre were watching me eat.

"Did you need a lemon sauce?" I asked.

"We do not partake in the food of humans." Petre didn't even try to mask the disdain in his voice. Lillian nodded in agreement, though I noticed her eyes lingering on the crab cake in front of her. "Blood is the only delicacy a vampire need taste. It is the perfect, the ultimate, the unequivocal joy. Everything else is but ash in the mouth by comparison."

Carefully considering his point, I waited a few moments more, then took another bite. Nope, definitely not ash. "Blood is quite delicious, but I've yet to lose my taste for the more familiar dishes of life. Maybe it's something that comes with time."

Petre kept looking at me as I scooped up another few morsels before finally responding. "Perhaps so. It is not entirely your fault for not knowing such truths, either. As an Abandoned, there was no one to teach you the proper ways of our kind."

"All things considered, I think I got off lucky being abandoned, if my other option was being taught by Quinn," I pointed out.

"Did you really call this damn meeting just for small talk?" Richard, who had been busying himself tucking away his own crab cake with enormous bites, dropped his fork to the empty plate below with a loud clatter. "I've got better things to do than listen to the vampires in town get to know some guy who does my taxes. Petre, if you pulled me into a useless meeting as an attempted show of power, I should warn you now that I won't take it well."

The whole room seemed to grow still at Richard's words. What he'd said was no idle threat. Power and authority were so important they verged on holy in the parahuman world, even more so with therians. A man in Richard's position couldn't afford to let himself be made an errand boy by some new vampires in town. Asking for a favor was one thing. Asking for a pointless favor to show they could make him do it was something different altogether. Depending on Petre's answer, they might soon have much more serious matters to deal with than some lowly accountant in their town.

"Our apologies, Mr. Alderson," Lillian said at last. Her subdued tone was a pleasant contrast to Petre's haughty nature; it was no wonder he kept her around. "Petre merely wished to get to know Fredrick before broaching our true business. Such is the traditional method to show respect and build a relationship. By all means, please feel free to leave if you like. We will certainly take no offense. Your gesture has been fulfilled merely by making the introduction."

Fear boiled in my stomach, tossing the crab cake to-and-fro. I knew Richard wouldn't want to leave me, but what if he couldn't think of a way to stay nearby without betraying that he saw me as more than a contracted employee? Giving away our friendship meant handing these people a bit of information, and I already knew that the less we gave them, the better.

"Much as I would like to, the fact remains that you asked me to make this meeting happen," Richard replied. "The accountant was barely ever in my service, but I did *have* to use him. It wouldn't look very well if I introduced you to one of my employees and then you went off and killed him. I have a reputation to uphold."

A bit hurtful, but it was hard to argue with the route Richard had taken. Making it about him and his reputation gave him adequate cause to stay nearby as a witness, without letting on that we were friends. If anything, Richard sounded like he detested me, which, I suppose, did fit the usual vampire-therian dynamic. Dealing with Petre and Lillian, I was beginning to think that perhaps I really had gotten a blessing in disguise by not knowing my sire for long. It had allowed me to shape my own relationships with other parahumans, rather than having them dictated to me.

"Very well, then. In respect to Mr. Alderson, we will move past the customary small talk, assuming that is all right with you, Mr. Fletcher," Petre said. I nodded my agreement, and he immediately continued.

"I called this meeting because I wished to know more about the vampire who survived in the same town that Quinn, the traitor, oversaw. The House of Turva needed to assess if you managed such a feat by wit or might. Now, I see that you had no hand in it. You were simply one of Quinn's experiments. What he intended for you, we may never know, but it seems you've made something of your life regardless. Since I do not deem you to be a threat, my clan has authorized me to make a gesture of friendship."

"That's appreciated, but unnecessary," I said, doing my best to head off this line of talk. One thing I'd learned from watching Richard, these sorts of gestures never came without strings. Whatever they offered, it would make me indebted to them, and that was the last place I wanted to be.

"Mr. Fletcher, as an Abandoned, I understand you might not know this, but to refuse a gesture of friendship is akin to declaring us your enemy." Petre didn't make it sound like a threat, which was exactly what told me how serious it was. When people moved past the bluster, it meant they weren't worried about your reaction. Things just were what they were.

"Oh? Then I do ask that you please forgive me. As you said, I have not been properly educated." I'd been backed into a corner; my only hope was that it would be something small and easily repaid.

"It is to be expected from an Abandoned," Petre replied. "As I was saying, the House of Turva wishes to make a gesture of friendship. After some inquiring, we heard that you were looking for a helper to swell the ranks of your growing company. Thus, it is my pleasure to present to you the newest employee of Fletcher Accounting Services."

He gracefully opened his hand, gesturing to Lillian, who gave me a small wave paired with a wide smile.

"Looks like you're my new boss, Fredrick."

3.

"I DON'T LIKE HER." KRYSTAL DIDN'T bother keeping her voice low; Charlotte could block the sound between walls so well that not even vampire ears managed to hear through them. My girlfriend was leaning back in her chair, arms crossed and a scowl etched into her face. "A little too nice, a little too charming. And what's with that 'Fredrick' shit? Getting pretty familiar pretty fast, if you ask me."

"Well, that *is* my actual name," I tried to point out, but the glare I received shut me down quickly.

"Missing the point, Freddy."

Dinner had wrapped up not long after Petre dropped the bomb named Lillian on me; he'd excused himself and drove off, leaving his fellow vampire behind. Under the pretense of handling some private business regarding his books, Richard and I had left Lillian in the dining room to have a quick consultation with Krystal. I'd hoped she could shed some insight on how to deal with the situation, but her ideas were . . . less than productive.

"I'm just saying, accidents happen all the time, and it's not like Freddy doesn't have a reputation for ending up in trouble. Maybe he goes on a call that runs a little long, and she gets stuck out in the sunlight while he barely survives."

"I know you're kidding, but just that joke made my blood pressure go up," Richard told her. "Petre is the number two in that clan, and he showed up to personally deliver Lillian as a token of friendship. If anything happens to her that smells even remotely suspicious, I'm going to have a ton of trouble on my hands."

"Think the Turva clan will get violent?" I asked.

"Worse. They'll drag me through meeting after meeting in diplomatic hearings." Richard shuddered, which made the chair he was seated on wobble violently. "I can handle a brawl or two, and my people vastly outnumber theirs. But when they invoke the treaties and pull me into that mind-numbing diplomatic bullshit, that's the real torture."

Krystal snorted, then looked up to the ceiling. "Charlotte, is she doing anything weird? Anything we could use as grounds for her being here under malicious intent?"

"She is sitting quietly at the dinner table, eating the cold crab cake left in front of her." Charlotte appeared between me and the doorway, wearing her usual antique dress. While Krystal and Richard seemed disappointed by the news, I found it a bit intriguing. It seemed Lillian didn't entirely agree with the Turvas' stance on blood being the only acceptable food for vampires to touch. Maybe there were other things they didn't see eye-to-eye on, as well.

"Charlotte, please book a room for Lillian," I instructed.

"Excuse me?" Krystal whipped her head around so fast that the fake glasses ended up cockeyed on her head.

"Like it or not, we're stuck with her for now," I explained. "Petre drove off in the car they came in, so I get the feeling she's not heading home anytime soon. I don't want to bring her to my apartment, so getting a room here is the best place to house her. Plus, if she *does* do anything suspicious, Charlotte will know about it and give us warning. We just have to make sure to tell Arch before he gets back from whatever assignment he's on; I doubt it would do well for her to realize she's bunking with agents."

"I can send a message to him," Krystal said. "And while I'm not crazy about sharing a house with that girl, I like it a lot better than having her try to crash with you. Not that I don't trust you, Freddy, but it would probably get awkward. This situation has "honeypot" written all over it."

Despite what you may expect, that term did not go over my head. I had taken in more than enough cinema about spies and subterfuge to know that a honeypot was when a covert operative attempted to seduce a target in order to gain information or trust. Unfortunately, knowing what Krystal meant just made it all the more awkward, as I considered that possibility for why Lillian was being handed to me as an assistant. It was a small mercy that vampires couldn't blush; I suspect I would have ended up on the receiving end of Krystal's wrath if my cheeks had suddenly gone red.

"Her plans are irrelevant. I intend to keep this relationship as detached and professional as I can manage." Krystal still looked a bit wary, though my words seemed to somewhat mollify her. "If anything, this might be a blessing in disguise. We all agree that she's most likely here as a spy, but knowing that means that we can control what she sees. After a week or so of working on accounts and doing filings, she'll realize that I truly am nothing more than an accountant, and can report her findings up the chain of command. I'll bore the House of Turva out of any interest in me."

Richard, Krystal, and Charlotte all exchanged a look. It was a brief one, but volumes seemed to pass between them in the span of that glance. After a moment, Richard rose from his chair to address me. "I'm not saying that's a bad idea, because it's not. But . . . come on, Fred. You have to know as well as we do that dealing with parahumans means a certain element of the unexpected. It wasn't even a couple of weeks ago you were trapped inside a pocket dimension with a pair of mages."

"Those . . . *incidents*, while unavoidable, happen few and far between," I replied. "How long do we really expect Lillian to hang in with me doing accounting work? A week, maybe two or three, at the most? Even if we do hit a chaotic incident, at most she'll see that the services come with a certain amount of risk, but that doesn't make me into a threat."

"No, but she might realize you're the vampire all those rumors are about." Krystal looked worried, which was all the stranger to see in her frumpy get-up. "They are still looking for that guy, too. The exploits got so exaggerated by the rumor mill that no one suspects it's you; however, if that vamp gets to see up close and personal what your job entails, she might put two and two together."

"So I stick to simple, easy accounts with minimal chance of things going nuts," I replied. "I think I've even still got some human clients I can check in on. This can work; we just have to bore her into submission."

"It's a better idea than refusing the offer and starting a feud with the House of Turva," Richard agreed. "Quinn really screwed you good, Fred. If you were actually part of a clan, they could intercede for you, keep others like the Turvas from just deciding that you were going to hire one of their people."

"From what I've seen, I actually think I prefer being on my own," I told him.

"Hey now, these people might be dicks, but there's something to be said for clans and tribes." Richard stood a little taller, which caused his sizable head to scrape against the bottom of the bedroom ceiling. "A lot of the ones who get turned lose their old lives, their old families, and end up alone in the world. Clans and tribes give them new people to turn to, and help in rebuilding their suddenly broken worlds. When done right, we're something of a surrogate family, and a lot of people need that."

"My apologies, Richard. I know how deeply you care for your people, and maybe if I'd been turned into a therian, things would be different. I just meant that, based on the vampires I've encountered, I think I'm a lot happier with how being abandoned turned out."

"And I think we can all agree that Fred has done an oddly good job at constructing his own makeshift family," Krystal added.

"Just to let you all know, Lillian has finished her food and is currently sitting at the table, looking bored," Charlotte reported. "Shall I bring her the next course?"

"No, we should probably head back to the table, anyway." I looked over at Richard, who'd ducked back down after bumping his head on the ceiling. "Will you be joining us?"

"Officially, I still need to make sure she isn't going to kill you," Richard replied. "Unofficially, if you think for one hot second I'm skipping out on Charlotte's cooking, you've got another thing coming."

I could hardly fault the man there, but as we headed for the door, I noticed we weren't alone. Krystal had fallen in behind us, only a few steps behind Richard, whose bulk blocked out the door frame.

"Um, Krystal? What are you doing?"

"Isn't it obvious? Since the official meeting is over, the other tenant in Charlotte Manor is going to head down and get some food." She adjusted her glasses and tugged on the oversized sweatshirt. "Besides, if Lillian is going to be crashing here, then she should probably meet your girlfriend sooner rather than later. If she asks, my place is being fumigated and that's why I'm living in a B&B."

"A supposedly haunted B&B," I pointed out. "And dating a vampire. Crap. What sort of parahuman are we going to say you are?"

"My grandparents were a quarter Fey." There was no hesitation in her explanation; clearly, Krystal had already thought this story through. "Still connected enough to the parahuman world that I'd have been raised around it, but my blood is so diluted that there's no longer much sign of magic. While I'd like to claim I'm a full human who found out about the world by chance, it's just too risky without knowing what she's been feeding on. If it's something that can perceive magic, then I'm sure to trip her senses, so putting in a little Fey ancestry will cover my ass on that front."

That was news to me; I didn't realize there were creatures out there that could sense Krystal's true nature. It really shouldn't have been, though. I'd learned time after time that the parahuman world was bigger and more complex than I could imagine. There were bound to be all sorts of different creatures with various talents out there, almost all of which a vampire could copy abilities from. That's what made us so dangerous, and so feared, even among other parahumans. Every time I met a new client, they were always a bit wary of me, never quite sure what I was capable of, and if I was looking at them as a source of income, or blood.

We made our way back down the hall, and Krystal grabbed my hand just outside the dining room door. She said nothing, though. With the doorway open, not even Charlotte could muffle the words away from Lillian's hearing. Instead, she just held me there as we watched Richard make his way into the dining room and roughly greet Lillian. It occurred to me for the first time that as long as my new employee was around, we were going to have to keep up the facade of Richard, of pretty much all my friends, not caring for me. The ruse would be for my protection, as I couldn't very well be marked as best buddies with a therian, or a mage, or a wielder of a Weapon of Destiny. All the same, even the idea of it felt lonely, and I found myself hoping Lillian would give up quickly so that things could get back to normal.

A tight squeeze on my hand reminded me that Krystal was still there, that she'd found a way to stay with me even with Lillian hovering around us. I felt a surge of love and gratitude for her, leaning in for a quick kiss while we were momentarily alone. She reciprocated warmly, then pulled away and carefully mouthed a single soundless word.

"Showtime."

With that, Krystal slouched her way into the dining room and let out a squeal of mock surprise. "Oh my goodness, Freddy didn't mention that his guests were still here. I'm so sorry to interrupt your dinner."

Awkward, deferential, and apologetic; this version of Krystal was about as far from the real one as she could get. Whether I liked it or not, the pageant had begun.

4.

"ARE YOU SURE I CAN'T COME ALONG?"
Albert stood in the doorway as I packed up my computer bag for the night ahead. Having managed to make it through dinner without anyone getting killed, I'd retired back to my apartment and spent the entire day working out a plan for the coming week. I'd gone through all my accounts, choosing the safest, least likely jobs to turn into anything exciting. Lillian was going to accompany me on boring client visits and assessments until she either quit or I ran out of dull situations to shove her in.

By this point, you're no doubt wondering why I didn't just stick my unwanted employee in front of a mound of paperwork and be done with her. The idea did occur to me—it was an obvious solution to the problem—however, it came with a serious drawback: if I let her handle any aspect of the real accounting, I'd be trusting her with my clients' confidential information. Since I didn't even trust her to know things about me, I certainly wasn't going to allow her access to any of my clients' private fiscal records. Better to drag her around town and risk my own exposure than allow her clan to get its hooks into the people who trusted me.

"No, Albert. I'm afraid it's too dangerous. Besides, I need you handling the more delicate work while I'm saddled with Lillian." Much as I might have enjoyed Albert's company, he was too high profile to bring along. The Blade of the Unlikely Champion took serious issue with being left behind, and Albert always seemed out of sorts when it wasn't close by, but one look at the ornate weapon and she might be able to figure out that he was the town's resident destiny-weapon wielder. And I really was leaning on him to handle a fair amount of tasks while I was busy. Parahumans didn't often go in for digital delivery, and there were several clients expecting contracts, budget projections, and filing receipts to be delivered in the very near future. Some of those, Lillian and I would be handling, but all the ones with the potential to get more . . . exciting . . . had to be entrusted to Albert. Neil would also be tagging along, in case he needed backup.

"You can count on me, boss." Albert saluted, then lowered his hand slowly as his cheerful expression became tinged with concern. "Is this lady really that dangerous?"

"She's probably stronger than me, whatever little that says, but it's not actually her I'm worried about," I told him. "It's her clan as a whole. If I can fall off their radar, be just an anomaly they know about but have no regard for, then that's our optimum situation."

"What's the bad situation?" Albert asked.

I jammed the charging cord, portable Wi-Fi hotspot, and array of flash drives into the top pocket of my brief-case. "Honestly, I'm not sure. Maybe they try to drag me into their clan. Maybe they do a hostile takeover of the business. Maybe they . . . encourage me to leave town." That actually wasn't what I wanted to say, but there was no sense in worrying Albert with the least likely option. Even if I struck their interest, the chances of them decid-ing to kill me were slim. I hoped.

"All I know is that I'd prefer not to deal with them at all, if possible, and that's what this week is about."

"Got it." Albert walked over to my desk, where I had neatly arranged all his assignments for the night. "But it's too bad."

"What do you mean?"

"You've been saying for a while that you needed more help. I just mean, it's too bad that this Lillian lady can't actually lend us a hand." It was hard to argue with Albert as we both stared at the mound of assignments I'd set aside for him. Had Arch been in town, I'd have never been able to lay such a heavy burden on my assistant's shoulders, but while the agent was gone, their training was on break. And he was right; the company did need to grow if I was going to keep up with demands. Just not like this.

"I'd far rather keep working overtime than accept any help the House of Turva wants to give," I told him. "This business might not be much, but at least no one else can lay claim to it. That's worth something to me."

"To me, too," Albert agreed, beginning to carefully scoop up his assignments and pile them into his backpack.

With my own accessories stowed, I said a quick goodbye, and then headed out into the crisp new night. The last of the sunset had only just fallen away, so the sky was still a bit lighter than usual. I did miss seeing the blue skies and sun, even if I was now able to glimpse them through enchanted windows. It wasn't the same, though. I'd never really cared much for standing in sunlight during my living days; mostly, I'd considered it an inconvenience. Now, I'd have paid an obscene amount for the experience. But that was life; everything was a transaction. Nothing came free. Ageless existence and mystical powers were a comparatively small price to pay for giving up the ability to tan. I just still missed the sun, occasionally.

By the time I arrived at Charlotte Manor, Lillian was already waiting on the porch. She wore yet another pantsuit, probably delivered by someone in her clan, and had a large purse with a yellow legal pad sticking out the top. Before I could so much as pop open my door to greet her, she rushed forward, opening the passenger side of my hybrid and climbing gracefully in.

"Something wrong?" I asked.

"Just excited to get started on my first day of work." Her smile was wide and infectious, but something in the way her eyes were twitching betrayed Lillian's anxiety.

"You sure that's all? Did something happen? Did Krystal say anything?"

"Krystal? Hell no. That girl barely even speaks; she's quiet as a barn mouse." Lillian glanced back at Charlotte Manor through the window. "It's just . . . I don't want to sound ungrateful—I really appreciate you putting me up somewhere parahuman friendly and with such good food. But you mentioned that place has a presence, and the longer I've been staying there, the more I can feel it. It's hard to describe, like everywhere I go, I know someone is aware of my movements and what I'm doing. It's kind of unnerving."

"Sorry you had to go through that." I shifted the car into drive and began heading back toward Winslow's proper city area. It was probably of note that she could tell Charlotte was paying special attention to her; it meant her senses were either exceptional or she'd been dining on something with high awareness. Either way, I'd have to ask the house to be more discreet in keeping watch. "When we get back, I'll have a sit down with the presence; see if I can get it to offer you a little breathing room. We've had dealings before, so I should be able to talk it into backing off."

"I would greatly appreciate that." Lillian leaned back in the seat, seeming to finally relax now that the manor was fading into the rear view mirror. "So, what's on the docket for my first day on the job?"

"Listening," I told her. "And taking notes. Right now, you don't have any of the training or certifications to actually do accounting work, so I'm going to teach you the customer service portion of the job. In a normal firm, there are reps to deal with most of that, but this is a small operation, so every employee has to be able to handle multiple jobs."

"Can do," Lillian replied. "I like to think I've got a way with people. I used to get compliments on my bedside manner, way back when I had a heartbeat."

"You were a doctor?" I asked.

Lillian chuckled, hard laughter tainted with something darker than mirth. "A nurse. They didn't let women be doctors back then. No matter how much we might have wanted it."

I looked at Lillian once more, realizing for the first time just how great the difference in our ages was. I didn't know much about the history of physicians—the best I could recall was that the first female doctor had been sometime in the mid-eighteen hundreds, which put Lillian's human life somewhere before that. She was at least a hundred and fifty years old, yet she looked not a day past twenty-five. As someone who was undead, you might have expected me to be more prepared for these things, but there is a huge gap between knowing you'll live without aging and actually confronting it while driving toward a highway.

"Sorry to hear that," I said finally, realizing I'd let the silence drag on a little too long. "Did you try going back into the field? Times have certainly changed since . . . whenever you were turned." I tried to steer around the subject of when exactly she was made into a vampire. Part of it was out of politeness, and the rest was because I couldn't shake the old adage of never asking a woman for her age from my head. I didn't know if it applied to the undead, but this was not the occasion to find out.

"Times have changed out here, but some clans are a little more stuck in their ways." Her eyes went wide at that, and she began speaking again so quickly she nearly stumbled over her words. "I mean, I've been busy helping my people. Not even the House of Turva runs itself. We all do our part to protect and watch over each other. It's truly rewarding, knowing that my work helps my family."

"And what kind of work might that be?" I asked. "I didn't get a resume from you, so it might help to know your strengths and weaknesses when deciding how to train you."

"Let's just say I'm a quick learner, and I've been around long enough to do almost every sort of job you can picture. Although, accounting will be a new one for me," Lillian admitted.

"Maybe that's why they lent you out. They want someone on hand who can balance the books." I carefully pulled through a green light and onto the ramp for the highway. Much as I loved Charlotte Manor, it was out in the boonies of Winslow and required more of a commute than I generally preferred.

"I'm not 'lent out,' Fredrick. I work for you now. No one is going to call me back and leave you high and dry. My clan takes its gestures of friendship seriously." She patted her legal pad gently. "You don't have to worry; I'm in for the long haul."

"How lovely to hear." I did my best to keep some cheer in my tone as I accelerated toward the city, hoping against hope that Lillian was lying her ass off.

5.

THE FIRST FEW APPOINTMENTS WENT AS well as I'd hoped, if not better. I introduced Lillian as my trainee to the clients, then got right to business. The curtness wasn't malicious; I simply didn't want her to have any chance to let them know about her affiliation with the House of Turva. Presumed alliances could be problematic down the line, and I liked to keep my business meetings on track. After all, the client was paying for my time, so the discussion should be centered around their needs. With two drop-offs and one potential client meeting under my belt, I began to feel more confident as I drove us out of downtown Winslow to the pleasant housing area where my next appointment was waiting.

This one was to be the softest of softballs, as I was supposed to meet with Amy to do a quarterly update on her supply receipts. We went through her logs, marking which materials were for jobs and which were for personal use or testing so that everything could be written off properly come tax time. It didn't really need to be done quarterly, but that was about as long as we could manage without Amy forgetting and tossing the receipts out or setting them on fire. While the actual meeting hadn't been due for another few weeks, I moved it up especially for my new employee's first night. The whole task was glorified inventory work; dull, methodical, and perfect to bore Lillian out of her skull.

We pulled into the driveway of Amy's modest, quaint-looking home. She lived with ample space and fences between her house and the neighbors, and none of them were aware that she had a top-end alchemical laboratory tucked away in the rear of the property. From the front, it appeared to be a totally normal, somewhat unremarkable dwelling.

Except, that was, for the frantic woman darting toward my car. Amy's face was smeared with soot, and her hair was flying in all directions. She began waving at me, then noticed the passenger staring in aghast confusion and quickly tried to tone down her panic. That, in itself, was worrying enough; Amy was usually on so many self-crafted potions that she tended to be the mellowest person I knew. If she was panicking, something must have really gone awry.

"Hey there, Fred," Amy said as I opened the door and climbed from the car. "So great to see you, really looking forward to the meeting, just one small thing that maybe we can chat about first? In private?"

As she finished speaking, the sound of something crashing behind the house rang through the yard.

"Now," Amy added, motioning for me to follow.

"Um . . . Lillian, the client has some confidential information to discuss. Please wait in the car, and do your best not to listen," I said. To her credit, Lillian shut the door and turned on the radio without a word of disagreement, which was a small comfort as Amy began dragging me around to the back of her house.

We'd just turned the corner when she dug through her pockets, pulled out a small blue vial, and threw it to the ground. The air seemed to warp around us, as if we were standing on the inside of a bubble.

"That should block her from eavesdropping," Amy said. "Soooo, we may have a bit of a problem."

"You don't say," I replied, offering her a handkerchief to wipe the soot from her face.

"I know it's not the best timing, but since you weren't coming by until late, I figured I had a little window of time to get some work done tonight," Amy explained, twisting the handkerchief around in knots on her fingers, the soot remaining uncleaned. "And Bubba has been up my ass about the enlarging potion, so when I finally had a breakthrough, I wanted to—"

"Hang on," I interrupted. "What's this about Bubba and a potion? He doesn't touch anything stronger than beer."

"This wasn't the recreational stuff. He was looking for real alchemy, the kind with the power to create change. You know how sensitive he is about his size," Amy said.

We all knew; it wasn't something Bubba hid particularly well. Despite his pride in being a therian and a weresteed, Bubba had insecurity issues about the fact that he was considered something of a runt. While Richard easily dwarfed most other therians in his lion form, Bubba was at the opposite end of the spectrum—he got smaller when he shifted. In fact, he was so small that he wasn't even technically a horse. He was a pony.

"He asked you to try and make a potion to fix that?"

"He's been asking me for months. Ever since Gideon got captured," Amy corrected, twisting the handkerchief even more. "And it's been slow going. I can craft a potion to make him bigger, no problem, but it's when you get into the permanent aspect that things become a lot more complicated. Anyway, I had an idea about distilling the essence from a Night Mare down and concentrating—"

"I'm sorry, a nightmare?" Much as I loathed to keep cutting Amy off, I wanted at least some clear idea of exactly what it was I was about to walk into.

Amy shook her head. "Two words. Legendary monster horse. Anyway, I got my supplies today, and decided to whip up a trial batch. I had Bubba take a drop, just a drop, to measure the effects. Good news: it sort of worked. Better than I'd hoped, actually."

Another round of crashing, this time accompanied by what sounded like hoof beats, tore through the night. Apparently, Amy's bubble only kept sound in, not out. Or maybe it turned us into ghosts, for all I knew; it wasn't as though her experiments were predictable.

"Okay." I pinched the bridge of my nose, trying to think of how I was going to explain this to Lillian. Just a casualty of dealing with mages? Maybe that would sell; magic users did have a reputation for being unpredictable. "Okay, what do you need from me?"

"I put together a second potion to neutralize the first one before I ever gave it to him, just in case, but Bubba's not in his right mind. He's tearing about, making it impossible for me to get to the antidote. Plus, even if I grab it, I might need some help getting it in."

"So, keep him distracted, then?" I asked.

"Pretty much. And maybe hold him down if I can't get a syringe through his skin." With that, Amy began dragging me again, out of the bubble (which popped at her touch) and around the back of the house to where her lab stood. She yanked me along, through the door, and into a scene of complete chaos.

Tables, beakers, and general supplies were on the floor, mostly smashed. In the middle of the room, crushing a table beneath his sizable hooves, was what I could only assume was Bubba Emerson, though not like I'd ever seen him before. No longer was he a runt; instead, the top of his body stood above my shoulders, and while I'm far from the tallest in the world, I'm not short, either. His normal sandy coat had been replaced by one of ash-black, like a burned-out log, and orange flames flickered along his mane and hooves.

Well, that explained the soot on Amy's face. Sort of.

"What did you try to splice him with?"

"Really not the important issue right now," Amy replied.

"How about the fact that your lab looks completely smashed, and I'm guessing that includes the antidote, too," I countered.

"Please, you think I kept that in the upstairs lab?" Amy nodded to a small wooden door that I was positive hadn't been there the last time I visited her, or on any of the previous occasions. "I need to get past him and down to where the dangerous stuff is stored."

"Lovely. And what if he breaks through the walls?" I asked.

Amy shook her head. "Not possible. I've had enough experiments go wrong to know the value of sound construction. This house is warded up, down, and sideways. He's not busting out anytime soon."

I began stepping away from Amy—there was no sense in even trying this ridiculous idea unless I kept his attention solely on me. When I was across the room, I pressed my fingers to my lips and released the loudest whistle I could manage. Truthfully, it was pretty unimpressive, but evidently it was enough to get the massive horse that was Bubba to look at me.

He stopped smashing up the table beneath his feet and turned to me, letting me see for the first time that his eyes were a dull red instead of a horse's usual glassy black. A snort came from his lips—mercifully not accompanied by a bout of flame—and his ears twitched as he stared at me.

"Hey, Bubba," I said, keeping my voice as calm as was manageable in the face of a giant, burning horse. Amy began to slink silently toward the wooden door. "Do you know who I am? It's Fred. Your friend. The guy who stocks your favorite beer in his fridge."

Another snort, but nothing aggressive. At least, not so far. Through my peripheral vision—I didn't dare risk a real glance—I saw Amy making progress, step by step, getting closer to the door. She was also getting closer to Bubba with every movement, so I kept talking, doing all I could to keep his attention rapt on me.

"It's okay. I'm here to help. We just need you to calm down a little. When this is over, we'll crack open a few beers and watch . . . whatever sport is on right now." I'd like to blame panic for making me blank on which sport was in season at that moment in time, but truth be told, I couldn't have named it even without my friend being turned into a monster horse.

"We'll find something on. Maybe a nice action movie, or a western. Amy has the fancy cable; there's bound to be options." At this point, I was mostly just saying whatever inane nonsense popped into my head. All that mattered was that I kept the sound going. As long as his attention was on me, Amy would be okay, and that was the important part. It almost worked, too. Unfortunately, Bubba wasn't the only one failing to pay attention to his environment.

The sound of crunching glass may as well have been a gunshot with how quiet the room was. Bubba let out a screeching whinny and reared onto his hind legs, twisting his head to see Amy, frozen in mid-sneak, her shoes lifting from the remains of a test tube. Faced with the split-second decision of how to handle the situation, she defaulted to the pair of options hardwired into every creature on the planet: fight or flight. Since her opponent was both an angry horse and a dear friend, Amy wisely chose the latter option, bolting the rest of the way to the wooden door before Bubba could get his bearings.

She barely made it, jerking the door open and slamming it shut an instant before Bubba careened into it. I expected the wood to buckle and splinter under the power of his charge, but it was Bubba who buckled instead, bouncing off the doorway like it was a block of steel. He shook his head, therian regeneration no doubt already patching up what little wounds he'd inflicted on himself, and then reared back again, trying to pound the entire wall with his hooves. It worked about as well as the charge, which was to say, not at all. Amy hadn't been kidding about the warding on her lab, and it was all paying off at that moment.

Finally giving up on the wall, Bubba turned back around to face me. The red in his eyes didn't seem quite as dull this time around, and before I could muster so much as a comforting word, he charged. There are few things in life quite like watching a sizable steed partially covered in flames come barreling down at you while inside a closed room, and for those wondering, I would highly recommend against experiencing it. Especially if you don't have vampire reaction speeds.

I leapt to the side, scarcely getting out of Bubba's way in time, even with my superior dexterity. He was so damn fast now, his natural speed having been upgraded along with his size, that it was all I could do to avoid his stampeding bulk. Whatever remaining tables and supplies had been behind me weren't so lucky; I heard him crunching them into debris as he turned back around. Amy's lab was big, but not so large that it left me many places to go when facing off against a burning horse. Another change from Bubba, and again, I was able to jump to the side. He bounced off the wooden door again, coming away from the encounter with even more anger in his eyes.

This couldn't go on much longer; I was barely surviving each attack as it was. My eyes flicked to the doorway, but I immediately realized I couldn't escape. If Bubba followed me through an open door, I'd be setting him free on the world, which would make catching and curing him far more difficult. If he didn't, then I'd be leaving Amy as a sitting duck the minute she returned from her lab. I had to stick it out if we wanted to help Bubba, but I couldn't keep running around like I was.

As I dodged Bubba for the third time, nearly catching the leg of my slacks on fire, an idea finally struck me. He might be faster and stronger than me, but he wasn't as lithe. Stretching my fingers out, wishing dearly that I didn't keep my nails so trim, I leapt upward, all the way to Amy's ceiling. The moment I made contact, I jammed my hands through the soft drywall, groping about for a beam to hang on to. For a second, I thought all was lost as my hands closed around nothing, but then I felt the wonderful sensation of something solid and grabbed on for all I was worth. Using my abs to lift my legs, I pinned myself to the ceiling like a fly.

It wasn't a great long-term solution—I'd have to come down when Amy emerged so I could do distraction duty again—but for the moment, it meant I was safe from Bubba's assault. He trotted about beneath me, staring up at me with those relentless eyes.

"Sorry, buddy, I just needed time—" It was my turn to be interrupted, as Bubba leapt up from the ground, far higher than a normal horse could, on a direct track for me. There was no chance of dodging; I was far too taken by surprise.

All I could do was gasp in shock as Bubba's hooves smashed into me, knocking me from the ceiling to the floor, where it would only be seconds until he started trampling me.

6.

OF ALL THE THINGS I WAS EXPECTING TO come next—stampeding hooves, lots of pain, perhaps even the smell of burning vampire flesh—what I did not count on was a blur in a pantsuit whipping through the doorway and slamming Bubba in the side. It wasn't enough force to knock him over—he was too strong for that—but it did push him off course, allowing me the precious necessary seconds to get back on my feet. Once I did, I was overwhelmed with equal parts gratitude and distress.

Lillian was backing slowly away from Bubba, never taking her eyes off the mighty steed as he gathered his bearings for another charge. "Sorry, boss, I got tired of waiting in the car."

"I'm not usually one for insubordination, but I suppose I'll have to look past it this time." While I'd have far rather recounted this tale to Lillian, which would have allowed me to glaze over the more dangerous parts and omit certain details entirely, her intervention had kept me from being trampled on the floor. Out of the two options, perhaps having to put a little more effort into my lies wasn't such a bad result.

"What's the plan? One of us distracts this thing while the other drains it dry?" Lillian asked.

"No!" I spat the word without thinking, my mind flashing back to that night with Colin. Lillian wasn't the type to hesitate, and if I didn't stop her right away, then Bubba might be in danger. "This is a client; he's just had a bad reaction to a potion. Right now, the alchemist is fetching an antidote, so all we need to do is keep him distracted until she arrives."

It didn't take any manner of expert to see the doubt and, worse, curiosity in Lillian's eyes. She voiced none of it, though, merely nodding her head stiffly and replying, "You're the boss."

After that, there was little time for talk, as Bubba tore after us once again. It was still hellish to try and dodge his assaults, but having Lillian in the room helped a great deal. We spread out instinctively, and even in the limited confines of the lab, he could only go after one of us at a time. That allowed the other to regroup and prepare for when his attention invariably waned— sometimes helped along by yelling when one of us was getting backed into a corner. Together, we managed to keep him smashing about without being trampled until the wooden door opened a small sliver and Amy's voice slunk out from behind it.

"How are we looking?"

"We're going to have to write off everything in here as collateral damage from a testing procedure, but otherwise, not bad," I replied. "My new employee stepped in to lend a hand, making the task far more manageable." While it sounded like (and technically was) praise, my real goal was to make sure Amy knew that we weren't alone before she let anything too important slip. Granted, there was little chance of that with Bubba as a far more eminent threat; however, I'd found it never hurt to be overly cautious. Especially not with my group of friends.

"Well, I brought the calm-down juice. Loaded it up and got it ready for injection, too."

"Do I want to know why you have that sort of equipment on hand?" I asked, keeping a careful eye on Lillian as she gracefully darted out of Bubba's path.

"Not every parahuman has a mouth, Fred. I have to cater to all sorts of clients," Amy replied, a bit more sharply than usual. Evidently, the experience of accidentally morphing her friend and seeing her lab torn to shambles had left her in a less-than-stellar mood, which I could scarcely fault her for.

"I didn't consider that," I admitted. "To the matter at hand, though . . . how do we administer the cure? Bubba doesn't seem too keen on letting anyone get close to him at the moment. At least, not unless he's trying to mow them down."

"Seeing as I'm just an alchemist and you're two strapping vampires, I'd say one of you is going to have to get the drop on him and jam it in. Catch." With no more warning than that, Amy flung open the door and tossed a metal syringe at me. My hand moved on its own, which was a great mercy, because if I'd had time to think, I surely would have let it clatter to the ground, rather snatching the cure out of mid-air. The moment my hand closed around it, the sharp scent hit my nose and caused it to wrinkle.

Silver. Not the whole device, but at least the needle. It made sense; therians were just as weak to the stuff as vampires—well, most vampires, anyway—and without knowing how tough his skin currently was, this was the only method to ensure the syringe broke through. All the same, I tried to look ill-at-ease holding such a thing, in case Lillian had picked up on the scent, as well. Since I wasn't technically touching it, I shouldn't be weakened; yet, all the same, it seemed prudent to show some discomfort. The absolute last thing I needed was for her to realize I'd found a way to shake off one our kind's biggest vulnerabilities.

"Lillian! Can you manage to make him hold still for a second or so? *Without* hurting him."

"Is this thing a therian?" Lillian yelled at me, bolting out of the way and whirling around so that Bubba would be charging past her into a corner.

"In normal form, yes," I replied.

"Stopping it without hurting it is probably impossible, but I can at least limit the damage to what their kind can heal. Will that work?" She couldn't turn toward me to ask; her eyes were unwaveringly on Bubba as he lined up his next attack. While I wasn't particularly fond of the idea, it seemed we were going to have to make the best of a bad situation. Better Bubba recover from a few bruises than any of us get serious injuries.

"Keep it as limited as you can," I instructed.

That was all the permission she needed. Bubba charged at her again, but rather than jump to the side, Lillian ran forward, meeting the challenge head on. Her posture dropped as she went into a slide, purposely putting herself down between those trampling legs. With movements so fast and precise I could barely follow them, Lillian threw a kick directly into one of Bubba's legs, just as his weight settled on top of it. I heard the snap and pop before I saw the knee bend, collapsing and bringing several hundred pounds of horse down with it.

Bubba's screech was awful, and I did my best to ignore it as I raced forward. He could heal fast—I'd seen that firsthand many a time—and if this version of my friend managed to get back on its feet, it would have a vendetta to settle. Wasting no time, I drove the syringe deep into his flank, the silver easily piercing his usually durable skin. Jamming the plunger down with my thumb, I didn't so much as wiggle the device until I was sure every drop of antidote had made it into Bubba's system.

The effects were visible almost instantly; a wave of brown washed out from the spot where I'd stuck him, overtaking the ashy black color of his altered form. As it spread, I noticed that Bubba was getting smaller, the terrifying horse turning back to my friend's true, diminutive form. His breathing was labored, however, and I could still see the broken angle of his leg even as his body morphed. Carefully, being sure not to antagonize him, I laid my hand on Bubba's neck.

"It's okay. I'm here. Amy's here, and you're going to be fine." The sound of plodding footsteps on shattered debris drew my attention, and I saw Amy walking over.

"Sorry about that, Bubba. Next time, I promise to filter out the aggressive tendencies inherent in their magic."

"How about we just not have a next time?" I proposed.

"Fred, do you know where the world would be if people gave up every time they had one little failure?" Amy countered.

"I'm okay with a lack of progress if the failures involve my friends being in danger." I could feel Bubba's racing pulse through his neck, but thankfully, it was beginning to calm down as his returned to his usual pony form.

"He would have been fine, eventually," Amy said. "It was a test potion, so none of the ingredients could have lasted longer than a day. I just didn't want him to get himself into trouble before it wore off."

"Excuse me . . . are you Amy Wells? Student to Gideon, King of the West?" Lillian had circled around behind us, and was standing by Amy with her hands clasped together in what was either real or very well-done mock excitement.

"'Student' might be a bit of a strong term. He just showed me a few things, mostly so I could make better products for him," Amy replied. After a second, her brow furrowed. "Wait, how do you know about that?"

"Oh, the House of Turva makes a point of researching everyone of significant status and power when we move to a new area, and as an associate of the King of the West, you, of course, caught their attention." I didn't know much about vampire culture, but this seemed like the sort of thing someone should probably be embarrassed to admit, and yet, it didn't leave even so much as a dent in Lillian's excitement. "I have to say, it's a real honor to meet you. People talk about how powerful your potions are for states around."

They did? I knew Amy was talented—the mere fact that Gideon was a client spoke to that fact—but I had never realized she was quite that well-regarded. It didn't seem to shock Amy much, though, as she shrugged off the praise in her usual blasé manner.

"Thanks, I guess. Sorry our friend almost smashed you."

"It was well worth it to meet such an icon," Lillian replied. If she took note of the fact that Amy referred to us all as friends, rather than business acquaintances, she didn't show it. Maybe I'd get lucky and she'd simply chalk it up to Amy being lazy with titles, or overly friendly.

Bubba, in the meantime, had fully transformed back to his usual weresteed shape and size, not so much as a speck of black or fire left on him. The glassy black eyes stared up at us, saying the apology that his mouth wasn't currently able to convey. For a moment, he began to warp, heading back to his human form, but before he could do more than start the shift, Amy whacked him hard on the nose.

"None of that, now. You know you heal faster when transformed, and that leg needs to patch itself up," Amy chided. She took a good look at the wound, which was already better than it had been moments prior. "Damn, your new assistant really got a piece of him."

"I'm actually a trainee, not an assistant," Lillian corrected. "But I do believe in fulfilling orders to the best of my ability."

Before I could tell her that some orders could be handled a little more gently, the sound of Albert's ringtone began blaring from my phone. Slipping the sleek device out of my pocket, I accepted the call and pulled the phone to my ear.

"What's going on, Albert?"

"Um . . . hey, Fred. I know this—" Albert was cut off by the sound of screaming in the background, at least one of the voices belonging to Neil. "Sorry, I know this isn't the best night for it, but I think I need your help on something. I was dropping off the packets, just like you ordered; only, when I got to the fifth one, instead of signing the receipt, the couple just started yelling at each other. Things . . . sort of got worse from there." Another bout of screaming, followed by what sounded like the thud of something dense hitting a wall.

"Neil and I are kind of stuck here," Albert continued. "And I could call the authorities, but I thought, since the papers got them fighting, maybe there was a non-agent way to fix this. 'Cause . . . well . . . you know."

I did know, all too well. He was smart enough not to say Krystal's name, but she was the authority he would turn to. And if Albert called in an agent, the situation was getting resolved. It just might not be in the most peaceful of methods. Aside from concern for my clients, I also had to worry about the reputation of my company. Being too closely linked with agents could be bad for business—a lot of parahumans tried to keep themselves as far away from the treaty-enforcers as possible.

Of course, even on the best of nights, I'd be hesitant to head into such a situation. With Lillian in tow, it was all the more problematic. Still, Albert was right. If I could figure out what in the documents had caused the issue and find a resolution, then it would be the best ending for everyone involved.

Except, possibly, me.

"Give me the address, Albert," I said, noting the interest in Lillian's expression. "We'll head there right away."

7.

IT TOOK US NEARLY TWENTY MINUTES TO
arrive at the destination, even with me breaking my
usual fastidious adherence to the speed limits (I went
up to ten miles over in some spots). I'd recognized the
address as soon as Albert gave it to me; even in my line
of work, the number of ranches I called on was minimal.
The Capra Ranch was to the north of Winslow, in one of
the most rustic sections. Unlike where Charlotte Manor
had been located, this piece of land was never attempted
to be industrialized, and in fact hosted a lovely farmer's

market on weekends that I would have happily attended, if it weren't held during the day.

Gerda and Oskar were the kindly couple who ran and owned the Capra Ranch—a satyress and satyr, respectively. I remembered driving out to meet them a few months back, their goat legs carefully hidden under thick overalls and custom boots. They had served me delicious cheese and asked me to carefully go through their costs and incomes to see why business was up, but profits were down. It had been a relatively simple job. All I had uncovered was that they were overpaying a few suppliers, hardly the sort of thing I expected to cause a ruckus. Yet, as I pulled my car around to the rear, I could clearly hear heated voices yelling at each other from inside the farmhouse.

"Please don't tell me to stay put again." Lillian's request came before I'd even gotten my seat belt off. It was prescient as well, because the next words out of my mouth were indeed going to be orders to sit tight while I handled this. "I'm here to learn about customer service, remember?"

"What's happening in there is hardly a standard part of the job," I told her.

"You do remember that we just came from subduing a rampaging therian, right? Seems to me it comes up often enough to be worth learning." Lillian took off her own seat belt and slung her bag over her arm. "Besides, you might need backup. Once satyrs get going on a tear, it's hard to calm them down."

"Lillian, I know the last stop set something of a bad precedent, but at Fletcher Accounting Services, we do *not* go into meetings planning on physically engaging our clients."

"No, but there's something to be said for self-defense," Lillian replied. "I promise not to lay a hand on anyone unless you tell me to, though. And don't act like you don't need the help. I know your assistant is stuck in there."

This, at least, didn't come as a surprise. I knew my own hearing well enough to expect that she'd been able to hear Albert's side of the call. I still scowled at her nonetheless. "Privacy and confidentiality are important aspects of the work I do. From now on, I expect you to tune out my business calls."

"Will do." Lillian looked as if she meant to say more, but a loud thud from inside the farmhouse made us both jump. "Sounds like we should really get in there."

Much as I tried to think of one, I didn't have a good reason to offer up for why she should stay in the car. I could hardly pretend to be worried for her safety—the way she'd brought down an augmented Bubba made it clear that, of the two of us, she would be more capable in dangerous situations. Not to mention the fact that, with no idea what I was walking into, having the help might actually make a difference again. Most compelling of all, though, was the fact that Albert and Neil were stuck in the middle of whatever was happening, and that meant getting them extricated came before anything else.

With a begrudging sigh, I nodded, and the two of us stepped out of my eco-consciously sized car. Moving quickly, I knocked once on the front door, which caused it to drift open, as it had evidently not been closed in the first place. This gave us an excellent view into the living room, and a sight so strange we were both struck by a momentary pause.

Gerda and Oskar, the two lovely people I remembered from our original meeting, were literally locking horns (which I was certain they didn't have when last I saw them) in the middle of the room. The furniture had been thrown about, and the dents on the wooden walls answered the question of what had been making the loud thuds. Backed in a corner, tucked behind what looked like the remains of a coffee table, were Albert and Neil. Albert had planted his sword, still sheathed, between the battling couple and them, while Neil was scratching some sort of rune into the coffee table and muttering under his breath. All of this came with the soundtrack of Gerda and Oskar both trying to yell over the other, so deep in anger and insults that I could barely piece together more than a few words of their dialogue, none of which I'd feel comfortable repeating in my retelling of the incident. I mean, there's swearing, and then there's two satyrs cursing at one another.

"Fred!" Albert popped his head up as he caught sight of me and Lillian in the doorway. Somehow, his one innocent exclamation got the attention of the battling couple, who yanked their horns apart and turned to face me.

"There he is!" Gerda yelled, voice nothing like the one she'd had when offering me glass after glass of sweet tea. "Tell this lying old bastard that the jig is up!"

"Fred, it's about damn time," Oskar hollered. "I've been trying to make your assistant explain to her that the truth is right there on the page."

"They've been screaming a lot, don't want us to leave, and I can't figure out what any of it is about!" Albert yelped.

"This accounting stuff is a lot more interesting than I was expecting," Lillian muttered, which was the exact opposite of what I wanted to hear from her.

All the voices were swirling around, trying to top the others and clamoring for attention. Rather than try and engage with any of them, I stormed into the room, grabbed the tattered (but not torn) packet I'd given Albert for delivery, and slapped it crisply against my hand.

"Gerda. Oskar. I want to help you, I do— "

My words were drowned out under a fresh tidal wave of yelling from each half of the couple, both trying to make their points so enthusiastically that they weren't even bothering with an explanation. In spite of their aggression, I remained calm, waiting until there was a lull and trying again.

"I can't offer any perspective on this unless—"

Another fresh wave of screaming. I continued to be patient, ready to wait for as long as it took to get them calmed down enough to explain the situation.

This time, however, they were the ones cut off. Not by words, but by the sudden audible crack of wood being fiercely splintered. We all turned to find that Lillian, still dutifully standing by the entrance, had driven her fist completely through the door with a single punch, and was now carefully brushing the splinters away from her unmarked hand.

"I believe Fred was trying to say something, before you interrupted him." There was no threat in her words, yet the hole in the door spoke volumes. Gerda and Oskar both seemed to shrink back, looking at her, and me, with an expression I'd encountered more than once since my transformation, and loathed more with every occurrence.

Fear. She'd reminded them that we were stronger, and now they were scared of her. Of us.

"Lillian, go wait in the car."

"But—"

"You are *done* here. Unless you want to be fired outright, go wait in the car. Now." It wasn't often that I found the nerve to be so forceful, but this was something I absolutely couldn't tolerate. My business, my very life, was built upon other parahumans looking past the reputation that other vampires had cultivated. I couldn't allow anyone to associate Fletcher Accounting Services with that kind of aggression, not unless it was a matter of life and death. Yelling didn't qualify. Sooner or later, voices got tired.

Lillian stared at me for several seconds, then spun around and left, presumably heading back toward the car. I looked at Gerda and Oskar, suitably cowed for the moment, and decided to capitalize on their silence.

"I am very, deeply sorry for that. Lillian is a new employee; though, one more stunt like that, and that won't be the case any longer. Fletcher Accounting Services is going to replace your door, and I'll be doing the next six months of budgetary maintenance for free as an apology. If you no longer wish to do business with us, I understand, and will happily get whatever new accountant you choose up to speed on your situation."

Some of the color that had drained from each of their cheeks began to return, and Oskar even took a step toward me. "Nah, Fred, you can't control what someone else does. We accept the apology."

"Thank you, very much," I replied. "Now, can we please, in calm and rational voices, discuss what in my findings led you to suddenly begin fighting with one another?"

"A fight? This ain't much of a fight. Barely even an argument," Gerda informed me. "Guess it might seem that way from the outside, though. We satyrs and satyresses are just passionate. And a bit stubborn."

"What caused the 'discussion' was that I looked through your pages and found out she's been double paying for the cow's feed," Oskar told me, his tone beginning to heat up a bit more. "Now, I know that's her cousin's company, so she's probably been paying twice just to squirrel a little money away from me. And the only reason she'd do that is if she was gambling again."

"Like hell that's what started it," Gerda shot back. "We started a row because *you're* paying three times what the fencing costs to your old drinking buddy who runs the company. And so help me god, Oskar, if you're back on the bottle, I'll break it over your thick skull. Again." From the way she was flexing her hands, something told me she didn't mean it as a figure of speech.

They were beginning to fume again, which was actually a relief, since it meant they weren't afraid I'd forcefully shut them down. Plus, now that I knew what the actual issues were, it allowed me to dig through the report and see how much truth there was to the claims. As the satyr couple started squabbling once again, I sat down in the sole remaining chair to dig through my compiled report.

Even as I worked, though, my mind was out in the car with Lillian. I didn't regret the choice I'd made in sending her away, but that didn't mean there wouldn't be consequences to it.

My night might very well end with a fight that would put the owners of the Capra Ranch to shame.

8.

IT TOOK A WHILE, BUT I WAS EVENTUALLY
able to piece together what had caused the errors. Double
paying for feed was an innocent mistake—both Gerda
and Oskar had thought they were supposed to set up
the automatic withdrawals from their bank account and
neither had checked with the other, causing the same
amount to go out twice per month. As for the fencing,
while the cost was exorbitant, it also matched the receipts provided by the company. I recommended that
they find a new vendor, as this one was clearly gouging

them. It was technically possible that Oskar was funneling cash through a friend to feed a secret drinking habit, but judging from the anger at hearing his friend was ripping them off, it seemed unlikely. That, or Oskar was a far better actor than I could have imagined. Either way, my work was done, and I liberated Neil and Albert, who were both handed cartons of baked goods from Gerda as apology for what she called "the slight inconvenience."

I saw both of them back to Neil's car—an old sedan most likely inherited from a family member who'd purchased cars back when they were made of thick metal frames and came with ashtrays in the armrests. It occurred to me as I watched their taillights fade down the road that I'd never actually met any of Neil's family. Albert's either, but that was understandable, as they all believed him to be dead. I knew I was stalling, avoiding heading back to my own car and facing the fuming vampire waiting inside. There was no getting around it, though. Not unless I was willing to abandon my car and run back to town—which was tempting, I will admit, but would leave Lillian for Oskar and Gerda to deal with. And that seemed like bad customer service no matter how I sliced it.

I rounded the farm house to see my hybrid still in one piece, which I hoped was a good sign. Lillian was sitting inside, staring out her window and away from my approaching form. She was still aware of me, her senses were too good for her not to be, but she was pretending not to notice. That was fine by me, as I would take frustrated silence over fury any day of the week. Popping open the door, I slid into my seat and started the car's engine. I said nothing as I put on my seat belt, giving Lillian ample time to open the conversation with an explanation or an apology if she so desired. When my silence was echoed, it became obvious that I was going to have to start things off.

"I'm sorry if my tone was too harsh in there. The situation was chaotic, and I had to try and salvage things as quickly as possible, which meant you had to leave. Still, I do wish I'd found a gentler way to voice that."

"Salvage things?" Lillian turned from the window, surprise overtaking the pinched annoyance she'd been wearing seconds before. "Fredrick, I had the situation perfectly in hand. They were silent, willing to listen, and ready to sign whatever you put in front of them. I fixed everything, and you cast me out for it."

"You didn't 'fix' anything," I told her. "You just made my clients afraid."

"They *should* be afraid." Her surprise was morphing to puzzlement before my eyes. "You are a vampire, one of the most feared and powerful types of parahumans out there. The very fact that they continued speaking when you entered the room was a slap in the face. All I did was restore the natural order. And without touching a single person, I might add."

I think I would have preferred it if Lillian had been at least a little miffed as she spoke. If she were angry, then I could have pretended the words came without thought and forgiven them as such. But Lillian wasn't mad. She didn't even seem overly prideful as she spoke of the natural order. The only emotion that came across was confusion, like I was the weird one. Which, when viewed objectively, I suppose I was.

"Is that what it's like inside your clan?" I asked. "Vampires are seen as the best, and the other parahumans are lesser?"

"Not the best, just among the top. We're aware of our abilities, and our limitations," Lillian countered. "As for the others, the satyrs and mages and therians, they are our food, Fredrick, just like the humans. A bit more difficult to hunt, but the nutrition is far superior. Or are you honestly saying that you don't use this job as a way to get in close to other parahumans so you can feed on them?"

Slowly, I lowered my head until the rims of my glasses were pressed against the steering wheel's leather. *That* was what she, what her clan, thought I was doing? Running an elaborate ruse to take blood from unsuspecting parahumans? Everything came into sharper focus now. Lillian wasn't here to learn about me, she was here to learn about my business. How it worked, and likely how it could be replicated. A blood-stealing venture that flew under the nose of a man like Richard was the sort of thing any worthwhile clan would be interested in.

"Lillian, I am going to say this once, and only once, so please listen carefully. I do *not* feed on other parahumans. Or regular humans, for that matter. I buy my blood through the Agency's supply system. My accounting business is not a way for me to drink from anyone. It's just an accounting business. Parahumans run businesses, and they sometimes need as much help as anyone else."

"I'm sure they do, but if you're not drinking from them, then why would you actually do this job?" Lillian asked.

"Because I like it. Because I'm good at it. Because it fills a very needed role in the parahuman community. Why do you think I was looking for new employees in the first place? There are so many of our kind out there who need the help I offer that there's more business than I can handle," I told her.

"Really? I mean . . . we just assumed you were either going to feed on the new employee or you wanted an accomplice to help make disposal easier," Lillian said.

"I assure you, that is not the case. What I need is another accountant, someone who can help with the workload." I raised my head from the steering wheel and looked at Lillian, who seemed oddly at peace with discovering she'd been lent to a real accountant rather than an ingenious blood thief. "There's nothing hidden about me or my business. What you see is what you get."

"That a fact?" Lillian leaned back, taking in my full profile. "While I'll admit it doesn't seem like you're eating people, you can't tell me there isn't something going on here. You happen to know one of the preeminent mages in the state, are good enough friends with a therian to care about his health even as he's attacking, and have what I'm pretty sure was a zombie on the payroll as your assistant. That's not normal for a vampire, accountant or not."

"What can I say? I was left without a clan." Putting the car into drive, I swung us around, heading away from Gerda and Oskar's ranch. "I didn't get a ready-made family, or a template for who I was supposed to hate, so I ended up making friends with anyone I got along with, regardless of their parahuman traits."

"So it seems. I am curious, though, since you've worked for Richard Alderson, have you ever had occasion to meet the King of the West?" She wasn't even trying to hide how closely she was watching my face for a lie. The other things were small coincidences, nothing that linked me to the vampire of rumor. If I had a good relationship with a dragon, though . . . well, very few vampires could honestly claim such a thing.

"I met him on the first night I met Richard, actually," I told her. "It was one of the absolute scariest experiences of my life, before and after undeath."

"He wasn't nice?" Lillian asked.

"He was *Gideon*." I shuddered involuntarily at just the memory of that night. "Have you ever been near a dragon? Had their attention focused fully on you? That aura of theirs is like nothing else. Your body begins to spasm as your brain loses all cohesive thought, filling only with animalistic screams of panic and terror. It left me so catatonic that I had to be carried from the building. When I went back to work on Richard's taxes, it was only something I could manage because Gideon wasn't there."

My words, carefully chosen, were all completely true. I just left out the part where Gideon came back to rescue Sally, giving me a drop of his blood so I could bring her home, and eventually filling me with more of it to later break him out of a magical cage. Disclosing all of that would pretty much mean the jig was up.

"I've met lesser dragons," Lillian said, after soaking in my story. "And even they were impossible to function around. I can't even imagine what the King of the West's aura would be like." She paused, watching the street signs go by as we drove back into a more developed neighborhood. "Do you really think there's a vampire out there who was able to withstand it? The rumors people have been passing along, about a vampire who won the dragon's respect . . . they must have a will of absolute iron, if they exist."

"I can't say I've ever met a vampire I thought was strong-willed enough to pull such a thing off." A bit self-deprecating, if honest assessment of my own abilities, but still not a lie. "All I have learned since I became undead is that this is a much bigger, stranger world than I ever realized when I was alive. Maybe there is a vampire out there who can stand up to a dragon's aura. If one of us can be happy as an accountant, that doesn't seem any less unreasonable."

"Still wrapping my head around that one," Lillian said. "This is really it? You just . . . do people's budgets and taxes and stuff? No intimidation, or forced feedings, or any of it?"

"I'm not sure how you think a business works, but I rely heavily on word of mouth for my clients. If I tried scaring them into doing what I wanted, or, heaven forbid, assaulted them, my reputation would fall apart within the span of a week. Which is why I had to come down so hard on you with Gerda and Oskar." I pulled onto the small loop that circled Winslow, heading back to Charlotte Manor. After that last stop, it seemed prudent to call it an early night before more could go wrong.

"No, I get it now. I'm sorry. What I did was out of line. It's just . . ." She tilted her head back, her dark hair bunching up on the headrest. "I've been with the

Turva clan for so long. More years by far than I was alive for. They're all about intimidation and power plays, the dominance of the vampire species. You live with that, surrounded by it all the time, and it's easy to forget that there are other ways to get by."

"Maybe it's a good thing that I won't be much help to them," I said.

"Yeah." A shadow that had nothing to do with the passing street lamps fell over Lillian's face. "Someone who could get them parahuman blood under the table would have been a lot more useful than just an accountant."

"Do I . . . should I be worried about not being useful?" My words hung in the air between us, the unspoken topic that had been present all night finally beginning to tear its way into reality. Lillian's gaze wandered out the window again, watching the few other cars out so late zip by as we puttered along at the speed limit.

"Probably," she said at last. "The House of Turva is moving into Winslow full force. They'll play nice with the therians and stick to the treaties, since the King of the West is here, but they've never been much for competition. If you had the backing of a clan, that would be one thing; there's a lot of politics involved when dealing with fellow clans. As an abandoned vampire, though . . . ." Lillian let her voice trail off. There wasn't anything more that needed to be said. I wasn't one of them, and without a clan to protect me, I had limited options. Be absorbed or be destroyed; those were my most likely scenarios. Absorption might not even be on the table.

We rode in silence the rest of the way back to Charlotte Manor. I wanted to press her for more, to ask about exactly what they might do. Part of me even wanted to ask her to lie, but that piece of me was foolish. Sooner or later, they'd realize the truth. Unless I actually started assaulting clients, it was an impossible façade to keep up. There was no sense in dragging Lillian down with me. She, at least, had given me a bit of warning.

Thanks to Lillian, if I wanted to, there was still time to book a ticket to Boarback.

That thought was heavy on my mind as I pulled into Charlotte Manor's parking lot. I was so lost in my musings that I almost didn't notice the unfamiliar gray minivan parked a few spaces up. It had government plates, and no windows aside from those in the front. Part of me wondered if the Turva clan was moving already, somehow getting the word that I was useless to them. Then, before my eyes, the back of the van was ripped off from the inside, revealing three white creatures with snapping jaws. If I lived a thousand years, I would never forget that sound. It haunted my nightmares, was tied to one of my worst memories. Dozens of those things had surrounded us the night Quinn kidnapped Krystal, the night he almost killed me.

The night I saw him tear out her throat, before I knew such wounds only made her stronger. Ghouls, that's what was leaping out of the van. Mindless appetites given physical form, they knew only hunger. And, before I could so much as yell, they were racing right toward my car.

9.

A WHOLE LOT HAPPENED IN A VERY SHORT span of time. I screamed at the ghouls' approach, while Lillian's hand dipped into her pantsuit and came out with a knife that looked like it was built to carve bone. The ghouls raced toward my car, their jaws clacking and eyes empty as they endeavored to lock those crooked teeth around our flesh. Gunshots rang through the night, turning two of the ghouls' skulls to mist and shattering my windshield. Because of the cracks, I could only barely see someone bolt around from the other side of the van, tackling the third ghoul and pressing a weapon to its temple. Another shot, and the monster went limp.

Lillian was out the door before I could say a word, so I forced my hands to grab the handle and yank it open, determined not to let her face whatever lurked out there alone. As it turned out, the well-meaning gesture was wasted. Not a single ghoul was left moving, or even with their skulls intact. What did greet us, however, was Krystal sitting atop the third ghoul's back, blood all over her sweatshirt as she removed her gun from the chunky mess that used to be its head. She glanced up, noticing Lillian and me for the first time.

"You're . . . uh . . . you're home early, Freddy. Kind of thought we had another hour or so before you showed up."

"We?" I'd barely gotten the question out when it was answered; Arch came walking around from the other side of the van, his own gun still out and ready to fire. I had a pretty good idea who'd taken out the first two ghouls with those perfect headshots; Krystal was good, but not flawless.

"You just smoked those things." Lillian was gazing at Krystal and Arch with a new expression, one I'd yet to see on her serene, always-certain face. Fear. Even if it hadn't been said out loud, she knew what she was looking at. The pieces were falling into place in her subconscious, and her sense of vampire superiority was crumbling quickly. "I thought you did software design."

"Would you believe I also play a lot of first-person shooters?" Krystal asked. Her glasses were gone, left off since she hadn't been planning on playing her part so soon, and the deferential attitude was just as absent. She was on the clock, which meant the real Krystal had re-surfaced, and there didn't seem to be much purpose in pretending otherwise.

"Fredrick, your girlfriend is an agent!" For a moment, I thought it was an accusation, which I was more than braced for. Then I caught sight of the panic in her eyes and the frantic gestures she was making. Lillian was trying to warn me, to give me a chance to escape. Even if I'd wanted to move, though, I couldn't. The sudden crushing boulder of guilt over deceiving her was weighing me down far too much to manage even a shuffle.

"Lillian . . . I know." Had I shot her, I don't think she could have looked more surprised. It seemed like we might get to find out, though, as Arch turned his weapon toward Lillian.

"It seems like this is the sort of conversation best had inside, wouldn't we all agree?" Arch's tone wasn't ex-actly what I would call cordial—he was still Arch, after all—but it was calm, which meant a lot since there were three ghoul corpses bleeding on the ground and he was holding a gun on one of us.

"Is that a threat, or a request?" Lillian spat, eyes never wavering from his weapon.

"Mandatory debriefing. You just witnessed three captured parahumans try to escape custody. We need get your account of how it went down for the record, and to make sure it doesn't happen again." Arch kept his weapon aimed, but nodded his head toward Charlotte Manor. "I can cite the treaty precedent, if you need it."

"How about everybody chills the fuck out for a second," Krystal suggested. "Lil, I know there's some explaining to do, so why don't you come inside and ask us whatever questions you've got. I'll get the manor staff to whip up some grub. Arch, put the damn gun down; she's not going to bolt into the night."

"What makes you so sure?" Arch asked.

"Because she's the one who really wants an explanation, which I'm offering to give her," Krystal said. "Plus, she knows we've got her name and clan, so running wouldn't do much good. If we told them we wanted to question her about something, the Turvas would likely hand over her head and say she broke an internal law. They're not big on their people talking to agents."

If any part of me had wondered about the idea of being pulled into the Turva clan, that perhaps it wouldn't be so bad, the fact that Lillian didn't dispute Krystal's theory quickly put those notions to bed. Instead of arguing, my fellow vampire simply turned and walked into Charlotte Manor wordlessly, leaving the three of us behind.

"Why in the hell didn't you give me a heads up you were coming home early?" Krystal asked.

"I didn't think about it," I said. "Tonight has been kind of . . . hectic."

With that, I launched into the story of what we'd dealt with so far: Bubba's transformation, the satyr couple's fight, Lillian's revelation of what the Turvas thought of my business. By the time I was done, Krystal and Arch had thrown the three ghoul corpses into the back of the van and jerry-rigged the door to stay shut.

"Guess the jig is officially up. No need to stay uncomfortable." Krystal yanked the blood-ruined sweatshirt off to reveal a black tank-top underneath. She popped open the barely working rear door and hurled the soaked garment into the back with the corpses. "What's the play now, Freddy?"

"I honestly don't know." The night had started with a plan. Maybe not a great one, but it had been there, an idea of how to handle things that might get me out unscathed. Now, though, all of it was in shambles. Lillian knew everything and would report it back to the Turva clan. There was always the chance that me dating an agent could buy some protection, but Krystal herself had said she was limited by the law. If they found a way to come after me without breaking the treaties that bound them, she'd either have to stand by or violate the law herself. Running seemed more and more like the only real option we had. And yet, part of me was still resisting. I didn't want to leave Winslow, even if every rational part of me screamed that it was the smart thing to do. If there was even a chance of staying, I wanted to try and uncover it.

"Let's just talk to her," I said at last. "Maybe we can find common ground, or reach an understanding, or something."

"Even if you can, she doesn't speak for the clan as a whole." Arch obviously noticed the surprised look on my face, since he continued with an explanation. "Krystal brought me up to speed on your situation."

"Arch, do I even want to know why you have a van full of ghouls parked outside Charlotte Manor?" I asked, realizing for the first time just how insane that really was.

"You might want to, but you aren't going to find out. It's confidential," he told me.

"In the future, if you could avoid bringing danger-ous creatures to suburban areas, I'd really appreciate it." I didn't even try to temper the sarcasm in my voice; my pa-tience for the day had worn almost completely through.

"Can't make that promise," Arch replied, unboth-ered by my tone. That was about par for the course with him, though; I'd been the silly one for expecting to make a dent in his stoic countenance.

"Let's just go get this done." I walked up the drive to the manor, Krystal arriving at my side seconds later. She said nothing, just took my hand and squeezed it tight, reminding me once again that she was there. If I hadn't already told her that I loved her, it would have burst from my lips in that moment. Curiously, having said those words to one another already, there wasn't any need to speak them as we made our way into the house. We both knew, just as we knew that however this all went down, we would face it together. Rain or shine, we were in it, side by side.

Lillian was waiting for us in the dining room, a slice of apple pie sitting untouched in front of her. One of the waiter versions of Charlotte stood quietly nearby, awaiting any order or request that Lillian might make. We took our seats, and seconds later another waiter arrived, setting pie down in front of both Krystal and me.

"Coffee, too, if you don't mind," Krystal requested. Our waiter nodded and headed into the kitchen, where he would wait as long as coffee normally took to brew before returning with the magically conjured cup. We didn't really need to pretend at this point, but I held my tongue. Charlotte's secret had no relation to mine, and it wasn't my place to give hers away without cause.

"You're him." Lillian's arms were crossed, and the stare in her eyes could have shamed a sociopath as she glared at me from across the table. "I can't believe I didn't see it earlier. That zombie had a freaking *sword* in his hands, but I thought he'd just picked it up from the junk tossed about. Friends with mages, therians, and dating an agent, plus your assistant had a Weapon of Destiny in his possession. You're the vampire everyone is talking about."

"I am." It felt oddly good to admit that. Even with things crumbling around me, stepping out of the shadow of deceit was freeing. "And I'm not. The things you've heard about me, some of them are true, but only in the most technical sense of the term. I didn't pretend to be someone I'm not, or lie about what I do for a living. I really am just a Certified Public Parahuman Accountant. Nothing more."

"Except that you've consorted with dragons, and brokered a peace with the leader of the therians," Lillian snapped.

"Like I said, technically true, but there were extenuating circumstances."

"Well, I'm listening," Lillian told us. "Explain the circumstances to me. Let's hear the truth behind the rumors."

My eyes darted to Krystal, who met them with a slight shrug. This was my choice to make, and while I knew she would back me in whatever I decided, she couldn't make the call for me. Giving Lillian information was dangerous. Everything I said, every weakness I revealed, all of it could be used against me. If that happened, though, was I really any worse off? Right now, fleeing was far and away the best option before me. Talking to Lillian wouldn't take that off the table, not with Arch and Krystal on my side. But it might open up a new path, one I couldn't see on my own. I was already on the brink of losing everything, why not roll the dice one more time?

"I'd say it all really started when I decided to go to my high school reunion . . . ."

10.

BY THE TIME I WAS DONE, THE PIE, along with a few cups of coffee and glasses of wine, had all long been put away. I didn't tell Lillian everything, the personal information and secrets of others never touched my tongue, but I did give her a good overview of what the last few years had been like. She was skeptical at first; however, after one story led to the next, she slowly began to come around and see how it was possible for me to have technically pulled off so many seemingly impressive achievements without actually being the vampire rumors made me out to be.

The one secret of my own that I skipped over was my immunity to silver. Showing her some trust, seeing if she might be willing to help me find a path to peaceful coexistence with her people, that was all well and good, but it wouldn't hurt to have a secret ace in the hole. The House of Turva not knowing silver didn't affect me could easily be the difference between escape and capture in a dire situation. I skimmed past it, wrapping up my tale with the events of the night Colin the vampire hunter had appeared.

"This was really not what I expected when Petre put me on the assignment." Lillian took a long sip from her glass of wine—a chardonnay that, while certainly of high quality, was far too sweet for my liking. "I figured a week or so to learn your operation, plus a few days for the seduction—"

"Pardon me?" Krystal didn't reach for her gun, but she did grip her coffee mug a bit tighter.

"I didn't know he had a girlfriend when they told me to come work for him," Lillian explained. "And do you think I really wanted to do that in the first place? No offense, Fredrick. You're a nice enough guy, but it's not like I'm keen on being ordered to seduce people I'm not even into."

"Then why do it?" I asked. My familiarity with the treaties and laws of parahuman kind was lacking in anything aside from the fiscal department, yet I couldn't imagine being part of a clan meant completely surrendering one's freedom.

"It's just the way things are done." Another sip, this time enough to nearly drain the glass. Seconds later, the kitchen door opened and one of Charlotte's many waiter forms appeared with a fresh chardonnay in hand. She might not have name-brand, but there was never a need to go thirsty while staying at Charlotte Manor.

"Do you know why I got turned in the first place?" Lillian continued. "It's because they were trying to get at a local politician of the time, collecting dirt to use so they could leverage control over him. And he supposedly had a thing for dark-haired women. That's it. I was given eternal life just so they could try and tempt some mayor into cheating on his wife."

"That is . . . really shitty," I said.

"Funniest part: it didn't even work. Turns out, he was gay. But of course, in those days, no one could actually admit to such a thing, especially not while in public office. The whole 'dark hair' thing was just a rumor; as far as I know, he never touched a woman, which suited his wife fine. They were what we used to call a 'good fit,' for the times."

"Speculation?" Arch asked.

"Very much confirmed." A bit of a smile appeared on Lillian's face—the first time since we'd been attacked by ghouls.

"Wait . . . ." Understanding set in at the sight of her grin, followed immediately by a fresh bout of confusion. "Then, why would they ask you to try and seduce me? I'll admit I'm not the most impressive of them, but I am still male."

"There's a lot of room between zero and six, Fredrick." Lillian chuckled to herself, polishing off the last of her glass and pulling over the new one the waiter had dropped off. "That Kinsey fellow had more sense than most of the others from his time."

"Steering the conversation away from how you were supposed to fuck my boyfriend, what, exactly, did your clan expect to come out of this?" Krystal asked.

Lillian paused, seemingly considering her options. "I suppose, since it's all a bust, there's no harm in telling you. We figured that you were probably running a successful blood-harvesting business, so the goal was to learn how that worked. On the off chance that you were on the up-and-up, though, I was supposed to charm my way into your client files to get account information for all the wealthy parahumans you'd worked with. Ideally, that would have been enough to scam or outright steal from them. Funding an entire clan's relocation isn't cheap."

"Don't suppose you'd be willing to say that to a judge in the Agency." From the grim frown on Arch's face, he already knew it was going to be a no, and was asking purely out of formality.

"Even if I did, I'm just a grunt on the ladder," Lillian said. "Everyone worth holding accountable would say they had no idea I was warping a gesture of friendship with such awful intentions. The most I could accomplish would be to incriminate myself."

"Which, seeing as you just confessed in front of a pair of agents, you technically already did," Krystal pointed out.

The table fell silent as we all nursed our respective drinks and tried to figure out where to go from here with the conversation. Arch and Krystal could haul Lillian in, but I couldn't see a way that would benefit any of us, especially Lillian. She was offering us information; repaying her with incarceration seemed like a poor trade. Finally, I spoke, determined to try and make some headway with the opportunity we'd been presented.

"Is there any chance of peace between me and the House of Turva?" I asked. "Knowing that I'm just some schmuck, with no blood business or real resources to offer, would they be willing to leave me alone?"

"No resources?" Lillian looked at me with incredulity, and Krystal's own gaze wasn't far behind. "Fredrick, you are quite possibly the most connected parahuman in the state, to say nothing of Winslow. Your lover is an agent, the powerful leader of the local therians calls you friend, you clearly have close ties to a renowned mage and the wielder of a Weapon of Destiny—who, apparently, is also best buds with a necromancer, of all things—and as the cherry on the sundae, you've earned the respect of an ancient dragon. If you called in enough favors, you could wipe out our entire clan."

"But I don't have those favors to call in," I protested. "And even if I did, I would never use my friends like that. They aren't assets to be tapped when I need something handled; they're people I care about."

"Oddly enough, I actually believe you," Lillian said. "Maybe it's because I've always been a bit of a softy compared to the others, or maybe you're just easy to read. Whatever it is, I honestly believe that you wouldn't try to use your friends, especially not to attack people. The problem is that almost no one else in my clan will buy that, and even if they did, they would still want to wipe you out before a century passed and you changed your mind. Time does funny things to us all, eventually."

"If I'm so connected and scary, wouldn't it make more sense to not attack me?" I was, admittedly, grasping at straws here, but with every word she said, Lillian seemed to seal my fate tighter. I was groping for anything that potentially offered hope.

"You're an abandoned vampire, Fredrick. There are at least a dozen or so ways the clan can annex you into it, at which point your life is more or less theirs, or they can just claim you've dishonored them and demand satisfaction. If they come through the treaties, then your friends can't help, not without calling down the Agency upon themselves."

Scary as Lillian's words were, they were made all the worse by the fact that I'd heard them before. That was almost exactly how Krystal had said it would go down, back when we were in Boarback and she'd first voiced her fears. I looked over at her and saw the sad resignation in her eyes. It was all coming true, just as she'd predicted.

"I've got a question," Arch interrupted, his hands twirling a cigarette between his fingers. Charlotte let him smoke in his room, but had banned it in public areas, especially where food was served. "Why are you telling us all this? Shouldn't you be scampering back to your leaders and letting them know the skinny on Fred?"

The . . . skinny? Sometimes I forgot how old Arch really was. But before I could comment on his word choice, Lillian gave her reply.

"If that's what you really want, I can. Or I can pretend things are going fine. Doesn't matter; sooner or later, they're going to find out the truth. Petre is nothing if not thorough. He won't stop digging until he finds the source of those amazing vampire rumors, and from the sound of things, there are certainly enough dots to connect him to Fredrick." She halted, running a pale finger along the rim of her glass, creating a high-pitched whine. "As for why I'm giving you the heads up, I suppose I sort of like the idea that one of our kind can actually form relationships based on genuine affection. In the House of Turva, the only worth you have is how useful you are. After over a century of dealing with that bullshit, I wouldn't mind seeing them take a failure or two."

"Are all clans like that?" I asked. Though my question was directed at Lillian, it was Arch who answered.

"Vampire clans are organizations, and they work in different ways, but most of them have some form of hierarchy and need to keep people productive. Inter-clan conflict is almost a staple in the vampire world, so those who don't shore up resources and numbers are leaving themselves open to takeover. The only thing that keeps them from building an army are the clan-size limits in the treaties, and, obviously, the conversion rate issue."

While I wanted to ask about what the heck Arch meant by "conversion rate issue," Krystal added on to his speech and steered my mind quickly away from the topic.

"Some clans are better than others. The Turvas are just especially aggressive, dickish specimens," she explained. "All of them come with strings and rules, though. That's why we built a condition into the treaties that exempts all vampire agents from their clan's authority. If we didn't, there would be no end to the special treatment and favors they'd be obligated to provide."

"Bad or not, they do offer protection," Lillian added. "Protection that you don't have, Fredrick. My advice would be to abandon Colorado now, before anyone else puts this all together. We'll be here for a long while, so as long as you leave the region, you should be fine. They might send a runner or two after you, but with an agent at your side, I hardly expect that to be an issue."

"Damn right, it won't be," Krystal concurred. She turned in her chair, laying a hand on my shoulder. "Freddy, you said that if you needed to run, you would. I hate to be the voice of caution, but it sure seems like if there was any time to skip town, this would be it. I can have the jet prepped within a few hours."

"Albert, Neil, and I would only be a half-day or so behind you," Arch added. "And I assure you, they would be well protected until they reached Boarback."

"What about Bubba and Amy?" I asked. "And Charlotte?"

"Amy Wells is a respected mage and student of the King of the West," Lillian told us. "The clan has no way to come at her that would not invoke retribution. Same for Bubba Emerson, employee of Richard Alderson, whom we must keep in our good graces to survive."

"As for me, I'm a fortress," the waiter spoke up, earning a sideways stare from Lillian, who still didn't know the true nature of the home she occupied. "I could easily keep a whole clan of vampires at bay, if they even decided to attack me. Which, honestly, seems unlikely. You already saved me, Fred. It's time to save yourself."

"From the mouths of magical houses," Krystal muttered. "We have to go, Freddy. You heard Lillian. There's no way they won't come for you."

No, actually, that wasn't quite right. What she'd said, what lay at the core of all of this wasn't the fact that I was a vampire. It was my being an unprotected vampire. Quinn the traitor, my sire, had screwed me once again by creating me as an abandoned vampire. But there might still be a way to keep myself—and my friends—safe, while staying in the town I considered home.

"What if . . . what if I joined a vampire clan?"

AN ACCOUNTANT IN THE CITY

1.

THERE WERE, ADMITTEDLY, FLAWS IN MY plan, issues that Krystal was quick and vocal to make clear. Aligning myself with a different clan of vampires might solve my current problem, but it would undoubtedly open me up to a whole slew of new ones. No clan came without costs, and to throw in with one would mean owing allegiance to people whose goals and ideals didn't always line up with my own.

Arch was the one who pointed out the more pragmatic issue: vampire clans weren't often keen on taking outsiders, and we would be working with a limited time frame. Even if Lillian hid what she'd learned from her people, sooner or later there would be a target on my head, and if I hadn't negotiated protection by then, I would out of luck.

Lillian, who I'd expected to be at least a little supportive of the idea, turned out to be my staunchest opponent, insisting that it was better to run as a free vampire than seek shelter in the cage of a clan. Her metaphor, not mine. The fact that she was the only one of us who was actually part of a vampire clan wasn't lost on me; yet, all the same, I couldn't bear to let the idea go entirely. Once I did, all that remained was running, and while I'd never had any issue with fleeing from danger before, something about this occasion just stuck in my gut. I couldn't explain it, but the idea of abandoning Winslow, of starting a new life in Boarback, seemed intolerable. Which was strange, all things considered, because I'd really liked our vacation there.

Eventually, the bickering wore down as dawn approached. It seemed prudent to get some rest and think things over. Arch and Lillian went to their own rooms, while I followed Krystal up the stairs to hers. We dressed for bed in silence, slipping out of our night's clothes—stained with blood and soot, respectively—and into comfortable pajamas. Keeping a small stash of clothes in her room had begun as a precaution and was quickly turning into a frequently needed asset. Sliding under the covers, I reached for her, but found she'd taken a perch near the edge of the mattress.

"Why are you doing this?" Her tone wasn't one of gentle concern, or frustration, like I'd been expecting. No, I'd heard Krystal pissed off enough to know what her anger sounded like, and there was quite a bit of it in her demand for explanation.

"I just don't want to leave town if I don't have to," I said.

"It's just a place. Buildings and streets and shitty, overpriced restaurants. Our families don't live nearby. Neither of us is even from here. I know you'll miss the friends who stay, but life means starting over sometimes. I've had to do it a lot, and no one was trying to kill me. So tell me, really, why the hell are you being so stubborn on this?"

"Honestly . . . I'm not even sure I know." Despite the fact that the room was dark, I could still see the ceiling perfectly as I stared up at it from the soft bed.

"Do you think it's brave? That refusing to budge is manly? Because it's not. It's self-destructive, and pig-headed, and damn it, that's *my* job in this relationship. I don't need someone who is unwilling to bend. You're supposed to be the sane one, Freddy. The one who makes the calls that are actually good for us." Despite the fact that her fury seemed to be growing, she scooted a bit closer to me, away from the bed's edge.

"I don't think it's brave at all. I know it's stupid, that I'm being stupid, but I just . . . you were wrong a few seconds ago," I said. "About us not having family nearby. We have Bubba, and Amy, and Charlotte, and Richard and Sally, and even Gideon, if you count him as the scary cousin with tattoos and a rap sheet. Yes, Albert and Neil would come with us, but we'd have to leave so much behind. Resetting our lives for a good cause or each other is one thing; I don't want you to think for a moment that I wouldn't be willing to do that. But I've never had something like this before. A community. A family that genuinely cared about each other. The idea of leaving it all behind is more than I can stand."

Krystal moved closer, wrapping her arm over my chest. "It's harder to run away when you have to actually leave something behind."

"Guess I never had anything worth missing before." I pulled her in close, holding her in the darkness that never seemed dark to my altered eyes. "Am I totally off base with this idea? Be brutal with me. If it's just going to cause everyone more pain, if it will leave us worse off, if you say it's a lost cause, then I'll let it go."

"You will?"

"I trust you, Krystal. With my life. And no one knows more about this stuff than you do—at least, no one in my social circle. Well, except maybe Arch, but he's got his own desires to look after. The point is, if you tell me there's no hope in coming out ahead on this, then I'll believe you. We can catch the plane to Boarback after dusk."

Instead of the expected and immediate barrage of reasons why that idea was idiotic, Krystal greeted my request with a long pause of silence. Most who knew Krystal Jenkins operated under the impression that she was impulsive, and that was a very accurate impression indeed. What many people missed, however, was that when a decision truly mattered, she showed more care with it than anyone else I'd ever encountered. That was why I didn't object to the silence as she thought the problem through; I merely listened to the sound of her breathing from a few inches away.

"Joining a clan just to stay in Winslow is an over-reaction," she finally began. "You're taking way too big of a jump to handle a problem that could be solved with just a sidestep of location. But the truth is that you're ageless now, Freddy. There will be more problems in the future, and running might not solve all of them. Belonging to a clan of vampires actually would be helpful in a lot of ways down the line. You understand that the act of joining opens up a myriad of problems all its own, but the clans thrive for a reason. At least as a member, you'd only have to deal with one clan's bullshit, instead of every House of Whatever that wants to hassle you."

"So, joining up now might not be worth it for dodging the Turvas, but it could pay off overall in the long run," I summarized.

"Maybe. You don't age, but I think we've both been around the block enough times to know that that doesn't mean something else couldn't knock you off the mortal plane." Krystal laid her hand on my chest, just above where my undead heart lay. "Though I'd make sure whoever took you regretted it, I've seen too much death to think even I could prevent it. No one is promised an eternity, Freddy. No one knows how long they get. You might be trading some wonderful years down in Boarback with me for kissing the ass of some vampire house's leader and scampering about at their every order."

"You do know how to make a compelling case for Boarback," I admitted. "But that seems like a worst-case scenario. We have a little time, here; Lillian said she'd keep the truth a secret for now if I asked. How about I at least do a little research into the vampire clans and see if there's one who aligns with my own general sentiments?"

A hot wash of air splashed over my chest as Krystal snorted. "Freddy, vampire clans are notoriously tight-lipped about what they do and what their long-term goals are. They file exactly the paperwork the treaties demand each year, and no more. Everything they can conceal, they do, from the Agency and from other clans. You can't just look that kind of shit up on the internet."

"Oh. I guess I just assumed someone would know something. I mean, Arch always seems to have the inside track on everything."

"When you've been around as long as him, you'll seem that way too," Krystal said. "But he's still an agent, which means he has way too much on his plate to keep up with the scheming and regime changes of every vampire clan out there. We have some analysts who do monitor what they can in that area, but pretty much all of that is confidential."

"Well, crud. There goes my brilliant idea of doing research." I gazed into the depths of the ceiling's tilework, wondering if I'd be able to get Charlotte a contractor to do updates from Boarback. With no way of knowing who I'd be throwing in with, my idea seemed dead in the water. I was willing to take some risk to stay near my friends and business, but blindly joining up with a vampire organization was a step too far. I might just as easily throw in with someone as bad as the House of Turva, if not worse.

"There might be one person who can fill you in, but you won't like it." Krystal muttered the words slowly, like she was pulling them out of her mouth by sheer force of will. "Someone who was around when the treaties were created, and got a sense of every clan's leader at the time. Someone who keeps an ear to the ground for schemes and rumors, and isn't beholden to any sort of confidentiality agreement. If he's willing, he could probably give you at least a basic understanding of most vampire clans."

Dense as I could sometimes be in regards to all things parahuman, the dots of this suggestion were large enough that even I could connect them. So far as I was aware, I only knew one person who was alive when the treaties were signed, which is to say, when America itself was founded. And he certainly would have been a part of the process, given the title he still held. Plus, since he was watching over a therian child, he would assuredly keep his ears perked for any sudden ambition or regime changes, lest they find their way to Winslow, Colorado.

"I have to go talk to Gideon," I said, trying to think of another option and failing miserably.

"Told you, you wouldn't like it."

2.

TO SAY THAT GIDEON AND I HAD A
complicated relationship would probably imply a familiarity that wasn't actually there. The first time we met, I'd
fallen under the sway of his draconic aura, as all vampires
did, and become a terrified, catatonic mess on the floor
who'd had to be physically hauled out. The second time,
I'd been kidnapped along with Sally Alderson, and he'd
given me a single drop of his blood so I could withstand
the aura and get her to safety. Our third meeting was the
strangest, though, in which I'd slipped into a magical

cage surrounding him and become a vessel for his magic so he could break free, all in order to stop the dragon who'd taken his place. That last one had actually been the most awkward of our encounters, and not just because it left me with the silver immunity as a side effect.

No, what had made that experience so strange was that, in conducting Gideon's power, I'd gotten a sense of just how strong he really was. If the draconic aura had conveyed how scared I actually should have been in our first meeting, I probably would have never recovered and instead just spent my undead life as a weeping mess on the floor. Knowing that power like Gideon's even existed terrified me in a way that went beyond fear of death. It was the first time that I'd understood just how great the divide between myself and the King of the West truly was. Powerful as vampires might be, we were still just augmented humans. Gideon was a living force of nature.

Some part of me suspected he knew what I'd seen, which was why Gideon had been absent every time I visited Richards in the months that followed. Perhaps it was out of deference to the fact that he didn't want me to give in to fear, or maybe he just didn't feel like dealing with me clumsily trying to kiss up lest he smite me with a thought. Whatever the reason, when I dialed Richard that afternoon and asked for a meeting with Gideon, I fully expected to be rebuffed. Even if he wasn't avoiding me, Gideon was still the King of the

West; he had every right to tell me his time was worth more than my petty requests.

Which made it all the more surprising when Richard told me that Gideon would see me at ten, after Sally went to bed. I should have been relieved—this meant my plan still had a bit of traction—and a small part of me was. It was just dwarfed by the far vaster side that was terrified at the realization I'd booked a meeting with an ancient dragon to ask his advice on which vampire clan I should try to join. My best hope was that he found it amusing and didn't take offense. Otherwise, the whole issue of my safety could become very moot, very quickly.

As the sun was nearing the edge of the horizon, Krystal and Arch came downstairs for our nocturnal version of breakfast, followed by Lillian a few minutes later.

"What's on the docket for tonight, boss?" she asked. She wore the same outfit as before, though it had been cleaned and pressed since she went to bed. Charlotte's laundering skills were like the rest of her hospitality abilities: flawless.

"Don't you need to head back to Petre and report on me?" I asked.

Lillian rolled her eyes while helping herself to the plate of eggs one of the Charlotte-waiters had set down in front of her. "I'm supposed to be covertly investigating you, remember? Wouldn't make much sense for me to run back to the clan every night. They'll be expecting me to hang around for at least a few days, worming my way in and getting the account details. I've probably got three more nights, this one included, before I need to report back and make sure things look like they're on track."

"Lillian, I wanted to ask you this last night, but there wasn't quite the opportunity," Arch said, exercising a lot more diplomacy than I usually saw from him. "If you cover for Fred, pretend you didn't realize he was the vampire Petre's hunting for, will there be consequences for you?"

"Oh yeah, Petre's going to be mad as hell," Lillian confirmed. "Even if he believes me that it was an accident, that's the same as failure in the House of Turva. They'll probably keep me off blood for a week or so as punishment."

It took her three bites of eggs before she realized we were all staring at her in silence. Lowering her fork, she let her practiced smile shrink by several degrees, if not fall away entirely. "It's okay. This isn't the first time I've disappointed my sire, and it won't be the last. I've had to go a month without blood in the past, so a few weeks is nothing. Sometimes, they punish me for things way beyond my scope of control. I'd much prefer to take this one for something *I* decide is worthwhile."

Though I heard her words, my mind was still reeling. A *month* without blood? More than two or three days and I would feel the thirst, and within hours, my body would begin to ache as the cravings grew stronger by the minute. During those first days, before I'd lined up my supplier, the most I'd made it was four days, and I could already feel the beginnings of my sanity fraying at the edges from the endless thirst and pain. I didn't want to imagine how much worse it got from there. Two weeks would have been a living hell. A month was more than I even wanted to wrap my mind around.

"Is there any way we can help you? Make it seem like this wasn't your fault?" I asked.

"Fault doesn't really matter. They just have to punish someone when there's a failure," Lillian replied, clearing off the last of her eggs moments before the waiter came through the door with a fresh plate for her. "Make an example for the rest of the clan. The House of Turva hasn't exactly kept up with the times in terms of motivational strategies. Like I said, though, it's fine. Far from my first time dealing with this."

"Maybe that's true, but it's certainly not fine." I did some mental math, thinking through what I was trying to accomplish, and how much time I'd need. Probably weeks, if I were to do things properly. Though, if properly meant someone else being punished for my longshot idea, it seemed I would have to cut a few corners. "In three nights, when it's time to report back, I want you to tell them the truth. That I'm the vampire Petre is looking for, that my accounting service is just an accounting service, all of it."

"You're giving up on the joining a clan thing?" Lillian asked.

"Not quite yet. I've got a meeting tonight that might shed some light on the viability of it. Regardless, I won't let you take the punishment for helping us. If I can't make it work in time, then that's on me, not you. Go back to the Turvas as a successful infiltrator. That's the very least I can do to thank you for all of your help."

"Freddy," Krystal said softly, "you do remember that trying to join a clan is already really hard for an outsider, right? Even if it were doable, you'd probably need weeks to convince them to take you on, jumping through hoops to prove you were worth a slot."

"If it's already nearly impossible, then trying to do it in three days instead of a few weeks probably won't alter the odds that much," I told her. "Chances are we'll still end up on a jet to Boarback. I just want to see this through."

I realized that Lillian was the one who'd fallen into silence this time, examining me carefully from her spot at the other end of the breakfast table. She'd even stopped eating, and was just pointlessly poking her eggs with her fork as she mulled over my words.

"If that's really how you want it, Fredrick, then I'll give them the rundown in three nights. But if you change your mind before then, just let me know. I made the offer, and I meant it; I can buy you more time."

"I greatly appreciate the sentiment, but I'm afraid the price on that offer is simply too high." Chancing a look at my watch, I realized that with the sun setting, I'd need to head out soon to make my meeting. While there was plenty of time until ten, Charlotte Manor was located some ways from town, and getting through the ceremony and security at Richard's office always took longer than I expected. Even after all my visits, they were still wary of letting a vampire into the heart of a therian stronghold.

"Beg everyone's pardon, but if you'll excuse me, I need to go get ready to head out," I announced, rising from the table, my own food barely touched. Even Charlotte's cooking couldn't settle the case of nerves I was dealing with.

"Just let me finish off this plate and I'll be ready to go." Lillian bent down closer to the table, fork in prime egg-shoveling position.

"No need, take your time and enjoy the meal," I advised her. "I'm going to have to leave you behind for this meeting."

"That's probably not going to fly," Lillian said. "Remember, I'm supposed to be your new assistant, your shadow, following you at every turn. What do I tell Petre if one of the clan sees you out on the town without me?"

"The truth," I replied. "That I was going to have a meeting with the King of the West. By now, they know enough about Gideon to be aware that he wouldn't tolerate a tag-a-long in one of his meetings."

"And if they ask how you're able to meet with him despite the fact that vampires can't handle their draconic aura?" Lillian pressed.

"Right . . . I forgot they knew about that." With everything on my plate, it was getting hard to keep track of how well-informed my opponents were.

"We just moved to a town with an ancient dragon; it came up in conversation," Lillian said. From across the table, I saw Krystal chuckle, and for a moment, I even thought I caught a smirk on Arch's face.

"Tell them Freddy dealt with a proxy." With her giggles dying down, Krystal had apparently decided to be helpful. "That's how the dragons dealt with vampires in the old days; they had a representative come stand in their place and have the conversation via telepathy enchantments with the proxy. Nowadays, most just use Bluetooth and a cell phone, but the tradition remains for the rare times when a dragon meets with a vampire. And since the proxy is essentially the dragon, you'd still have to show it the same respect by not bringing an intern along."

"Trainee," Lillian corrected.

"Spy, if you want to be a dick about it," Krystal shot back.

"Right then, let's just say I dealt with a proxy." Something told me that if I didn't right the conversation to a more productive path quickly, it might spiral beyond saving. "Lillian, will that sell upstream?"

"Don't see why not, though maybe it's best if you just try not to get spotted by any other vampires," she suggested. "The less I have to talk to Petre before it's decision time, the better off you are."

"Well, I've managed to spend most of my life slipping around unnoticed," I said. "Maybe just this once, it can be an asset."

"Personally, I think it's the sweater vest. Who pays attention to someone wearing a sweater vest?" Though Krystal was the one to speak the words, it didn't escape my notice as I left the dining room that everyone else at the table seemed to be nodding along in agreement.

3.

TO MY SURPRISE, WHEN I ARRIVED AT Richard's building, I wasn't shown up to his penthouse/throne room at the top like usual. Instead, I was frisked by therian security, who glared at me stonily while checking to ensure I hadn't brought any weapons with me. This pat-down was far less extensive than usual, I noticed, probably because while a firearm might be an issue for Richard, all it would do to Gideon was annoy. When security was finally done, I was taken up a different elevator than the one I normally used, to a floor that looked familiar—though all the generic office floors seemed that way. I was escorted down a hallway, coming to an office near a corner, and I suddenly realized exactly where I was before the door had even opened.

This was the room where Gideon had been held captive several months earlier. Where Bubba, Amy, and I had hunted him down, breaking into the magical cage while therians from another tribe slammed on the door, trying to kill us before we could free him. Even if I hadn't been able to place the dull gray carpet and open layout, I certainly recognized the broken remains of the cube where Gideon had been trapped. They were there, just as I'd last seen them when fleeing the building. All that was different was that now a desk and a few chairs were set up in front of the twisted metallic remnants of a trap strong enough to ensnare a dragon.

Sitting behind the desk, drawing in a coloring book, was Gideon, whose child-like appearance belied the tremendous power and knowledge resting inside him. The door whispered shut behind me, and I realized that the therians had left me alone in the room. Not even they liked to be around Gideon any more than was strictly necessary. Since I didn't have the luxury of fleeing, I decided to say something and start things off. Given how nervous I was, I hardly think I can be blamed for grasping the easiest conversational option available.

"I thought you'd have cleared that out by now." I nodded to the massive remains of his cage, as if he didn't know what I was talking about already.

Setting down his crayon, Gideon looked up from the coloring book with a stare meant to scrutinize. It was unsettling to see on a child's face, though I was slowly getting used to that effect when dealing with Gideon. It beat his aura any day of the year.

"Interesting." Slowly, Gideon hopped off the chair, raised to its highest so he could see over the desk, and approached me. Every step was tentative, as if he thought I might bolt should he move too fast. Eventually, he got within a few feet, close enough that I could reach out and rumple his hair, were I so suicidally inclined. "This has already proven to be a fascinating meeting. I wasn't sure you'd be able to withstand my aura anymore."

"Why wouldn't I? You gave me your blood," I reminded him.

"Indeed, and far more than a drop on that night." He gestured absentmindedly to the cage's remains, never taking his eyes off me. "But from the reports I received, all that power had been used up, burned through in my escape. The effects of such gifts are temporary, as you must know by now. Even the drop I gave you would never have lasted so long, were you the sort to actually use your abilities. When the draconic power in your veins is tapped out, so too should go your immunity to my aura. Yet here you stand, unbothered by my presence."

"I do still find you very intimidating," I said, not sure if I was trying to reassure Gideon that I was still meek and cowardly or that he had more than enough mojo to be terrifying.

"That is because you are a being of logic," Gideon replied. "Of course you fear what is stronger. Nonetheless, this makes for a fascinating study. Never has a blood-eater tasted so much of a dragon before—at least, not a dragon of my power—nor have they been used to wield their magic. It seems there are some lingering aftereffects, aside from just the ability to dine with proper silver."

"You knew about that?"

Gideon turned and walked back to his desk, motioning for me to follow. "You saved me that night, Fred. Not my life, no, but certainly my pride. And, more importantly, perhaps you even aided Sally by freeing me. True, I am not the kindest or most cuddly of creatures in the world, yet even I see fit to look in on those who have done me a good turn. I even agree to take their meetings, if I'm curious enough."

"And I appreciate that," I said, taking a seat in one of the open chairs in front of the desk. Again, my gaze slipped to the cage, and I could see Gideon's violet eyes tracking my own.

"I keep it here to remind anyone I meet with how futile it is to try and go against me," Gideon said, offering the explanation to my opening question. "Almost none know of your part in my escape that night, which makes it all the easier to build my reputation. Defeating another elder dragon's carefully constructed trap is no small feat, and the name of Gideon has only grown more feared since I accomplished it."

"Do you really need intimidation tactics? I mean . . . you're *you*." That was, sadly, the best way I could think to phrase my thoughts in the moment. I didn't want to fall over myself and gush; besides, we both knew I'd seen how deep his well of power went. The idea of using intimidation tricks felt like ridiculous overkill.

"Strong as I am, there are others out there who are my equal, if not my better," Gideon said. "Though these methods are not for them. Should we ever clash, the very landscape of the Earth would be changed, which is why we all tend to avoid each other as much as possible. No, I keep it here for the smaller threats, the nuisances. So many that would waste my time and their lives never do, simply because I show them the futility of such actions. Power is useful, Fred, never doubt that, but far more useful is the perception of power. I've lived a very long time, and I can say with certainty that the easiest fights to win are those that never start."

Since Gideon had just offered me the perfect segue, I hurriedly leapt for it, determined to make the most of my time with him. Curiosity had gotten me in the door; there was no telling how long it would keep me there.

"It's interesting that you bring that up, because I asked to meet you for essentially that purpose. I'm sure you know about the arrival of the House of Turva in Winslow—"

Gideon's mouth pinched into a visible sneer, so I raced forward before he could cut me off.

"—and they've become interested in me as either a subject or a rival. Since I'm an abandoned vampire, there are many ways for them to come at me through the treaties, so I thought it would be worthwhile to look into joining a clan of my own. But no one knows a lot about them and their inner workings, except perhaps you, so I came here seeking counsel about what you knew of the various clans."

The sneer had faded as I got further along, turning back to the same scrutinizing expression I'd seen when first walking in. He was searching me for something; though, what it was, I had no idea.

"Fred, do you believe that you and I are equal?"

"Absolutely not, sir." My eyes widened, and I momentarily faced the very serious possibility that this might be my last few seconds of life, undead or otherwise. Offending a dragon like Gideon was not the sort of thing many lived to tell about. "I am keenly aware of how much more powerful and important you are, and I'm so sorry for wasting your time with my request. It was a move of pure desperation, and—"

"I think, perhaps, that something was lost in translation here." Gideon was still calm, which wasn't as reassuring as it should have been. I had no doubt he could kill me without any emotional fluctuation whatsoever; the only thing I'd ever seen rile Gideon up was Sally's safety being threatened. But he also hadn't made any aggressive movements, and that was somewhat more heartening. "What I mean is, do you believe we are equal for the turn you did for me in this very room? That my debt to you is paid in full?"

"Oh . . . then yes, I do. Our bargain was fulfilled. You asked for freedom, and I asked you to save my friends. We both honored the agreement, so I didn't think there was any debt between us."

Gideon's eyes, for the first time since I'd met him, fell a few inches toward the ground, almost like he was a bit embarrassed by something. "You are incorrect, both on what I swore and on the topic of our equality. Though I accepted it in the heat of the moment due to limited time, the truth is that, that deal was not a fair one. I asked more than I gave, and while dracolings may take pleasure in such slights, we dragons hold ourselves to a higher code. Stealing, pillaging, ransacking, all of that is fair game, but in our bargains, we always seek to find equilibrium. There is still some debt between us, Fred, and that is the real reason why I took your meeting. I despise inequality, and I would like to remedy it as quickly as possible. So then, would you like me to take care of your problem?"

"That's why I came here," I said, no doubt visibly relieved. Gideon wanted to pay me back and I wanted to pump him for information, so this would work great for both of us.

"No, you came here for a temporary measure that would only incur more trouble for you. I'm not offering to tell you about the blood-eater clans. I'm offering to solve your problem. These creatures stepped foot in my town, and no doubt, they are scheming all manner of mischief. It will be little more than a slap on the wrist for me if I wipe them out."

And that was when I finally realized what Gideon was actually offering. He would purge the entire House of Turva, kill every last one of them, just because he felt some debt to me. That was possibly the most terrifying prospect I'd ever heard, all the more so because I knew too well just how easily Gideon could do it. One word from me and by the morning sunrise, there would be no issues. No House of Turva. Likely, no other vampires would come to Winslow for a century or so after such a display. And, ashamed as I am to admit it, there was a fleeting moment where I wanted to let him do it. Take away all the fear, and worry, and stress these invaders had caused. Mercifully, it lasted no longer than a moment before reality came crashing back in. Even if I believed that this would really be the end of it—which I didn't— the guilt I'd feel over all those lives would utterly dwarf whatever issue I was dealing with currently.

"I'm grateful for the offer, really I am, but I think that might be a touch extreme. I'm sure the House of Turva has plenty of good people in it who don't deserve to die just because I was scared. Besides, there are only so many vampire clans, right? The Agency is bound to be a little miffed if you wipe one off the map," I said.

"It would get replaced eventually; every half-century or so, one ballsy blood-eater founds a new clan that actually manages to stick around. But it is not my place to dictate how I repay my debt," Gideon said. "If information is what you want, then I'll give it. Just know that this does not fully settle things between us. Perhaps you'd care for another few drops of blood?"

"Thanks, but no thanks. Your power is way too potent for me to handle. I kept snapping things in half for a week last time I got a drop." I hadn't meant it as a joke, but I caught site of Gideon snickering anyway.

"Very well, then just information for now. Though I doubt it will give you what you need, I shall tell you all

I can remember of the various blood-eater clans dotting this county's landscape," Gideon said.

I yanked out a pen and pad of paper from my briefcase as Gideon started talking, jotting down every detail I could as quickly as he laid them out. There would be more questions later, when I knew enough to have an idea of what to ask about, but for the moment, I was content with simply absorbing a small bit of the ancient dragon's expansive memory.

4.

"TWENTY-EIGHT ACTIVE VAMPIRE CLANS IN America, four of which were founded after the actual creation of the country and treaties. Of those, twelve have some pretty repugnant ideas about humanity as a whole and are kept in check only by the laws, which rules them out right off the bat. Two are pro human and vampire relations, but have a lot of bad history with therians. Three are openly about vampire superiority over other parahumans. And the other eleven are either too secretive or small to make waves in any direction, though there's always a bit of scuttlebutt around them."

I finished running down the list, pages of more detailed notes summarized into these simple bullet points. I'd spent all night and halfway through the morning talking to Gideon, cooped up in that windowless office as he went through exhaustive explanations of every vampire clan he could remember. It had been a disheartening affair, yet I pressed on regardless, sure that it would be the next clan he mentioned that would finally fit my needs. Eventually, he ran out of things to share, and I had Krystal come pick me up, since her truck was fitted with enchanted windows to block out the sunshine. Back at Charlotte Manor, I'd taken a big meal and spent hours reviewing the notes, looking for something, anything that I'd managed to miss.

"To be fair to all the respective houses of vampires out there, it looks like the core of Gideon's knowledge came from when the treaties were being drawn up, and that was over two hundred years ago," Krystal said. "There were a lot of unpopular opinions held by humans back then too, which have changed with the times. I'm sure some of these have grown at least a little."

"Enough to where it's safe to petition them for membership?" I asked.

"Oh *hell* no, are you kidding me? Jumping in bed with a clan you know next to nothing about is freaking

crazy. Even if they'd make room in the quota for you."
Krystal, unlike me, was still eating, having decided that
since she might be leaving Charlotte for some time, it
was a good excuse to avail herself of as much cooking as
possible. Currently, she was working on a half-devoured
piece of chocolate pie, though I had no doubt it would
fully vanish within the next few minutes.

"Right, the quota. You and Arch mentioned that
last night. What's the deal with quotas?" Even as I asked,
I remembered another term they'd used, one which stuck
in my head. "And for that matter, what does 'conversion
rate issue' mean?"

Krystal set the fork she had partially raised to
the side of her plate, my first clue that I'd touched on
something more serious than I realized. "Quotas are
straightforward. The treaty limits how many vampires a
clan is allowed to have at any given time. This is based
mostly on how long a clan has existed, though it does
cap out at a certain point. It's part of how we ensure
that the need for blood never outpaces the supply. Conversion rate . . . well, that's the reason vampires didn't
manage to take over the world before the treaties. The
truth is, being turned into a vampire is far from a fool-
proof thing. Of the humans that vampires attempt to
turn, a shockingly small amount actually make it over."

"Do I want to know?"

"Since actually testing it clinically would require killing a lot of people, the Agency has never done formal research, but based on what we've learned from the older clans, our best guesses put it at a little less than one in every ten," Krystal told me. "No one knows what makes the difference; it goes across all genetic markers that we can find, and seems to hit male and female equally. Just a lottery that gets played with someone's life on the line."

"Wait . . . that can't be accurate." Already my memory was whirling, back to when Lillian had told us a small bit of her history with the House of Turva. "Lillian said she was turned just to seduce some politician. Why would they do that if there was a good chance she'd die?"

"Because they didn't care." Krystal's tone was so blunt it could have fallen from her mouth and cracked a wineglass. "Vampires are allowed to try and turn a certain amount of people each year—that's how they reproduce, so it was well worked into the treaties—but that comes with knowing about the failure rate. And back then, things were messier, less organized, so not everyone kept to their numbers like they should have."

I sat in silence for a long moment, staring at my stack of notes, waiting for some solution to pop out at me. "Just when I think I couldn't possibly want to be affiliated with these people less, I learn more about them, and suddenly, it's all I can do not to run screaming into the night."

To her immeasurable credit, Krystal resisted the urge to say that she'd told me so, picking up her fork and turning her attention back to the pie instead. I let her eat as I perused the notes, slowly realizing with each turned page that my hopes were growing dimmer. Logically, my best bets were the four newer clans, formed after the treaty, but if membership was limited by seniority, then my odds of getting in with them were all the slimmer. Not to mention, I was assuming they would be more akin to my way of thinking, since they were newer, but I also had the smallest amount of information about them, which increased the risk of me choosing poor allies.

"What's the quota for new clans?" I asked. It was a pointless question that would lead nowhere, yet I asked it all the same. Some part of me, it seemed, was determined to examine every avenue of this idea, regardless of how fruitless I already knew it to be.

"Not a hundred percent sure," Krystal said. "I'm pretty sure it's ten to start, then ramps up for the first few decades, and after a century, the rate slows down a lot. You can always check the books, though. That would definitely be in them."

She had me there. I was just being lazy with my desperation. Slipping my laptop out of my briefcase, I woke it from hibernation mode and pulled up one of several saved PDFs on the hard drive. Though Charlotte Manor now had excellent Wi-Fi, I'd been left without signal one too many times not to keep these tomes saved locally. To a layman, these documents merely looked like material for the most boring role-playing game on earth. *Spells, Swords, & Stealth: Modern Justice* was ostensibly a court-like tabletop game notorious for its insanely complex rules about parahumans living in the modern world. In truth, it was the actual bible of treaties, laws, and revisions which governed the parahuman part of our country. Hidden in plain sight, where anyone was free to see it, in what I always considered to be one of the Agency's more cunning moves.

Though I usually occupied myself with the books regarding accounting law, a close call—in fact, one inside Charlotte Manor—had shown that it was worthwhile to keep all of the books on hand, just in case. After a few wrong files and a quick search, I finally found what I was looking for. The actual laws about founding new clans were surprisingly lean, and it took no time to skim down and find the information about quotas.

"Looks like new clans get capped at ten parahumans—wait, that can't be right. It should say 'vampires.'"

"They tried to keep the language as generic as possible, just in case we ever hit a snag," Krystal explained. "There have been a few vampire offshoots over the centuries—mages experimenting and creating things that were close, but not quite, vampires. Since 'parahuman' is a word that covers everything, most of the treaty uses it wherever possible, just in case we get some surprises down the line."

"That is an impressive amount of foresight," I said. "Anyway, they get ten spots at their founding, then they get another five slots after twenty-five years, another five at fifty, then five more at seventy-five years, and one last group of five at a hundred. From there, they gain ten new slots every fifty years for the next two centuries, and then ten every hundred for a millennia." My brain quickly did the math before I even noticed I was adding the numbers up. "So, the most any clan can have is a hundred and seventy vampires?"

"Sounds about right," Krystal confirmed. "Though, of course, we've got the clanless ones to account for too, like those in the Agency, or abandoned ones like you. Still, you can see how precious those slots are, especially for the younger houses."

"No kidding. A clan with only ten vampires would be crushed by the ones with a full roster," I said.

"There are some checks and balances for two houses dealing with one another, but yeah, not many of those last too long," Krystal confirmed. "Starting a new clan generally means you either have real ass-kickers with a lot of connections and mojo, or you're aligned with someone powerful enough to give you protection."

"Seems to be the case." I read through the document again, noting that although the limits on how big a clan could get were well defined, down to the parahuman, actually starting one was relatively easy. A new idea, built on the ashes of my old one, started to bloom. This was insane, obviously. Completely so. Even worse than my first idea. But . . . it couldn't hurt to do a little research. Could it?

"If Lillian wakes up, let her know I'm on the phone," I said, rising from the table.

"Calling the Sheriff to tell him we're heading down?" Krystal asked.

"Not quite yet." My fingers were already flipping through my phonebook as I sought out the familiar name of an old friend. "First, I need to talk to a lawyer."

5.

Note: As I was not present for what occurred next (I was busy in a meeting with Asha to further my own plans), I must allow another to momentarily take up the tale. In this case, Charlotte was chosen, as she has both an excellent memory and a knack for seeing more than most.

STRICTLY SPEAKING, IT IS NOT THE PLACE of a house to interfere. We exist to offer shelter from the storm, warmth from the cold, and a sense of security to those staying within our walls. That is the philosophy of all proper houses, even if some aren't as keenly aware of it as I. And that is the directive I was created with, when those mages empowered and enlightened me all those decades ago. So I said nothing as they drove themselves deeper into madness and greed, courting an inevitable death at the hands of angry agents. I merely did my duty, filling their bellies with food and wine, keeping the beds neatly made, and stopping any who might intrude.

Then the agents came, with cunning plans and stronger magic. And I sat alone for a very long time, ensnaring any stray guest I could just for a small semblance of company, something that could remind me of when I'd been more than just a house, I'd been a home. It was a lonely stretch that I can scarcely look back on without my windows growing foggy. But on the day when someone proposed my very destruction—what should have been the worst, possibly even final, evening of my life—salvation arrived. Fred protected me, gave me the rights to my own property, and for that alone, I was grateful. But then he went and did something I'd long given up hope of ever feeling again: he gave me purpose. First Arch, then Krystal, and, bit-by-bit, laughter and conversation filled my empty halls for the first time in so long I could barely withstand it, I was so happy. There was a reason to burn the candles again, as he and his friends routinely came for dinner or lodging.

It is not the place of a proper house to interfere. But I am not just any house, and I have had my rooms emptied before. That is not something I wanted to experience ever again. So perhaps that is why, when Fred ran out the door with Lillian in tow and Krystal called my name, I came to her, ready. That shrewd look on her face left no doubt of what she would want from me, and despite all the notions of decorum and privacy I knew I should maintain, I put up no resistance as she asked for it. I materialized in the form they thought of as the real me, a lovely young woman in a gown I'd seen and fancied on one of my residents. It was as good a form as any, and I somewhat enjoyed the sense of familiarity in her eyes as I appeared at her summons. True to form, she wasted no time in getting down to business.

"What was Fred talking to his lawyer about?"

"Based on what I could overhear, it seems he's decided to take a new approach. Rather than just joining an existing clan, I believe he intends to found one of his own." Though I couldn't make out Asha's words through the small phone—so much tinier than the rotary versions we once possessed—Fred had been the one doing most of the explaining.

Krystal sucked in a sharp breath through her teeth and let it out as an equally sharp whistle. "Fuck me, that's what I was afraid of. He had that look in his eye, you know? The one where he thinks he's cracked the problem. I was hoping it meant he'd given up, but with what he just finished reading . . . shit. Shitty shit, shit, shit. This isn't good."

"It does seem like it would remedy the issue, does it not?" I'd dealt mainly with mages and elderly couples between my creation and bed-and-breakfast days, so vampire society was not something I had extensive knowledge of.

"Only in the most technical of senses. A clan with one member is no better than an abandoned vampire in practicality. He's far from the first of his kind to get this idea, and there's a reason so few new clans survive. There are plenty of ways within the treaties for the houses to squabble with each other." She stared down at the empty plate in front of her, and for a moment, I considered having another part of me bring out more pie. I hesitated, though, as Krystal was generally one to make it clear when she wanted something.

"There's probably no stopping him, either. When he gets these ideas, it's like all the smart parts of his brain just shut down." Krystal reached into her pocket and yanked out her own phone, thumb racing across the flashing screen. "Charlotte, I hate to impose, but would you mind putting together some dinner and coffee? You're going to get an influx of guests in the next hour, and I'd like to soften them up with some good food, at the very least."

"Of course. Let me know when you're ready for the meal to be served." I vanished then, though that was merely for her benefit. Though they rationally knew that I was everywhere at once within these walls, the act of seeing some specter or other tends to unnerve people. Perhaps they felt they weren't being watched if they couldn't see the eyes. Not that they had anything to worry about; a proper house knows the value of silence and decorum. With forgivable exceptions where the safety of one's guests are involved.

Over the next hour, I opened my doors several times to many familiar faces. Neil and Albert were the first to arrive, the latter courteously wiping off his shoes and urging the former to do the same. Then came Amy, who stared up at me as she entered, no doubt examining the spell work that wove through every beam and stud of my being. Bubba was next, and along with him, I was surprised to see the massive Richard ducking down to fit through my door frame. I wondered if I had any rooms big enough to accommodate him, should the meeting run long, and then resolved to fix that lack of hospitality as soon as possible. Arch made his way down from his room eventually, having finished the paperwork he'd been dealing with for several hours.

With the last of the guests present, I began serving the soup course, as Krystal brought everyone up to speed on Fred's predicament. Most knew the basics, but between clarifying questions and recaps, I was putting down the fish course before she was done telling them about the latest twist, that it seemed Fred was trying to form his own vampire clan.

"Well, that's surprisingly stupid," Arch noted, as one of my waiter selves filled up his water glass. A cigarette was being rolled between his fingers as usual, but though I kept watch, I never caught him breaking our lease agreement. Once I had the time, I was hoping to add a smoking lounge for those with small nicotine sticks or old-fashioned pipes like my creators had smoked.

"I'm sure he thinks he's got some angle on it; Fred's rarely one to overestimate himself," Krystal snapped defensively. "But, this time, he's biting off more than he can chew. If he tries to meet the House of Turva on even ground, they'll tear him apart. Worse, they'll see it as a sign of aggression, and that makes our plan to disappear more complicated."

"Sheriff Thorgood can more than handle one clan of vampires," Bubba pointed out.

"True, but he shares the same weakness we do—come through the treaties, and he may have to back down," Arch countered.

"If you think Leeroy Thorgood is backing down from anyone trying to hurt his residents, you don't know him that well," Krystal said. "No, my concern is that eventually Fred will want to leave Boarback. Maybe for a trip; maybe for somewhere new to live. Whatever it might be, if Fred creates a grudge between himself and the House of Turva, then they'll lie in wait until opportunity strikes. Boarback is supposed to be our refuge, not our prison."

Slowly, Albert raised his hand in the air, waiting to be called on. Eventually, Krystal noticed and gave him a small nod. "Maybe he won't be able to pull it off so soon. If I've learned anything working for Fred, it's that paperwork can take a long time to go through. You said he has only two nights left, so time might fix the problem for us."

"Much I wish I could believe that, having seen Asha and Fred work together up close, I've got no doubt in my bones that they'll find a loophole or expedition clause or somethin'. Nobody knows paperwork like those two," Bubba said, shaking his head gently.

"I could petition to block it, since he'd be founding in my town," Richard volunteered. "That might slow them down enough to force the issue. I hate to do it, but if it's for Fred's own good, then it would be the right call."

Krystal drummed her hands on the table, considering the proposal. "Too risky," she said at last. "Even if you can block him, the Turvas might still find out he tried to form a clan. At that point, he's in just as much shit, but without even the thin veneer of being part of a clan to protect him."

"It is possible to render the discussion moot." Neil had been uncharacteristically silent as he listened to the issue's discussion, his eyes glancing over to Albert on occasion, and Amy more frequently. "Fred and I haven't always gotten along well, but I don't want to see him killed. So, what if I were to bind him like that night at the LARP? Grab him as soon as he comes back in, leave him catatonic, and then put him on a plane."

"I don't think Fred would care much for that," Amy told him.

"Oh, no question about it, he'd likely despise whoever did it to him, which is why I volunteered," Neil said. "We're already on poor terms; it doesn't really matter as much if Fred hates me. I can even pull it off alone, so that the rest of you have deniability."

Though I said nothing, Neil's plan did seem to have some merit to me. It kept Fred safe, minimized risk, and kept the backlash limited to one person. Those thoughts stayed with me as I cleared plates and readied the steak, however. It was not my place to intrude.

"I am not proud of how tempting that offer sounds." Krystal pushed her empty fish plate away and reached down, pulling up a thin device that I'd learned was a tablet, which essentially seemed like a big version of those new phones, except that it didn't make any calls. "The truth is, I do have something of an idea on how to help Fred. Not to stop his gambit, to make it actually work. But, and this is the part that I know makes me a shitty person, I can't be a part of it. I have to ask something huge of you all, while I can't do the same." She pressed a button on the side and the tablet's screen began to glow as my waiters made their way to the back.

"Charlotte, can you send one of the staff over here or just show up yourself?" Krystal called, looking around the ceiling like I was going to suddenly pop out. "This concerns you, too."

My dress-clad form appeared near her, ready to serve my guests as always. "What can I do for you?"

"Pull up or create a chair, I guess." Krystal tapped her screen gently. "I want to get your feedback on the plan, even if you don't choose to join in."

My form shuffled uncomfortably, a bit of my feelings accidentally leaking through. "Respectfully, I'm not one to usually give feedback. I make contracts with guests and fulfill them. I keep my residents safe and comfortable. That is the duty of a house."

"Well, this time, I'm going to ask you to make a choice," Krystal replied. "This won't be a request, or a contract, or any of that. But depending on how things go, this might change a lot of stuff. For you, and for your current guests. You deserve the right to have some say in it."

I said nothing, merely nodding slowly while, in the kitchen, my waiter selves materialized food. I should have been in there, shapelessly watching over them, not out here dealing with matters that I likely had no real right to involve myself in. A proper house was silent, stoic, and took no action in its residents' lives.

But, as I was slowly discovering, I was not such a proper house as I might once have thought myself. And if it meant my halls were not forcibly emptied again, I could find a way to deal with that. So I sat and listened as Krystal outlined her idea, which seemed, by all accounts, just as—if not more—crazy than Fred's. I didn't say that at the time, of course.

After all, that would have been impolite. Besides which, I was far too busy falling in love with the half-mad idea.

6.

**Note: As this chapter starts after both my own meeting and the one I was, at the time, unaware of, I will resume the telling from this point. Suffice it to say that unless you have a deep and abiding fascination for the complexities of paperwork, there is little being skipped over that would be worth recounting. **

LILLIAN AND I MADE IT BACK TO Charlotte Manor less than an hour before sunrise, having pushed our time with Asha to the utmost limit. The hours flew by as she and I worked to make something impossible into a reality, all while Lillian pitched in with her experience from being part of a clan. We made our way in through the door hurriedly, noting that the sky was already growing light, only to find the elderly version of Charlotte—the one I considered the greeter— waiting for us.

"Hello, Fred, Lillian. Can I prepare anything for you?"

"I wouldn't say no to some steak and coffee," Lillian replied, without a moment's consideration. "After watching Fred and his lawyer go through paperwork all night, it's going to take a little caffeine to keep me perky past sunrise."

"I'm on it. And for you, Fred?"

"Some light fish, if you have it," I told her. "And wine. I'd very much like a nice glass of red. Are Krystal and Arch around?"

Charlotte shook her head, her hair not swaying in the slightest as she did. "They were both called away shortly before you arrived. Neither offered their destination, and I find it best not to pry into the business of agents."

"Can't say I disagree with that policy." Lillian let out a long yawn and stretched, putting her arms overhead like a pale cat reaching for the ceiling. It was a gesture I'd grown quite used to during the past several hours, as she'd had no qualms about demonstrating how bored she was while Asha and I poured through stacks of laws and documents. That said, her help had also been invaluable, as the only one among us with practical knowledge of vampire clans.

The old woman lifted an ancient phone, ostensibly to put a call into the kitchen, and I knew that the moment we sat down in the dining room, dinner would be served. I tried very hard not to think of it as a last meal while Lillian and I made our way down the hallway. It wasn't, after all, even by the most pessimistic of standards. There was still one more meal to eat, regardless of how things played out afterward. It would be, without question, the most uncomfortable dinner party I'd ever hosted, but by necessity, there would be food. What came after that, however, was completely up in the air. I'd done my very best, and chosen to take a gamble that at least had the potential to see me through.

While Charlotte's waiters brought out our drinks and dishes, I found myself wishing Krystal was there. There hadn't been time to consult her while Asha and I tried to determine what was even possible, and then how to accomplish it, but now that things were settled, I'd have preferred to get her up to speed. True, most of the dice were already cast, though a few could perhaps still be altered with a fast enough call to Asha. Honestly, though—and I feel awful admitting this—part of me was also glad that Krystal had been called away. Despite it being my best odds for survival, I knew she wouldn't entirely agree with the path I'd taken. When it mattered, she would support me, just as I would her, but that didn't mean I wouldn't get a long chewing out when everything was on the table.

For the moment, at least, the only table I had to concern myself with was Charlotte's, and that one was currently hosting our entrees, along with a cavalcade of sides neither of us had shown the presence of mind to request.

"You know, even with this place being haunted, the service is freaking incredible," Lillian commented, as she dug heartily into her rare steak. The need for blood in her beef wasn't vampiric in origin; Lillian simply appreciated a quality meat cooked only enough to add flavor, not steal it away.

"Charlotte Manor is the best kept secret in Winslow," I said, knowing full well that Charlotte was listening. "My only complaint is that the prices are too low. For food and service this excellent, I really wish she would charge a fair amount."

"Money is useful, but it's not the goal of our establishment," one of the waiters, usually silent as a church at midnight, said politely as he topped off my wine glass. "We see our rewards in other ways."

Which was the same argument Charlotte had used before when I encouraged her to increase her prices. It was a long-running discussion we'd had many times since I took up the role of her business manager. One day, I hoped to break through to her, but she could be surprisingly stubborn on certain issues. Then again, houses weren't exactly known for being easy to budge, so perhaps I was at fault for being surprised she had dug in so hard.

"Would you please let everyone know that there will be a dinner party tonight?" I told the waiter. At this point, keeping Lillian in the dark about Charlotte's true nature was a matter of time rather than secret-keeping— the explanation just took too long. "We'll invite guests to join us at eleven, so please have refreshments on hand for . . . ?" I stopped, looking across the table to Lillian, who began doing quick math on her fingers.

"For a meeting like this, Petre will come, and he'll want to bring some muscle under the guise that they're assistants and lawyers, but he won't want to seem like he's walking in ready for war, just in case. With Petre included, no more than four would be my guess. Add in you and me, that makes six. Then there's Krystal—"

"No more than six," I told the waiter. "Much as I would like to have her around, I'm almost certain that bringing an agent to a meeting like this comes with all manner of implications. Krystal is my girlfriend, but she is also her job. It's not my place to drag her into this situation. Plus, having an agent at the meeting would be a bit like showing up at a negotiation and setting a loaded handgun on the table. It lends an air of inauthenticity to any advocacy of peace."

"Not even going to invite your other friends?" Lillian asked.

I picked at my fish, moving my fork slowly from side to side. "More of the same. It pulls them into a problem that isn't theirs. Like I said before, my friends aren't assets, and I won't treat them that way."

"Then you better really hope this gambit goes well," Lillian replied. "It's a new one, I'll give you that, but Petre doesn't usually care for surprises. For what it's worth, I'm pulling for you, even if I won't be able to actually help if it all turns to shit. It probably won't, though. Petre prefers to be more methodical than just murdering someone at dinner."

"Thank you. It's worth quite a bit, actually. I never would have made it this far without your help." Lifting my glass, I exchanged a brief clink with Lillian's coffee cup. It was strange, knowing that someone I was quickly growing to consider a friend would stand idly by if I was being torn to shreds, but I understood. My research into the world of clans had done nothing if not show me just how dangerous vampire society could be. I'd barely managed on my own for a few years, and that was only through the help of my amazing friends. To face that world completely alone, without any sort of aid or clan backing her, would be akin to a death sentence.

"So, just to be clear, you're sure you want me to put in the call during the day?" Lillian asked. "If we wait until nighttime, Petre can still make it over easily. During the day, though, there's the slim chance that he might hire some non-vampire goons to come try and solve the problem."

"Despite the quaint looks, Charlotte Manor is extremely difficult to break into," I assured her. "And it's a small risk. I'm just asking for a meeting, after all. Petre seems like the business-minded type. I think he'll want to show up and see what I'm offering before he decides to try and kill me."

Since the time for Lillian to check-in was almost at hand, we'd decided that she should come clean about what she'd uncovered. Today, while the sun hung overhead, she was going to call in and report all about how she'd realized I was the vampire from the rumors, though the rumors had been exceedingly misleading. She'd also let Petre know that I was requesting a formal meeting with the House of Turva, though I ostensibly wouldn't tell her the exact details of what it concerned. At that meeting, I would lay everything out for Petre. If it worked—which I was pinning all my hopes on the prayer that it would—the night would end peacefully and I'd be able to remain in Winslow.

If I failed, then I might get killed, and even assuming I survived, running would be the only recourse left. Albeit, not in the way that Krystal had initially proposed.

Lillian finished off her meal and coffee, and then rose from the table. "All right, I'm going to go try and yank all the paperwork discussion out of my head before making the call. If anything goes off-plan, I'll knock on your door and let you know."

"I'd greatly appreciate that." As Lillian left the dining room, I polished off the remainder of my fish and picked up the wine. Though the sun would be rising soon, and I should get as much rest as possible for the coming night ahead, I found myself with no inclination to close my eyes just yet.

Charlotte emerged from the dining room in the form I considered to be her true one, even though it was no more real than the waiters she had scuttling about. Moving delicately, she took a seat at the head of the dining table and turned her attention to me. "Going to bed?"

"Not quite ready," I told her. "I think I'll try to wait for Krystal to get back."

"She might be gone for some time," Charlotte cautioned me.

"That's all right. I have almost nothing else to do. All the pieces are in motion now; until tonight, I have no real part to play. Oh, except . . ." I reached down for my briefcase, popped it open, and pulled a business card from its depths. Sliding it across the table, I waited until Charlotte had picked it up to continue.

"In the event of my death, whenever that may come, I've made arrangements for Asha to manage your business until such time as a suitable replacement is found. She would come by to explain everything if the occasion arose, but I felt like you should hear it from me, just so you knew she was on the up-and-up. You can trust her."

"Didn't I hold this woman hostage and threaten to kill her?" Charlotte asked.

"Water under the bridge. Well, mostly under, anyway. Regardless, she agreed to take on the responsibility, and that means she'll see it through," I assured Charlotte.

"Thank you." In a motion, the card vanished, though I had no doubt it was tucked away safely somewhere inside the expansive estate. "You didn't need to worry about me, you know. There's already a lot on your plate."

"It's really nothing, something I should have gotten done ages ago. Most of my clients can find new accountants, but I'd be doing you a disservice if I left you in the lurch." I took a long drink from my wine, and behind Charlotte, a waiter appeared with a fresh glass in hand.

"Please do your best to survive this dinner party," Charlotte told me. "I've got no desire to get accustomed to working with someone new. Plus, cleaning all the blood off my floor would be a real pain, even for me."

"Have no fear, I plan on doing everything I can to survive the night."

That seemed to satisfy her, and we sat in silence for some while afterward. I went through three more glasses of wine while I waited for Krystal to come bursting through the door, yelling about some out of control parahuman she and Arch had brought down. She would be loud, and messy, and total chaos, and I wanted to see her like that again. Just once more, before it all came to a head.

Eventually though, I gave up, heading upstairs and climbing into bed alone.

7.

THE PAPERWORK WAS SITTING ON THE BED,
messengered over midway through the day. The dinner
was being prepped, not that most of the diners would be
touching it, and the clock was ticking down, with less
than half an hour left until my guests arrived. And yet, I
was stuck, fumbling with a tie I'd knotted countless times,
my fingers so numb with nerves that I couldn't manage to
get the cursed thing properly around my neck. All I could
think of was the impending meeting, the clan of vampires
on their way to Charlotte Manor, and with every passing

second, my longshot seemed less and less likely to succeed. It was like my hands knew it, and were purposely refusing to finish the knot, keeping me from going downstairs and facing my own execution squad.

At least the rest of my suit was pressed and ready; the delivery service Asha recommended had really been top-notch. I didn't own a lot of suits; they were mostly used when I went to formal occasions or courted more professional clients. Still, like any good entrepreneur, I had a few, and I'd been wearing ties for the vast majority of my adult life, which made it all the more frustrating as I sat in the bedroom, still alone after a day of waiting, trying to figure out where I kept going wrong.

"Someone is feeling fancy tonight."

I jerked my head around. In my preoccupation with the tie, I hadn't even noticed the door slip open, let alone the familiar face it had revealed. Krystal stood there, in the same clothes I'd last seen her in, bloodshot eyes betraying the fact that her assignment had kept her up all day. I didn't care in the slightest as I rushed forward and embraced her. Deep down, I'd begun to grow truly afraid that I might not get to see her again before the dinner. While I didn't actually think Petre would kill me outright this evening, it was a risk, and if it happened, then my greatest regret—aside from getting murdered—would have been not getting to tell Krystal goodbye.

"Yeah, I missed you, too," she said, from deep within my tight hug. "Sorry, day's activities took a lot longer than I thought they would."

"It's more than fine." Pulling her through the door, I closed it, and then allowed our bodies to part. Much as I wanted to hold her, getting her up to speed was the first priority. "There's so much to tell you, and not much time to do it. Firstly, the House of Turva is sending—"

"Petre, who Lillian told all about you, and you boys are having a formal sit-down to discuss the new situation." Krystal grinned—that wildcat smile that spoke of danger and secrets not yet seen. "Who do you think you're dating? I've got my ear to the ground about everything that even thinks it might have fangs right now. And yes, that includes your Hail Mary with Asha, too. I'm fucking air, Freddy. I'm everywhere."

"So . . . you already know everything?" I plopped onto the bed, a sudden rush of anxiety leaving my body. I'd been bracing for this all day, nearly as much as the meeting itself, and she'd already found out everything on her own.

"You, my little overreaching boyfriend, decided to found your own vampire clan. Thanks to a lot of loopholes and paperwork, you even managed to gain temporary authorization until a full review can be conducted. Still, it's enough to give you some treaty protection for now, and you're hoping that will be enough to keep the House of Turva at bay."

"Actually, there's a bit more to it than that," I said.

"Geez, Freddy, I told you I'm in the loop. Do we need to sit here and hash out every freaking detail? By my count, you've only got a little bit until your guests show up, and you should be ready to meet them when they arrive. Don't start something this important off by slighting another clan." She leaned down and poked my poorly knotted tie gently. "And what's with all this get-up?"

"You've seen me in a suit before," I reminded her.

"Yeah, for the job, or when we went somewhere swanky. Why are you dressing up for these shitbags?" Her hands moved quickly, pulling apart the tie's interwoven areas until it hung limply on both sides of my neck once more.

"I thought it would be only proper. I want to show them respect."

"This isn't a business meeting, Freddy. It's a pissing contest. Don't try to impress them, make them try to impress you. Dress in a way that's comfortable, familiar, and lets these bastards know exactly who you are." Krystal yanked the tie off, crumpled it up, and tossed it into the corner.

"You think I should stick with the khakis and sweater vest?"

"If it ain't broke, don't fix it." She leaned in, kissing me firmly and running her hands through the hair I'd just recently finished combing. "Go meet these people as yourself. That's my advice. And I hope you'll take it, since we both know you're about to insist I not join you for dinner."

"Did Charlotte tell you?" I rose from the bed as I spoke, beginning to unbutton the crisp white shirt and eyeing my closet for something with a bit more life to it. I'd long ago brought a small stash of clothes, given how often I slept over at the manor, and it was preparation that paid off as I surveyed my choices.

"She offered to serve Arch and I meals in the sitting room, so that was a bit of a tip-off," Krystal replied. "By the way, I accepted the offer, but he didn't. If this is a formal meeting between the representatives of two vampire houses, an agent has the right to sit in and bear witness. That should make sure things stay peaceful, and Arch has a long-standing reputation for remaining fair and unbiased, so they won't have any room to bitch."

"Will Petre be okay with that?" I found a light blue cotton button-down and tossed it over my torso.

"Who gives a shit? Part of the fun of being an agent is getting to swing our dicks around when the occasion strikes. It's all in the treaties, so Arch is allowed to be there. Which means if Petre has an issue, he'll take it up with Arch, and no vampire lives to be that old by being stupid enough to pick that kind of fight."

With the shirt on, I swapped out my dark suit pants for khakis, and then topped it all with a gray sweater vest. I did feel more comfortable, more like myself, and it seemed to have helped with the nerves. Turning to face Krystal, I held out my arms and did a quick spin. "How do I look?"

"Like Freddy. Like the man I love. Like someone who's going to make it work tonight." Just like that, she was across the room and kissing me once more, though this time, she left my hair alone.

"You're really okay with all of this?" I asked once more, just to be certain. "It's going to change things, you know."

"Aren't you the one who told Albert about how everything changes, and sometimes, it makes our lives a lot better?" Krystal reminded me. "I'm not super thrilled with the plan overall, and I've got a plane on standby if it's needed, but I'd be lying if I said I wasn't a little impressed. You went to all this trouble, just to avoid running."

"It wasn't that I didn't want to run," I told her. "I just didn't want to leave so much behind."

"Well, then, get your cute ass down there and go fight for your town." She smacked me on the butt and pointed me toward the door. "Oh! And Charlotte is doing place settings; make sure you get the seat designated for you. I left you the extra special cutlery, just in case."

"You realize this is supposed to be a peaceful discussion, right?" I asked.

"Freddy, if you don't come ready for war, then you'll never manage to bargain your way to peace. Now scoot, I've had a long day, and I need a shower. When it's all wrapped up, I'll come join you, and we can go from there." With that, she disappeared into the attached bathroom, shutting the door firmly behind her.

I took the cue and headed downstairs, two envelopes of documents tucked securely under my arm. With a brief detour to the dining room to drop the papers off at the seat with a white placard bearing my name, I headed to the front hall, where my guests would soon be arriving. Lillian was already there, as was the old woman version of Charlotte. The former was wearing a new outfit, and she gave me a discerning glance as I walked in.

"Didn't feel like dressing up?"

"This is a business meeting, and you've seen that this is how I dress for business." Though I expected to feel a wave of self-doubt over the fact that I'd gone too casual, I actually weathered the comment decently. Krystal was right, feeling centered with myself and who I was mattered more than impressing these people.

Arch stepped in from outside, the lingering wisps of cigarette smoke still clinging to his form. "Looks like your guests are here. Three in the car that's pulling up, no idea if more are lying in wait on the road."

Though, from most people, such thoughts might have seemed paranoid, with Arch, I knew it was just him thinking tactically. He strode past us, on track for the dining room, where he'd no doubt be waiting to oversee the meeting. It was quite comforting, actually, to know he'd be there. I'd never really expected the night to devolve into violence—Petre seemed the type to be more cunning than that—but having Arch on hand made it all the less likely.

I stood as straight as possible while the three figures made their way up the porch stairs, finally pushing through the front door. Petre was flanked on either side by thick-necked vampires dressed in impeccably tailored dark suits. They were tall and strong, likely nurtured by a healthy diet of therian blood. Despite the size difference, Petre himself still stood out the most, his pale blue eyes taking in every detail, like he was deciding which nearby knick-knack would be best suited for killing us all.

"Mr. Fletcher, a pleasure to see you once more. I trust your new employee is working out well?"

"Quite well. She's been a tremendous help, and I think she'll only grow more useful as she's trained." We exchanged bows, and I looked to the hulking slabs of undead muscle near him. "And may I ask your friends' names?"

"They are unimportant, only here to assist me with details. Please, ignore them. I try to whenever possible." Petre smiled, his fangs just the slightest bit extended. He was enjoying this, and didn't mind letting me know. I hoped he kept his good humor when the situation changed. "I must say, Mr. Fletcher, I've been doing my research, and you are quite the interesting character. Tell me, what do you consider a higher honor, having won the esteem of a dragon, or having bedded an agent?"

"Ah, right, the rumors. Those do come up on occasion. That's part of why I called you here for a meeting. But how rude of me, let's head to the dining room. No point in standing about the hall when there's comfort and drink to be had." I motioned down the hallway, hoping I'd kept the temptation to sneer at him off my face when he talked about bedding Krystal. This was the game I had to play if I wanted to win the right to stay in my town. I wouldn't let him beat me so soon.

The night was just beginning, and I had a few cards of my own to surprise him with.

8.

TO HIS CREDIT, PETRE WAITED UNTIL THE drinks were poured and a plate of appetizers was set on the table before getting down to business. Somehow, a part of me doubted he'd have shown such courtesy if Arch hadn't been sitting there, helping himself to the bruschetta while the rest of us stewed in anticipation for what was to come. Once the agent was eating, however, Petre clearly felt the time had come.

"I'll be brief, Mr. Fletcher, as I'm sure you have much to do with your evening. Having learned what we did about your incredible achievements over the past few years, the House of Turva has decided to do something we'd previously ruled out: offer you membership in our clan." Petre held out a hand, and one of the nameless goons sitting to either side of him slipped a large piece of paper into his fingers. He set it down and slid it expertly across the smooth wooden table, where it halted inches from my plate.

"Feel free to look things over—and that goes for you as well, good agent—the pertinent information is all there. We extend this as an olive branch to one who has been left alone for too long. However, as an abandoned vampire, you have little means to refuse the invitation. We wouldn't want fear of something new to make you miss out on such a wondrous opportunity." Petre smirked, a small gesture that wasn't even properly suited for the amount of gloating he obviously wanted to do. No doubt, he expected this to be an easy win. Maybe he even hoped to walk out tonight with his new pet accountant—taken right out from under an agent, no less.

"It is a very kind, generous offer," I replied, careful to keep civil. I was pushing my luck more than enough without adding a personal grudge to the mix. "Unfortunately, I must refuse it. Renowned as the House of Turva is, I'm afraid the invitation comes a bit too late. You see, I am no longer an abandoned vampire. I've already joined a clan."

Petre's small smile receded back into his sour expression as I reached under my chair and pulled out my first envelope of documents. Rather than slide it like Petre had, I merely held it up, allowing one of the waiters to take it from my hand and walk it over to the other side of the dinner table. Petre snatched it and ripped open the top, eyes darting down the pages as he took the information in. I used the brief moment of silence to take a deep gulp of wine from my glass. This next part was going to require all the fortification I could muster.

"Surely this is some poor attempt at humor." Petre dropped the documents carelessly, as though he could no longer bear them sullying his fingers, and several slipped from the table to the floor below. "A temporary authorization for a one-person clan? That is what you would choose over the millennia-old House of Turva?"

"I'm really more of a modern vampire anyway, not much for older styles," I replied. Not exactly the most neutral way to decline, but it was hard to tell someone you didn't want to join their club without hurting their feelings in one way or another.

"This is preposterous." Petre's eyes danced to his muscle, who stirred at his gaze, but then his attention turned to Arch and the activity came to a standstill. He calmed himself, looking back at me and speaking with forceful intention in every word. "Let me tell you something, Mr. Fletcher, as I'm sure you didn't truly understand what you were doing. Founding a clan is not something to be done lightly. Even assuming you correctly jump through all the hoops to be recognized under the treaties, what you have done is form a new a clan in territory currently being controlled by another, much larger house. The agent here can attest that such situations are very rarely amicable, and there are no shortage of treaty-sanctioned ways for us to deal with a rival on our territory."

Petre paused, waiting for Arch to say something, either in agreement or disapproval. Instead, Arch merely nodded to a waiter for more water, staying devoted to his role as overseer and refusing to get unnecessarily involved.

"I'll give you one more chance, Mr. Fletcher." Petre wasn't even hiding behind the veil of civility anymore. He leaned forward halfway from his chair, and as he spoke, I caught sight of his fangs, further extended than they had been in the hallway. "Throw off these ridiculous notions. Submit to the House of Turva now, while the doors are still open to you. Or is it truly your intention to fend off an entire house of real vampires with a clan consisting solely of yourself?"

And here it was, time to hit him with the sucker punch that would determine whether or not this plan was a total bust. "As a matter of fact—"

"As a matter of fact, you're bad at counting, fuck-face." Krystal's voice rang through the dining room, cutting me off and causing Petre's goons to start in their chairs. She was no longer dirty or tired; in fact, she seemed to blaze with a light all her own as she strode into the room. Her rough boots stomped on Charlotte's wooden floors, and the gun belt strapped to her hip jingled slightly with every step. I'd seen this Krystal before, only in fleeting glimpses, but it was unmistakable for any other version of her. This was Krystal in full-on, ass-kicking-agent mode.

"Who in the nine hells do you think you are, interrupting a private meeting?" Petre motioned to the goon on his right, who started to stand. A very audible click filled the air, and all eyes turned to Arch, who'd produced a gun and had it expertly trained on the vampire halfway out of his chair.

"I'm going to have to insist that you not make any aggressive moves toward an agent. For everyone's safety." With his free hand, Arch helped himself to the last of the bruschetta, and a waiter whisked away the plate as if there wasn't a gun suddenly out at the table.

"Sit down," Petre hissed to his muscle, glaring at Krystal with a sudden influx of fear. A few seats over, Lillian grinned, taking a sip of her wine for the first time. She obviously couldn't meddle or show me support, but the sudden appearance of Krystal had caused all our controls to slip a bit.

"I see, so you're Mr. Fletcher's lover." Petre seemed to be regaining his self-control. He did know how to roll with the punches; I had to give him that. "Then, as an agent, you'd know that you are not permitted to interfere in conflicts that adhere to treaty conditions. Bluster about all you want, but if you so much as put a toe out of line in defending this one-vampire clan, I'll have your badge."

"First off, there's a lot of shades of gray in those treaties, and you shitbags aren't the only ones that can use them." Krystal leaned forward, stopping inches from Petre's face. Whatever aura of confidence and intimidation he'd spent centuries perfecting was wasted on her as she met his sneer with a grin. "And secondly, I just told you that you counted wrong. Freddy's not the only member of his clan."

"Ahem. Um. Is that my cue?" We all turned to find Albert, standing in the dining room doorway, talking to someone out of sight further down the hall. Evidently, he received an affirmative answer, because he stepped forward and looked the entire dinner party in the eye, one by one. "Fred—I mean, Mr. Fred, also has me."

"Am I expected not to notice that's a zombie?" Petre asked. At this point, I think he was temporarily more confused than anything else, which made two of us. While I'd certainly come to the meeting with a crazy, long-shot plan, this hadn't been part of it. So when

Krystal began to explain, I was paying just as much, if not more, attention than my adversary.

"Notice all damn day if you want. We checked the treaties up, down, and sideways. Any newly founded vampire clan has ten parahuman spots. It's just that none of you ever bothered using them for anything besides vampires."

"Why would we?" Petre turned from her to me, clearly under the misimpression that I was in on this spectacle. "Is that the best you can do? Padding your ranks with a mere zombie?"

Two heavy footsteps were the only warning we got as a new figure arrived in the doorway, this one far less concerned with protocol. Neil was decked out in a full set of robes, similar to the ones I'd seen the mages wear during Albert's fight with the chimera—though his were darker, and he clutched a black tome in his thin hands. From how tightly he gripped the book, it was clear he was annoyed, even before he began to bark at Petre. "Watch your mouth, or I'll make you rip your own tongue out."

In a few steps, he'd joined Albert by my chair, resting his free hand on my assistant's shoulder, near where the top of Albert's sword poked up. "This 'mere zombie' happens to wield the Blade of the Unlikely Champion. Show some damn respect." He paused, apparently remembering that he was supposed to do something other than just stick up for Albert. "Oh yeah, and I'm a member of the new clan as well. And no, I'm not a vampire, either. I'm a necromancer. I'm the puppet master who can pull all your undead strings."

"You align yourself with the ones who can control us. How desperate are you, Mr. Fletcher?" Petre asked.

"I mean . . . honestly, right now, I'm a lot more confused than I am desperate," I admitted. My eyes turned to Krystal, even I as heard heavy footsteps making their way to the doorway. "What is going on here?"

"I told you I was in the loop," she said, unabashedly savoring the surprise on my face. "It was easy to figure out. And when I talked it over with everyone, they agreed that this was doomed to fail if it was just you. So we decided that if you were willing to go to this much trouble to stay with us, then the least we could do was have your back. Officially. Well, they can. I'm an agent, so we're not really allowed to belong to any organization."

"But . . . but I didn't want any of you to be drawn into this." Now that I finally understood what was going down, my mind was reeling, so forgive me if perhaps my word choice wasn't quite as keen as it should have been.

"We know you didn't. And we know you'd never ask us to do somethin' like this. Which is prolly the exact reason we all agreed to." Bubba's thick, deep voice resonated from the doorway as he walked into the room. "And for y'all in here who don't know me, I'm Bubba

Emerson. Therianthrope and currently a member of the tribe led by Richard Alderson."

"This is getting beyond ridiculous," Petre snapped. "A therian cannot belong to a clan and a tribe at the same time."

This time, when the footsteps echoed, there was no mistaking their owner. Bubba might leave a hefty boot print, but no one in the room, or probably the city, carried the same kind of bulk as Richard Alderson. He ducked his head to step through the doorframe, and suddenly, the entire atmosphere seemed to change. Up until then, I'd have guessed that Petre considered himself to be dealing with annoyances, something he'd have to pick apart later. Richard, however, was a peer. This man wielded most of the power in Winslow, power the House of Turva very much didn't want turned against it.

"As it turns out, parahumans can belong to multiple organizations, assuming the leaders of each permit it," Richard told the room. "I personally signed my agreement to Bubba's dual status this afternoon. Fred, you have any objections?"

"I'm just trying to keep up at this point," I replied. "But since it seems like this happening with or without me, Bubba is free to be in both organizations, if it's what he really wants."

"Didn't think you'd mind," Richard said. "Also, Petre, though I obviously cannot join Fred with the others, you should know that my tribe has submitted an official mutual cohabitation and alliance agreement to Fred's new clan. I'm sure I don't need to tell you what that means if you decided to declare war on my friends."

"I also wouldn't count on the mage community for much support, unless you're playing nice." Amy had wandered in, practically unnoticed by any of us amidst the sea of vast personalities already present. "Since I joined the clan too, I reached out to a few friends in the spellcasting community. As of now, anyone on unfriendly grounds with my people can go elsewhere for all their magical needs."

Petre was fuming, unsure of who to stare more angrily at, though I was certainly getting the most frequent bout of his attention. "And who the hell is this woman?"

"That would be Amy Wells, sir. I mentioned her in my report." It was the first time Lillian had spoken since we sat down, and from the barely suppressed mirth on her face, I could only imagine how long she'd been waiting to slip a few words in, twisting the knife as she watched her superior lose control.

The rage on Petre's face seemed to dim. He glared at us, more sullen than furious now, bathing us in unmasked hatred. "This is quite the coup, Mr. Fletcher. You present yourself as such a caring, innocuous man, but when the moment arrives, it seems you have no trouble throwing the might of your allies around."

"Yo, dumbass, have you really not caught on yet?" Krystal snapped her fingers in front of his face, forcing him to look up at her. "Freddy didn't ask us for this. We snuck around behind his back, meeting with his lawyer as soon as he left, getting the paperwork sorted and everyone officially registered. He would never use us to scare you. We made that choice all on our own, and it's because we're not his allies. We're his friends."

"Technically speaking, as of now, we're also his family," Amy added. I noticed that tonight, in one of the few occasions I could recall, Amy had no strange auras, glows, or magical effects around her. She'd shown up stone-cold sober, which meant more than words would ever convey about how important she considered this evening.

"Fine, you're all friends, you're all family. It doesn't matter. The oldest of you is what? Perhaps a few decades old? I've been playing politics for centuries upon centuries." Petre rose from the table, his goons following suite. Only Lillian hesitated. "You think an alliance with a therian will protect you? Or a little inconvenience from the mages? I am beyond patient, and I will find a way to gain retribution for this slight. And what will you do, Mr. Fletcher, when I strip away the protection of your precious family? How will fend for yourself when there is no one else to stand for you?"

"You know, I was actually getting to that, before my friends came charging in and did the most amazing, caring thing I've ever seen." It was my turn to stand, because, with the momentum on our side, I had a new idea, one I'd have never dared try before. But the night was going well, and all of a sudden, pressing that luck didn't seem quite so foolish. First things first, though, it was time to get my last card, what I'd thought would be my trump, down on the table.

"Feel free to come after me any way you see fit, Petre." I reached back under the chair and grabbed one last document, this one kept apart from the others for good reason. "Just know that, when you do, you're attacking more than just me. As of last night, Fletcher Accounting Services has officially signed on to do freelance budget auditing for the Agency."

9.

IT WAS MY TURN TO SMILE AS EVERYONE
else in the room stared with unexpected shock at the
revelation, which I actually found quite confusing. Some
had wide eyes, others gasped, and Krystal was opening
and closing her mouth repeatedly, as though she kept
deciding what to say and then changing her mind at the
last moment.

"What? You said you were filled in all the way. You're
the 'fucking air,' remember?"

"I meant I knew about you starting a vampire clan," Krystal snapped, my prompt finally giving her a set of words to start with. "But you signed on as an *Agency* contractor? How did you even know that was possible?"

"You mentioned it when we were in Boarback," I reminded her. "Said it came with a lot of perks. I did some digging and found out that that included a certain level of protection. *That* was my plan tonight. You didn't all really think I was planning to keep a whole gang of vampires at bay just by starting my own clan, did you?"

"Did Asha know about this?" Krystal demanded.

"Sure, she's the one who helped me put it through." From the look on everyone's faces, ranging from uncertainty to betrayal, I gathered it was something she hadn't mentioned during their meeting. While she technically shouldn't have, and given that she had let them all join my new clan in secret, I had a hunch that she'd have given them a heads up on the contractor thing if they'd asked. "Wait, did you all barge in declaring that you already knew everything and wanted to help?"

"Well, we let Krystal do most of the talkin'," Bubba admitted.

"Still, even if I told her we were up to speed, you'd think she would have mentioned it," Krystal mumbled. "Freddy, do you have any idea what you've done? Being connected to the Agency is not exactly all smiles and tickle-fights, even if they just want you to crunch numbers.

The reason the job comes with protection is because a *lot* of parahumans hate us, and aren't shy about taking it out on the people who work with us."

"Indeed we do," Petre agreed. Truthfully, in the moment, I think we'd all nearly forgotten he was even there. "Mr. Fletcher, when I believed you had turned your allies into pawns to stave off being absorbed into our clan, I thought you a manipulative, cunning bastard, but at least I respected that. Throwing in with the Agency, however, is an unforgivable decision. You would scamper under the protection of those that murder our kind, all for little more than accepting the nature we were born with."

"We only kill the ones who break the law." Arch hadn't completely put his gun away; instead, it was resting near his dinner fork, one motion away from being swept up again.

"Petty, pathetic laws that we were strong-armed into agreeing with," Petre replied. All the anger was gone from him now; in its place was cold, empty hatred. There was no question about it, I'd definitely made myself an enemy this evening. It was a terrifying thought that I would dwell on endlessly later. For the moment, however, I tried to focus on the fact that he probably couldn't hate me anymore when I made my big move.

"Tonight, you have done more than slight the House of Turva," Petre continued. "You have betrayed your own kind. To take the sacred tradition of a clan and allow the common parahuman riffraff within its ranks was bad enough, but to then cast your lot with the Agency just for a small modicum of protection . . . Fredrick Fletcher, you are no vampire to me."

"You know, I think I'm okay with that," I replied. "If being a 'real' vampire means being like you and your clan, then I'm fine being considered something else. Hell, I'll take it as a compliment. Because here's the thing, Petre: your kind of vampire might have a giant clan with lots of people to take orders, but as Amy pointed out, my kind has a family. If that's the deal, then I'd rather be a failure of a vampire any day of the week."

"Let's see if you can hang on to that sentiment when the House of Turva begins picking you all apart." Petre turned to the last seated member of his party and called to her. "The work is done, Lillian. Let us return home for the night. There is no longer any need to serve such a useless man."

"Lillian, stay right there." I spoke before she even had a chance to pull her chair back, keeping Petre's attention on me. This was the part I'd been trying to build toward, the thing I'd wished for, but never would have had the courage to try without my friends filling the room behind me. "Not to be rude, but I believe Lillian was given to me as a gift of friendship. Or does the House of Turva often rescind its gifts when it suits them to do so?"

"We do when we no longer wish for any sort of friendship with those we were dealing with," Petre snapped. "I am willing to leave here tonight peacefully, Mr. Fletcher. Do not test my generosity any further than that."

Krystal actually laughed at that point, short and harsh and so emasculating that even I felt wounded by it, despite the fact that it was aimed at Petre. "Are you really trying to pretend that *you're* the one who is choosing to resolve things peacefully tonight? Freddy might be naïve, but the rest of us can do the math. If you throw so much as a sharp look at someone in this room, the three of you would get beaten halfway to your final coffins. As for Lillian . . . hey, Arch, you know protocol better than me: what's the deal with taking back an official gift of friendship?"

"Legally complex, and often varies case by case," Arch replied calmly. "It's a tedious ordeal, usually more trouble than it's worth for both parties. Still, if you both want to go down that route, I can make some calls to start the paperwork."

"Or . . ." The idea poured from my mouth as fast as it formed, my eyes on the untouched place setting only a few feet in front of me. "We can settle it here and now, like real vampires. How about a test of strength, Petre? That should appeal to your proper ways."

"You wish to fight one of us?" Though I'd expected him to be annoyed, Petre instead seemed cautiously intrigued. He was probably imagining getting to snap me in half while my friends looked on, but I had something different in mind.

"Oh no, nothing that barbaric. Besides, with the amount of parahuman blood in you, I know I wouldn't stand a chance. I meant a much more personal, ego-driven strength. Strength of will. Krystal, do you or Arch happen to have any silver daggers on you?" I asked.

Without pause, Arch reached into his jacket and produced a gleaming silver blade. Everyone in the room (except Krystal and the mages) shrank back visibly, though my reaction was purely for show. Catching Petre's eye, I nodded to the dagger resting in Arch's hand.

"It's a simple game. We take turns holding the dagger, and whoever can bear it the longest is the winner. No amount of blood either us might have in our system is going to help with that." Technically, my words were true, as the blood in my system had absolutely nothing to do with how this could play out.

"Let me guess, if I win, Lillian comes home, and if you win, she stays?" Petre asked.

"No," I said, looking at Lillian past Petre's glowering countenance. "If you win, Lillian goes with you. If I win, Lillian gets to choose what she wants to do. Maybe she'll still go home to the House of Turva. Maybe she'll ask to join my clan, which she's welcome to do. Maybe she'll want to be an abandoned vampire for a while and see how she likes it. But the decision will be hers to make."

Petre chuckled under his breath, turning to meet Lillian's uncertain eyes. "I think you ensnared this one too deeply, my child. He thinks to win you a freedom you don't want. Very well, Mr. Fletcher, I will play your game. But I have a condition: we will need two silver daggers, and we shall hold them at the same time. This way, there is no dispute about who drops first, and neither of us has the advantage of a goal to beat. You might think me foolishly prideful, but I'm not so dumb that I think you'd choose a contest you didn't have a good chance at winning. Perhaps your pain tolerance is abnormally high, or you simply believe in your heart that you can do it. Regardless, I will not give you any needless advantages."

"I'd say that's more than fair," I agreed. "Arch, do you have another?"

The blade was in his hand before I'd even finished the question. Rising from his seat, Arch walked toward Petre, and I made my way over to join them. The rest of the room backed up, giving us ample space. This was as much because we were near silver as out of desire to let the contest occur uninterrupted.

"These blades are both silver," Arch announced. "I'd like you both to briefly touch, smell, or do whatever you need to confirm that, just so there are no accusations later on." Petre carefully touched his thumb to both daggers, showing no outward sign of pain, but keeping the contact brief. I did the same, though I made myself appear to be hiding a wince each time.

"I will lay these in your bare palms simultaneously. You cannot touch, bump, or in any way physically interfere with the other. The first person to release their grip on a blade is the loser. Any objections or questions?"

Petre and I both shook our heads and held out our hands. Arch didn't bother repeating himself; instead, he laid the blades across our flesh, releasing his hands once we'd gotten a firm grip. The silver still tingled a bit as I clutched it, unlike a normal metal, but I wasn't flooded with pain and weakness the way it had once affected me. Even being near the stuff had worn me down to near human levels; chains of silver over my clothes had held me more than once. Actual skin-to-metal contact had burned, like touching something that was just a bit too hot at first, but with every passing second, the pain had grown steadily worse. Silver-insulated magic interrupted it, and for a vampire, that meant being brought back to the corpses we truly were.

At least, that's how it was affecting Petre. For me, it was just the tingle, nothing more. It was possible Petre hadn't been wrong when he said I wasn't a real vampire anymore. Whatever Gideon's magic had done to me, it must have changed my body in a pretty fundamental way for silver to leave me unbothered. Being different wasn't so bad, though. Especially not when it gave me the opportunity to help my friends.

To his credit, Petre held out for a full minute before his composure began to slip. The steady hand holding his blade wobbled first, by only a few degrees, then progressively more and more as his placid expression melted to one of focus and pain. His gaze wavered between his own hand, mine, and my face, where he found an utterly untroubled expression. If I was going to go to all the trouble to make an impression, I felt like it should at least be a strong one.

"You have . . . good . . . pain tolerance." His teeth were clamped together as his hand shook violently. All of his instincts were undoubtedly screaming at him to throw away the dagger, yet he was halting them through sheer force of will. In that moment, I dearly hoped I never had to face off against Petre in a genuine contest. The way silver used to hurt, I couldn't have managed what he was doing for even ten seconds.

"I just have a really good reason not to let go," I replied, voice steady and calm.

"Even if you . . . win . . . she'll . . . come home."

"You think so? Maybe you're right. Why don't you drop the dagger, and we'll find out." The truth of the matter was that I didn't know if Petre was wrong or not. Lillian had certainly voiced frustration with her clan and the desire to not take their orders, but ours was still a motley lot to throw in with. She very well might choose to stick with what was familiar and at least relatively safe. But . . . they'd kept her from blood for a month before. That wasn't punishment, it was torture. If there was even a chance she'd grasp for freedom, I owed it to her. Without Lillian, I never would have gotten the time and intel to create my own clan in the first place.

Despite my words, Petre kept hanging on to his blade. Another minute passed, and then another. At long last, as his whole arm was shaking, Petre let the dagger clatter to the floor. He'd made it three minutes and change, judging by the antique clock hanging on the dining room wall. Honestly, I was incredibly impressed at such a feat of willpower, even if I couldn't afford to show it. For good measure, I waited several more seconds, making sure that Petre's fallen knife was completely still, before releasing my own to join it.

"And Fred is the winner," Arch declared, not so much as even one bit of enthusiasm or showmanship in his voice.

Petre was staring at me with a new look, something between respect and doubt, as he reached down and pushed his finger against my dagger. Instantly, he jerked his hand away, all his tolerance for pain used up on the amazing display he'd just put on.

"This is a trick," he said. "Are you wearing some sort of enchantment?"

"Everyone knows you can't enchant against silver," Amy supplied helpfully from over my shoulder.

"Then a plastic, or a coating of some sort." He grabbed my hand, and even though my friends all seemed to move closer, I made no motion to stop him as he examined my palm for some method of defeating the dagger.

"Like I told you before, I just had a really good reason to not let go." With that, I pulled my hand away and walked over to Lillian, still seated as she patiently watched the contest unfold.

She smiled, taking a moment to look over my hand herself before speaking. "That was pretty impressive, Fredrick."

"I like to put on a good show," I replied. "And hey, I won. Which means that what happens next is up to you. Go with Petre, stay with us weirdos, or strike out on your own."

"Before I decide, can I ask you something? Why go to all this trouble for someone who was sent to spy on you?" Lillian asked.

Turning slowly, I pointed to my group of friends. "The first time I met Neil, he tried to sacrifice me and a bunch of LARPers for more power, and Albert helped. Amy had accidently created a bunch of monsters that nearly killed me more than once. Bubba got us drawn into a gambling debt that could have had us working for slave wages in Vegas. Charlotte threatened to kill a whole house of guests if one of the people didn't off themselves. And Krystal is the catalyst the dragged me into all of those dangers, along with a whole lot of others. Honestly, as far as first impressions go, you made one of the best of the lot. You saved me from a vampire hunter, and spying doesn't really stack up to attempted murder. As for why I'm doing it, well, I think we're friends. And if you haven't noticed, this is a group of friends that tends to stick together."

"You are, without question, one of the oddest vampires I've ever met." Lillian sighed. "But damn if this doesn't seem like a lot more fun than doing yet another honeypot in a few weeks." She stood from her chair at last, walking over to Petre and looking him square in the eyes.

"It would shame the House of Turva to rescind a gift of friendship, especially to a clan with such power and connections. Your pride has blinded you to this, Petre, but I can still see what is best for our people over my ego. I will stay with Fredrick Fletcher, and continue working for him as a member of his new clan. Thus, the friendship between our two houses shall remain intact."

Petre's eyes narrowed further with every word Lillian spoke. "Our leader—"

"Our leader will see that I made the right decision, when you tell him of everything that has happened here tonight," Lillian said, cutting Petre off. "The alliance with Alderson's therians and Wells's mages is too much to have turned against us in this fragile time. Go make your report, Petre. And when they side with me, I hope you learn some humility during your fasting."

Though he was barely repressing a snarl, Petre turned from Lillian, motioning to his cronies to follow. Krystal, Arch, and I walked after them, making certain they found their way to the exit. None of the three tried to stray, but after his goons had walked through the door, Petre turned back to face me.

"No doubt you consider this evening a victory, Mr. Fletcher. You've gotten everything you wanted, and we are being sent slinking away. Allow me to offer some advice, though, as one with far more experience: a single win can easily be nullified further on. Do not consider this matter settled just because of one well-played maneuver."

"Petre, I thank you kindly for the advice. Now allow me to return some of my own," I told him. "Winslow, Colorado is not a place for malicious threats and blood-soaked takeovers. This is a good place, where good people, human and parahuman alike, try to make their homes. And I welcome you to it, because that's what you do when new neighbors arrive. Just remember that if you want to make trouble, you're better off looking somewhere else to do it. This is *our* town, and we won't just sit around if someone tries to ruin it. So be good neighbors. It'll make things easier on everyone."

Petre opened his mouth to reply, but before a word came out, the front door slammed closed in his face. A moment later, Charlotte was standing there, her usual formal gown ditched for something that looked like a party dress from the flapper era.

"If you're all about done, I have a giant feast prepared, and it seems like we've all got quite a bit to celebrate."

10.

"BE HONEST WITH ME, ARE YOU A LITTLE bit sad that we didn't have to move to Boarback?" I set the new laptop atop a modern desk, sleek and vastly more stylish than I would have ever chosen for myself. But this wasn't about me, and it sort of fit with the room Charlotte had provided. This sizable chunk of space on the manor's third floor was so bare that I half-suspected she'd created it just to fill our needs. I'd never gotten a good grasp of exactly how much control Charlotte had regarding what existed within her walls, and this was no occasion for me to look a gift horse in the mouth.

"Sad isn't really the right word," Krystal replied, pulled a stack of files from the cardboard box and setting them carefully down next to the filing cabinets. If she knocked them over, then everything would have to be re-sorted, and that was a task neither of us wanted to undertake. "Part of me would have enjoyed it, and I think you'd have learned to love it there too, but this is what's best for everyone, us included."

"Best" might have been an optimistic term, but I didn't raise any objections. Over the last few days, we'd seen all the paperwork continue making its way through the system, and as of yesterday, most of my temporary authorizations had been approved. Though the House of Turva had raised a few objections here and there, they lacked our passion and gift for paperwork, which made clearing their minor obstacles hardly any challenge. Things were settling down now, and with the threat of immediate, looming death momentarily pushed away, I'd had to turn my attention to more pragmatic issues. The largest of which was my office.

While I'd greatly enjoyed working from home for a long while, the truth was that I could no longer justify such a system. Between Quinn and Colin, too many people had broken into my apartment over the years, no matter how many security measures I implemented.

Now that I knew the House of Turva had been interested in my client's records, it would be bad faith for me to store them in a place so easily accessible through force. Thus, Krystal and I were handling part four of the Fletcher Accounting Services home office move. As of two days prior, I was leasing office space through Charlotte, meaning that my files—both digital and hard copy—would be stored in the safest location I had access to. Truth be told, Krystal was on me to let the apartment go altogether and move in myself, but I wasn't quite ready to make that jump yet.

However, it had made sense to change the housing situation of someone else in the company. Much as I enjoyed having Albert around, renting him a room at Charlotte Manor made things easier, as he split his time between Arch and me. Now, he wouldn't have to come to my apartment to handle any filing; everything he needed would be under the same roof. And the same held true for my company's newest employee.

"Knock, knock. I've got a lawyer with a hefty brief-case, boss." Lillian pushed open the door, clad in a long skirt and strikingly green blouse. Though I'd told her she was free to do as she wished, the elder vampire seemed oddly taken with my line of work. Perhaps it was some debt she felt compelled to pay off, or maybe she merely wanted something a little more humdrum after the hecticness of her previous tasks. Either way, I needed the help, so I didn't object.

"Fred, you're lucky we go back so far. I would not put in these kinds of hours at the drop of a hat for just anyone." Asha barreled past Lillian at the doorway, dropping her own briefcase down next to the laptop and popping the latches to reveal three large stacks of documents. She yanked all of them out, setting them carefully on the desk before shutting her case and moving it onto the floor. "These are the newest pages for review, not that you can change much at this point in the process, but rules are rules. Check them over and have the signature pages back to me by tomorrow night."

"That's a tight deadline," I said. In my line of work, I was no stranger to loads of tedious paperwork, but this was quite the task even by those standards.

"Yeah, well, when you say 'put the fastest rush possible on everything,' you're going to get some tight deadlines. And some heavy briefcases." Asha was glaring, all but daring me to complain after the endless barrage of work I'd put her through.

In what I considered a wise decision, I let the issue of the deadline pass, taking a peek at the documents on top of each stack instead. These were to be the last in a long line of smaller batches, making my new clan finally official. Idly, I flipped through several pages, letting my eyes skim the hundreds of lines of inky text. One piece, bigger than the others, caught my attention, and I yanked the page free from the stack.

"Asha, please don't hurt me for saying this, but I think there's been a mistake." Carefully turning the document around so that she could see it, I pointed to the bold letters that were at least three fonts larger than anything else on the page. "Right here, where it lists the official title of the new clan. This is supposed to read House of Fletcher."

"Oh, yeah. I changed that," Krystal called from the other side of the room. "Cashed in a few favors, said there was a mix-up, and got the name updated. House of Fletcher seemed way too stuffy for this crowd, you know?"

In a smooth motion, Asha snatched the page away from me and read the new name, her grip tightening on the pages. "House of Fred? That's what you had the clan's name changed to?"

"Fits much better, don't you think?" She finished unloading her box and kicked the empty cardboard across the room, where it joined many of its already un-packed brethren. That done, she strolled over to where the rest of us were standing, giving me a quick peck on the cheek. "I can have it changed back if you really want. I mean, you're the one who has to live under the name. But come on, House of Fletcher? Bleh. Lillian, is that the clan you want to be associated with?"

"Hey, I came from Turva, so pretty much anything is an improvement after that," Lillian replied. "Although, for what it's worth, I do sort of agree with Krystal. House of Fred seems like a better fit."

Two against one was hardly insurmountable odds, but when half of that equation was Krystal Jenkins, I knew better than to fight without cause. "Asha, could you run it by the others and see what they think? Whatever the majority wants, that's the name we'll use."

"Feel free to double check, but I shopped the idea around before I made the calls. Everyone either didn't care or agreed with me," Krystal said.

"Is there any reason why I wasn't one of the people you shopped it to?" I asked.

"Because then it wouldn't be a surprise. Geez, Freddy, you're supposed to be smart, try and keep up here." Given the sort of mischief Krystal often liked to cause, I decided to consider it a boon that she hadn't altered the name to House of Freddy.

"If I have to run down opinions, I'm at least going to help myself to some food first," Asha declared. "Charlotte, set a place for me, please. And put this one on Fred's tab; it's the least he can do."

"I still can't believe this is a living house," Lillian muttered as she watched Asha head out the door. In the time since dinner with Petre, we'd brought her up to speed on almost everything about our group that she'd missed, the true nature of Charlotte Manor included. "Charlotte, would you set a place for me, too?"

"Hold on a minute," I said, holding up my hand. "Have you done your studying for the day?"

"Like . . . all of it? 'Cause you gave me a shitload to work through each day," Lillian pointed out. "And that's on top of all the online classes I'm taking."

"You're the one who wanted to get your accounting certifications as fast as possible. That workload will allow you to handle the basic exams in just a few months, but only if you stick with it," I told her. It was, admittedly, a very aggressive timetable, far more ambitious than something I'd have undertaken when just starting out. Lillian, however, had little patience, despite what one might expect from a vampire as old as she was, and had insisted on racing ahead to become a full accountant.

"Fine, fine, you win. Charlotte, can you have someone bring me a meal up here? And some blood from the fridge. I'm going to need actual sustenance to get through this workload." Lillian glared at me, but I took no offense. We both knew she was the one actually keeping herself on track. I just served as a convenient reminder and occasional foil.

As Krystal and I left the office, heading downstairs for night-lunch before another round of unpacking, I wrapped my arm around her shoulders and pulled her close. She matched my affection, squeezing my torso so hard that a living me might have gotten bruised ribs.

"Any word on how long it'll be before I'm contacted to start work?" I asked. Thus far, the Agency had accepted my contractor application and said they would be in touch. Other than that, I was left completely in the dark as to what the cost of aligning myself with them would be.

"Still nothing so far; at least, that's what I've been told," Krystal replied. "We don't always have work for our contractors, and I don't know that we've ever brought in an outside finance person before, at least not for a long time. They're probably trying to figure out what to do with you. Maybe they'll never think of anything, and you won't have to take any jobs."

"My luck isn't that good," I said. "But when the jobs come, they'll just be accounting. I triple checked everything before applying as a freelance contractor; they can only offer me work in the specified field. Plus, I doubt even the Agency has found a way to turn number crunching into hazardous employment."

"Let's not put too much faith in that theory." Krystal squeezed me once more, just before we reached the bottom of the stairs. "You may have really stepped in it this time, Freddy. You are damn fortunate that I'm always around to keep you safe."

"You've got a point. Maybe my luck isn't so bad, after all." I kissed her there, at the bottom of the stairs, before we went to join the ruckus of a dining room I could already hear from down the hall. I'd taken a big gamble, binding myself to the Agency, and while it seemed like the right call for the moment, there was no way to know if it would work out okay in the end.

All I knew was that, no matter what came next, we'd be facing it together. Me, Krystal, and the small family of misfits we'd been blessed enough to gather together.

ABOUT DREW

Drew Hayes is an aspiring author from Texas who has written several books and found the gumption to publish a few (so far). He graduated from Texas Tech with a B.A. in English, because evidently he's not familiar with what the term "employable" means. Drew has been called one of the most profound, prolific, and talented authors of his generation, but a table full of drunks will say almost anything when offered a round of free shots. Drew feels kind of like a D-bag writing about himself in the third person like this. He does appreciate that you're still reading, though.

Drew would like to sit down and have a beer with you. Or a cocktail. He's not here to judge your preferences. Drew is terrible at being serious, and has no real idea what a snippet biography is meant to convey anyway. Drew thinks you are awesome just the way you are. That part, he meant. Drew is off to go high-five random people, because who doesn't love a good high-five? No one, that's who.

CPSIA information can be obtained
at www.ICGtesting.com
Printed in the USA
LVOW11s0712170917
548588LV00002BC/23/P